Riding Tall

Kate Sherwood

Copyright 2019 by Kate Sherwood

Published by Kate Sherwood

Cover Art by Leah Kaye Suttle

Print ISBN #978-1-988752-15-0
ebook ISBN# 978-1-988752-16-7

Second Edition Issued 2019

CHAPTER ONE

"COME ON, Mr. Bowerman," Joe said with what he hoped was a charming smile. It wasn't easy to be firm and still pleasant, wasn't easy to seem respectful but still go after what he wanted. This was the sort of job he'd always sent his twin brother to do, and there was a reason for that. But Will had his own concerns now. This was Joe's problem. "I know it's not as tidy as it could be, but we're working on it. The elementary school didn't have a problem with the setup."

"You're asking us to register a student for whom you are not legally responsible and who has no fixed address." Mr. Bowerman shook his head as if he were saddened by Joe's irresponsibility. The man had been a vice principal at the school when Joe had attended, and then been transferred elsewhere, to the town's general relief. Now he was back as principal, inching his way toward a retirement that couldn't come soon enough for his students. He hadn't been flexible when Joe had been a student, and he certainly didn't seem to be mellowing with age.

Joe tried to be calm as he repeated what he'd already told the man three times. "She has a fixed address. *Our* address. She's staying with us."

"*Staying*," Bowerman said pointedly. "Not *living*. That doesn't sound like a fixed address to me. We can't create schedules for every *couch surfer* in the district, you know." He pronounced "couch surfer" as if simultaneously proud of his use of the vernacular and somewhat disgusted by its feel in his mouth.

"Lacey's not couch surfing. She's here for the rest of the school year, at least." Joe wanted to make his point a little more vehemently, probably with a bit of volume. The school had a legal obligation to educate the students within its catchment area, and Bowerman should just admit that and stop wasting Joe's time. Yeah, it'd feel good to do a little yelling right about now. But Bowerman seemed like the sort of guy who'd hold a grudge. Joe wasn't worried about himself, but Ally still had most of a semester in the school and would be needing support for scholarships and graduation awards. There was no point in making things more difficult for her. "We're hoping to have the paperwork sorted out in the next few weeks. Jean Carpenter's the social worker on the case, Andy Stark is onboard—"

"We don't take instructions from the provincial police," Bowerman scoffed.

Joe tried to ignore the interruption. "The aunt down in Sarnia has said she's happy to be rid of both girls. There's nowhere else for them to live and nowhere else for them to go to school. Lacey needs to get registered here."

"Once the paperwork's in place—" Bowerman started, but now it was Joe's turn to interrupt.

"They're saying weeks for that, at best. It could be longer. Lacey's already missed too much school, and this is her last year— her marks really matter."

Bowerman looked pitying again. "Lacey Walton's marks *don't* really matter. She's not heading for postsecondary education. She'll be lucky to pass."

"Okay, well, maybe her marks weren't great in the past, but she's a smart kid. She can do better if she gets more support at home. But if she *is* a weak student, that still means she shouldn't be missing a ton of school while we wait for things to get formalized. She needs to be in class."

"We're not a day care, you know. We're not here to solve your childcare issues."

Joe frowned in confusion. "She's seventeen. She doesn't need a babysitter." He wished Will was there. Or Mackenzie. Yeah, Mackenzie would definitely understand what was happening here. The guy could read people like Joe could read animals. If Mr. Bowerman were a stubborn steer refusing to go into a chute, Joe would know how to handle the situation. He wouldn't push too hard, he'd try to figure out what the steer was thinking. Was the animal scared of something? Was he seeing an obstacle in the chute that Joe hadn't noticed? "Lacey was okay when she was here last time, wasn't she?" Joe didn't know about any problems, but he'd mostly heard Ally's stories, and it was quite possible his sister had cleaned things up to protect her friend.

Bowerman raised an eyebrow. "Well, here we get into one of the problems with a casual arrangement without paperwork. Until I have documentation of your legal relationship with Lacey, I'm afraid I cannot discuss any aspect of her history with you. The privacy legislation is *quite* clear. I also couldn't discuss any aspect of her *current* behavior. So if she acted up and needed to be suspended, who would I contact? If a teacher had a concern...?"

"The teachers aren't going to be stubborn jackasses about it," Joe said. His calm was definitely slipping. "They'd call *me*. If *you* want to follow the letter of the law, I guess you could call the aunt in Sarnia, but good luck getting through the alcoholic haze— apparently she drinks worse than her brother did. That's why Lacey's back up here, and that's why she's going to *stay* up here, and that's why she's going to be attending this school." Joe had tried to see things through the steer's eyes, but cattle had never tried to use *privacy legislation* to defend their stubbornness. But if the animals *were* just being stubborn, if Joe had done everything he could to figure out the problem and still couldn't see it, well, then he just needed to be firm with them.

He straightened up out of the uncomfortable plastic chair on the visitors' side of the principal's desk. "Lacey will be here tomorrow morning, ready to go to class." Joe had already talked to the guidance counselor, a shy girl who'd been a student at the school the same time he was, and she'd assured him she could put a schedule together for Lacey in no time. But he wouldn't mention that to Bowerman. Instead, he glowered. "She needs to be here. You're legally required to educate her, so stop wasting everyone's time. If she isn't in class tomorrow, I'll be in your office again, and I'll wait out in the front for as long as it takes to get her registered, and I'll tell every parent who comes in just why I'm there, and then *you* can try to explain to them why you're trying to deny a teenager her education."

Joe remembered too late about Ally's scholarships and awards. Well, he'd just have to work extra hard to make sure there was enough money to make up for their loss, because he wasn't backing down now. He stared at Bowerman, letting the principal see that he was dead serious, and then, when he was sure the point had been made, he shrugged. "I hope it doesn't come to that. I'll tag along with Lacey tomorrow to make sure she's set up okay, and if she is, everything's good." He decided against offering his hand and instead just smiled politely and said, "See you in the morning," as he headed for the door.

His phone rang as he was striding through the parking lot. He pulled it out, saw the name on the call display, and felt his shoulders relax. "Hey," he said quietly.

"Hi," Mackenzie said. Joe heard a lot of noise in the background, and Mackenzie raised his voice as if to drown out the din. "I'm still in the city. This job is going long. I'm not going to make it back tonight."

And Joe's shoulders tensed again. But he forced himself to keep his voice calm. "Oh. That's too bad. You're going to stay at Kristen's?"

"No, they're putting us up in a hotel. Hopefully a good one."

Joe leaned against the side of the truck. "Did they say why they couldn't get it done? Did something go wrong?"

"Nothing big. Just one of those things." Joe could almost hear Mackenzie's shrug. He obviously wasn't too worried about this. He wasn't upset about spending a night in a hotel instead of coming home to Joe.

So Joe shouldn't be worried about it either. Things were going well with Mackenzie, but that didn't mean the two of them had to be together all the time. Independence wasn't a sin. "Okay, have fun. We'll see you tomorrow night."

"Or maybe the next morning," Mackenzie amended. "If tomorrow goes long, I'll be too tired to drive that far. I'll stay with Kristen if they don't put me up again."

Joe swallowed hard. It felt like the beginning of the end. He'd known it all along. Mackenzie was only visiting the country; he belonged in the city. Joe was going to get his heart broken. It was coming.

Or, just possibly, he was insecure, paranoid, and neurotic. "Sounds good," he said. "Drive safe."

"You bet. Hey, how did it go at the school?" But before Joe could answer, he heard a voice in the background, and Mackenzie said, "Oh, they're ready. I've got to go. Give Griffin a good-night kiss for me, okay?"

And that was it. The call disconnected. Joe looked at his reflection in the blank screen and tried to find his confidence. Mackenzie wasn't starting to slip away. He just had a modeling job, and he was wisely choosing not to spend hours on the highway if he wasn't going to be alert. Everything was good. When the phone rang again, Joe smiled in anticipation, but it wasn't Mackenzie's number displayed on the screen.

He hit the button to talk to his youngest sister. "Ally, are you calling from class?"

"Are you standing in the parking lot of my school staring at your phone?"

"I was standing in the parking lot of your school *talking* on my phone."

"That's not what *I* saw. But anyway, did you get it all figured out? Is Lacey coming to school tomorrow? What's her schedule?"

"I'm working on it." He looked up at the school, trying to find his sister's face in one of the windows. "Seriously, though, are you calling from class? Your teachers let you get away with that?"

"Bathroom break," she said unconcernedly.

"I'm pretty sure those are supposed to be for going to the bathroom."

"I'm *in* the bathroom. So there."

"You'd better not be peeing."

"Yuck!"

"Okay, I agree. Now you should go back to class. But before you go, can you tell me—is there any reason the school wouldn't want Lacey back? Were there problems last year?"

Ally's answer took longer than it should have. "Not *problems*, exactly. I mean... she did *not* have a stable home life, you know! She had a lot of challenges!"

Joe groaned internally. "Ally, listen to me, okay?" He paused for her to object, but she didn't, so he continued. "I'm on her side. I want to help. But I'm not going to be able to do a very good job of that if I don't have all the facts I need. Okay?"

"Yeah," she said reluctantly.

"So you should make one more call before you go back to class. Get in touch with Lacey, let her know that we're going to be having a talk this afternoon. Me and her, and you can be there if she wants. Okay?"

"Yeah. But be nice, okay? You *know* that family was a mess! Can you imagine living with them and not having some issues? I mean, it's not easy to get to school on time when your parents are passed out in the bathroom so you can't shower! And then if you *do* make it in and somebody gives you attitude for being late, maybe you'd slip up and give a bit of attitude back, right?"

"It's not going to be a trial. I'm not looking to change the past or punish anyone for it. I just need to know what we're dealing with."

"In a nice way," Ally tried.

"You bet," Joe said with enthusiasm he wasn't feeling. "So call her, *briefly*, and then get your ass back to class. And if anyone gives you attitude for talking on the phone when you said you were going to the bathroom, you had damn well better not give them any attitude back."

"You're no fun," Ally groused.

"I've got errands to run this afternoon. Pick up Austin at the end of the day, and I'll meet you at the elementary school, give you both a ride home. Okay?"

"Okay. But you should call Austin's school and let them know the plan. The new secretary over there doesn't really understand our family dynamic. I think she thought I was trying to kidnap him the last time we didn't get on the bus."

"Excellent," Joe sighed. "Okay, I'll call. Have a good last class."

He was in the truck and about to pull out of the parking lot when his phone rang again. He didn't recognize the number. "Joe Sutton," he said into the phone.

"Joe, it's Margaret Varney. We've got cattle in our hayfield." The Varneys owned the farm next door to the Suttons' place. They didn't raise cattle.

"Damn it." His mind raced, trying to find a way this wouldn't be his problem. "They're black?" he asked. There was one other cattle operation in the area, and they raised Herefords. If the cattle were red and white, they belonged to that farm. If they were Black Angus....

"They're black," Margaret confirmed. "It's not a big deal—it's the field we sell to you, anyway. Your guys are probably leaving some nice organic fertilizer behind. But that field isn't fenced, and the road's got some blind turns right around there. I wouldn't want them to get out on the road and get hit."

No, Joe wouldn't want that either. "I'm in town, but I'll be out there in twenty minutes or so. They're in your side field, the one by the maple bush?"

"That's right."

"I'm going to stop at the house and get a horse and a dog to help me round them up, so that'll add a bit of time. Less than forty-five minutes, okay?"

"I'll keep an eye on them," Margaret promised.

She was a good neighbor, lucky for Joe. Still, this was a nuisance. His errands obviously weren't going to happen that day, but he'd be back in town the next morning to drop Lacey off. Assuming that went well, he'd have time afterward. If it *didn't* go well, he supposed he'd be pretty damn busy with his threatened campaign against the school.

He got stopped by a train at the level crossing on the edge of town and pulled his phone out to call Ally. She wouldn't be getting a ride home that afternoon. He should have known better than to plan it.

Should have known better. The words played in his mind, and he tried to relate them to cattle and picking kids up after school. They had nothing to do with Mackenzie. Things with him were fine. Joe hadn't made a mistake there.

He tried to ignore the nagging voice that told him he *had* made a mistake, a huge one, and he was going to suffer for it. Every day that passed, every extra drop of affection he let fall into the already huge pond of his feelings for Mackenzie. Every drop was going to burn like acid when Mackenzie left him.

"Shut up," he growled to himself, forgetting he'd dialed the phone and was holding it to his ear.

"That's charming," Ally replied. "You called me to tell me that?"

"Sorry," Joe muttered. He needed to pull himself together. The whole world didn't need to know about his insecurities. "And why aren't you in class?"

"I was visiting! And maybe I could sense that you'd be calling me back."

"Stop visiting and get to class. I thought I'd be leaving a message. I just needed to tell you that plans have changed."

"Don't they always?" Ally replied. The attitude was close enough to Joe's own that it startled him. Was his cynicism rubbing off on his little sister, or were they both just realists who saw the world as it truly was?

But he didn't have time for philosophy; the train was almost past. "Take the bus home, okay? I'll explain later." He hung up the phone once he heard her assent and started driving as soon as the crossing gate lifted. He needed to keep moving. He'd learned that long ago, when he'd first taken responsibility for the younger members of his family. If he stayed still and let himself think, it would all start pressing down on him. The responsibilities he'd never asked for, the pressures he didn't need, the goddamned cattle in the neighbor's hayfield... it could be too much, unless he kept moving and refused to think about it. This was his life, and there was no escape, so he might as well just get on with it.

Thinking about Mackenzie made things better. Sure, Joe was up here and Mackenzie was a couple hundred miles away, living the glamorous life, but he'd come back. Joe kept his brain moving past the little voice reminding him that one of these times Mackenzie *wasn't* going to come back, because there was no point dwelling on that, either. This time, at least, Mackenzie would probably be back. Joe could just focus on that, and it made everything else a little easier to accept.

Chapter Two

"No wonder you're in such a hurry to get out of here," the makeup artist gushed. She was looking at the photo in Mackenzie's wallet: Joe sitting on top of Misery, the man grinning while the horse pinned her ears back. "He's *gorgeous*. And he's, like, a real cowboy?"

"A rancher," Mackenzie said with a nonchalant shrug. "I think technically the cowboys are the hired hands. He owns the place."

"Wow. That is *so* sexy!"

"I know. It's killing me to be down here."

"Why *are* you?" she asked with a furtive glance around them. "I mean, this isn't exactly the cover of *Vogue* we're shooting. Wouldn't you be happier up with him?"

"I would be," Mackenzie admitted. "But it's hard to make any money up there."

"So who cares? Let the rich rancher take care of you!"

Possibly Mackenzie had overstated things, or at least allowed the woman to develop a slightly exaggerated understanding of Joe's wealth. He wasn't going to correct her, though. "I want to have my *own* money," he said. "For independence, you know? I don't want to be a kept boy." He'd been that for too long, and even if he knew Joe wouldn't be an asshole about it, he refused to go back to that dynamic.

"Wow. You're stronger than I would be." She took one more

wistful look at the photograph, then turned her attention back to Mackenzie. "And you're looking pretty gorgeous yourself," she said with satisfaction. She lowered her voice to say, "It's a bit sad that we're doing a vampire shoot this long after the trend crested, but you could suck my blood anytime."

"Thanks, I guess." Mackenzie smiled at her. It *was* sad that they were doing a vampire shoot. It was sad that he'd pissed away the best years of his potential career just because Nathan didn't like him working, and it was sad that he was now too old, according to his agent, to break into the top ranks of the modeling world. Well, it hadn't just been the age, if Mackenzie was being honest with himself. Carson, his agent, had been kind, but clear: *You're a good-looking man, Mackenzie. Very, very handsome. But you're not exotic. You're not special. There are a thousand other Mackenzies out there, looking just like you do. All of you very, very handsome. I can get you catalogue work and local ad campaigns. You know the drill. It can be a career, but I'm being honest with you. I don't think you're going to the top. You're already too old for your type, to be honest. People want eighteen-year-old twinks; they don't necessarily want what they turn into ten years later.*

Carson had been talking about *advertisers* not wanting him anymore, but Mackenzie had still been tempted to pull out his wallet and flash Joe's picture in the agent's face. *Joe* wanted him. That was what mattered.

And Joe hadn't been impressed with Mackenzie's past as a kept boy. *I don't want to date someone who chooses his fucks based on the size of their bank accounts.* Sure, they'd been in the process of breaking up when Joe had said that, but that didn't mean the accusation wasn't valid. Joe looked after himself *and* every orphan and stray that wandered into his environment; he wouldn't have much respect for a grown man who couldn't even make a living. And Mackenzie wanted Joe's respect. He wanted to be Joe's partner, not just another dependent.

So he smiled at the makeup artist and glowered at the photographer, trying to look dark and dangerous in his leather wear. He wondered if any of the material came from Joe's cattle.

"Does black leather come from black cows?" he asked one of the assistants while the photographer was monkeying with his camera. She looked at him like he was insane and stepped a little further away.

It was past eight by the time the shoot ended. Mackenzie wanted to have a hot shower and then crawl into bed. Into *Joe's* bed, ideally, but that was a three-hour drive away and Mackenzie was supposed to be back on the set at ten the next morning. No Joe for him. So he'd settle for the hotel, even if he *was* slated to share a room with another model, who seemed to be channeling the vampire vibe just a little too deeply. He'd been flown in from New York and seemed to think that meant he was the star of the shoot. Hell, maybe he was. Maybe in the years that Mackenzie had been goofing off, this clown had cornered the market on "smoldering vampires who wear a lot of leather" modeling.

"You heading over?" Mackenzie asked with a friendly smile that was only a little fake. "Want to share a cab?"

The guy looked at him as if he was insane. "To the *hotel*? It's eight o'clock!" His smile was pitying. "It's a little early for bed, don't you think?"

Well, that was a good point. Mackenzie needed to get himself back on his city clock. "All right, then," he said with what dignity he could muster. "I'll see you later, I guess."

"Wait," the vampire said as Mackenzie started to turn away. His sullen expression morphed into something Mackenzie couldn't quite identify. "I thought maybe you'd show me around. I don't know Toronto very well, but it's a good-size city, right? I mean, I don't expect New-York-caliber nightlife, but there's clubs, right? Things to do, people to fuck?"

And now Mackenzie recognized the man's expression. The vampire was trying to leer at him. Mackenzie forced himself to keep a straight face. "There's both," he agreed. "I could suggest a few places to you."

"You don't want to show me?" The vampire pouted about as

well as he leered. "That's not very hospitable. I thought Canadians were friendly."

"Polite," Mackenzie corrected. "The stereotype is that Canadians are polite." And the fact that he wasn't laughing at this clown was proof he was living up to his nationality.

"Hmm... you say *polite*, but I hear *boring*." The tone was teasing, but there was a bite behind it all. "Is this because of your boyfriend? I heard you talking about him." The vampire shook his head. "Myself? I will not tolerate a possessive, controlling man." He looked Mackenzie over. "I guess once you get a bit older it's easier to accept, but I'm still young! I need to have fun! You remember what that's like, don't you?"

Mackenzie had no idea how he was letting himself get dragged into this. "Joe isn't controlling. And, yes, I remember how to have fun!"

"Yeah?" Now the vampire smiled, and it was actually a fairly attractive expression. Mackenzie had no idea why the kid didn't use it more often. "So prove it!" He wasn't flirting anymore, just playing, like a puppy darting in to nip and then dance away. Actually, the kid kind of reminded Mackenzie of Griffin when he'd been young. Skinny, with floppy hair and pointy white teeth.

"Are you going out like that?" he asked. "All the leather? The eyeliner? It's a bit...." He saw his chance for revenge. "Are people still dressing like that in New York? That look is really over up here."

The kid raised his eyebrow. "New York is all about irony. You know?"

"Nope," Mackenzie said blithely. He was too old for this nonsense, too old to be worried about what some punk kid thought about him. But there was something depressing about the thought of going back to his hotel room all alone, and so early. "We can get something to eat, if you want. Maybe downtown. There's a pretty good gay village. You'll find lots of places to have fun down there."

"And I'll persuade you to stay and have fun *with* me," the kid promised.

They were out in the suburbs and had to phone for a cab. Mackenzie almost called the whole adventure off right there. He wasn't making that much money from this shoot, and now he was going to blow some of it on cab fare downtown, spend more on a meal and at least one drink while he was down there, and then pay for cab fare right back to the burbs for his stupid hotel room. It wasn't a good idea.

But as the cab made its way down the Don Valley Parkway, his attitude started to change. By the time they got off the DVP and started working their way through the crowded streets, he was feeling energized again. The tall buildings, the crowds, the sense of being in the center of things, where anything could happen... he hadn't realized how much he'd missed it all.

He directed the cab to stop outside one of the places he'd used to go when Nathan wasn't with him. Nathan hadn't really appreciated the more alternative styling of the place, and the conceited waiters, merely annoying to most people, had enraged Nathan. He wasn't a man who'd tolerated any challenges to his own dominance. Mackenzie smiled as he thought of bringing Joe there. Joe wouldn't *love* it, maybe, but he'd be a good sport. And he'd probably think the waiters were hilarious. Joe was confident enough in himself not to let someone else's perceptions affect him.

The vampire had been looking out the window with interest, and when he turned back to Mackenzie, his eyes were bright. "Yeah," he said with satisfaction. "*This* is what I was looking for!" He jumped out of the cab like Griffin chasing a ball, and Mackenzie was left to pay the fare.

By the time he was done with that, the vampire was already posing by the window of the bar, looking for and receiving admiration. Yeah, the kid was good-looking. Mackenzie wasn't going to argue with that. But he wished Joe was there instead. Damn, *that'd* give people something to look at. Joe's shoulders alone were enough that Mackenzie could probably make back his cab fare by offering five-second looks for ten bucks a pop. And there'd be repeat customers even at that price, because five seconds really wouldn't be enough to appreciate all that soft skin and hard muscle.

But Joe probably wouldn't be a big fan of the idea. Spoilsport. Mackenzie was smiling as he pulled the door open for the vampire.

The waiter came, and Mackenzie was about to order a beer when he remembered that he'd never really liked beer when he lived in the city. He'd developed a taste for it since it was all Joe ever seemed to have in the fridge, but it wasn't his traditional preference. He'd drunk vodka martinis with Nathan, but he hadn't really loved those, either. "I'm looking for a new favorite drink," he told the waiter. "Can you bring me something I might like?"

The vampire looked horrified at Mackenzie's lack of trend sensitivity, but the server was obviously pleased to have yet another opportunity to demonstrate his superiority. And that proved to be Mackenzie's downfall.

It was a Tuesday, and one of the first really cold days of the year, so the bar wasn't as busy as usual, and apparently the servers and the bartender seized on Mackenzie's innocent question as a challenge. Instead of coming back to the table with one full-sized drink, the server brought a tray of shot glasses, each filled with a different-colored liquid. "Taste test," the server declared. "These are our top sellers. I expect you'll find something delicious in there, but if you don't, we'll keep track of what you like or don't like, and we can refine the selections for the next round."

"It's science," the vampire said approvingly.

Mackenzie tried not to think about the possibility of a next round. There were twelve shots on the tray already. They probably weren't all straight alcohol, but even if there was a lot of mix in them, his plan for a meal and an early night was fading fast. "I'm going to need some food," he said. "Something to help soak up the alcohol."

"Pasta special?" the server asked with a halfhearted wave at a chalkboard near the front of the restaurant. It was too far away for Mackenzie to read, but apparently the server had chosen to specialize on drink-seeking and wasn't interested in helping with food choices that evening.

"Okay," Mackenzie agreed.

"Carbs will make you bloat," the vampire said disapprovingly, "and we're shooting tomorrow. I don't want your big soft tummy ruining the shots."

Mackenzie had a moment of wondering what the hell was going on. How had he ended up in this bar, with this asshole, trying to find a new drink that he'd never have a chance to order when he went back to his regular life.... Then he took a cautious sip of the first drink on offer, and the moment of doubt passed. "That's delicious," he said, and then he finished the shot. "What is that?"

"I'll tell you at the end," the server said. "You should taste them all first."

"Science," the vampire said again, and Mackenzie sipped the next drink to avoid saying something he'd regret.

The second drink was tasty as well, although not quite up to the standards of the first. The server was standing there, watching Mackenzie drink and taking note of his preferences. Apparently all the drinks were supposed to be consumed at once?

"Excuse me," someone from a nearby table said, and the server and the vampire scowled him in unison.

"I'm helping this table right now," the server said, shocked by the other customer's rudeness.

The vampire just hissed, "It's *science!*"

Mackenzie took another drink, and then another. The flavors were starting to blur together, but that was okay. Apparently he wasn't quite as dedicated to pure research as the other two were. He just wanted to finish this, get his pasta, and go back to the hotel.

Round about drink number nine, his resolve started to weaken. He was getting drunk. There was no way to deny that. It seemed wasteful to consume all that alcohol and then just go back to his room and pass out. The money, the calories, the effort of coming all the way downtown—all for nothing, if all he did was finish dinner and climb back into a cab.

He finished drink ten and had almost convinced himself to extend the evening, experienced a brief moment of self-doubt when drink eleven tasted of black licorice, and then knocked back drink twelve with enthusiasm. He nodded happily. "Number one is number one," he said. "Can I have another one of those? Full size? And what was it, anyway?"

"Raspberry cosmopolitan," the waiter said as if he was imparting the wisdom of the ages.

"I'll have one too," the vampire said as he drained whatever it was he'd been drinking. He looked at Mackenzie, then grinned and looked back at the waiter. "Better make them doubles."

Mackenzie didn't object. The shots hadn't been all that big or strong, but he was definitely drunk. And after a certain point, there was no point in trying to fight against the current. Better to just let yourself be swept along and see where you ended up. He was pretty sure the night's destination wasn't going to be anywhere all *that* special, but maybe he'd at least have some fun on the way. He was two hundred miles away from the man he loved, but at least he had alcohol. And a vampire. Yeah, it was going to be one of those nights.

CHAPTER THREE

"It was one of those nights," Mackenzie said. He was standing just inside the barn, watching as Joe untacked Misery. The mare had tried to bite Mackenzie the first two times he'd gone near her, and he'd never given her a third opportunity. Joe couldn't blame the guy; he was new to horses, and trying to learn, but Angel or Devil were really more his speed.

"I still don't quite understand. You ran into the Russian guys *after* the vampire model passed out, or was he still around and talking to them?" It didn't really matter, but Joe was trying to wrap his head around it all. Mackenzie had just gotten back from the city and come up to find Joe at the barn, so this was their first chance to catch up. Except Mackenzie wasn't really all that useful when it came to figuring out how he'd been spending his time.

"I honestly have no idea. Everything after the third club is a total blur."

"And you still managed to work the next day?"

"That was the best part!" Mackenzie grinned like a little kid. "The photographer *loved* it. He said we'd looked too healthy the day before. He wanted a sort of dark, decaying look, and we were both *totally* able to give it to him."

"You got lucky," Joe said. It wasn't his place to lecture Mackenzie about any of this. The guy was a grown man and he made his own decisions. Mackenzie going on a bender hadn't hurt Joe or his family, so it really wasn't any of his business. Still, it sucked to think that Mackenzie cared about his career enough to leave Joe behind, but not enough to keep his drinking under control.

"Speaking of *getting lucky*," Mackenzie said, "You think there's any chance of a quick trip to the house? The kids are all at school, right?"

"They are," Joe agreed. There'd been no more resistance from the school when he'd dropped Lacey off the day before; everything seemed to be going smoothly, at least for the time being. He leaned his saddle against the barn wall and tugged the rope to untie Misery. He had lots to do, as always, but Mackenzie *had* been away for two nights, and Joe *had* missed him. Maybe there was time for a quick visit.

He led the mare to her pen and watched her walk straight to her favorite patch of sandy dirt. He never spent a lot of time grooming her after a ride because no matter how clean he got her or how carefully he massaged away any possible itches, this was always the first thing she did when he let her go. Her knees buckled, she lowered her muscular body to the ground, and she rolled, staying balanced on her spine for longer than any horse he'd ever known, twitching from side to side as if she was trying to erase any possible evidence of human contact from her skin.

"She looks like she's going to get stuck," Mackenzie said from surprisingly close behind Joe.

"She never has. But I put those boards along her fence, there, to make sure she doesn't get a foot caught in it."

"You take good care of her."

"She's valuable. A total bitch, but a hell of a good worker."

They watched the horse until she clambered to her feet and shook the dust off. Joe turned to go back to the barn, but Mackenzie didn't follow him. "You okay?" Joe asked.

Mackenzie's expression was strange. "I can't help noticing

that you didn't exactly leap at the 'go to the house' suggestion." His smile seemed a little forced. "I think this is the first time you've turned me down. I was just wondering whether there was a reason for it."

"I didn't turn you down," Joe protested. Sure, he hadn't thrown Mackenzie over his shoulder and sprinted for the bedroom, but there was some middle ground, surely. "I needed to look after the horse. She's not an ATV; I can't just park her and go do something else."

"The horse is taken care of," Mackenzie said calmly, "but we're still here. Not at the house."

Joe looked at Mackenzie. There *was* something wrong, he realized. A tiny bit of resentment, probably something stupid or petty, but enough that he hadn't jumped at the chance to make Mackenzie feel good. He coiled the lead rope in his hands and tried to figure out the problem, but nothing came to mind. Probably best to ignore the whole thing, he decided. So he smiled, slow and easy, and stepped closer to Mackenzie. "You seem really interested in *the house*. And we have a nice soft bed down there, no doubt. But is it really the *bed* you're interested in?"

For an awkward moment it seemed like maybe Mackenzie really *was* interested in just the bed, like he'd been planning a nap and Joe had twisted it all into some sexual innuendo. But then he raised his eyebrows and looked around slowly. "Where'd you have in mind, cowboy?"

"*Not* a roll in the hay," Joe said quickly. "That's really itchy. And it's kinda cold out here. How about... blowjobs in the feed room?"

"Sexy?" Mackenzie said, his voice laced with doubt.

"Focus on the blowjob part," Joe recommended.

Mackenzie nodded slowly. "Yeah, that helps. Okay, I'm up for it." He stepped aside and waited for Joe to precede him into the barn.

But Joe didn't move right away. Instead, he waited, watching

Mackenzie, then said, "You have no idea where the feed room is, do you?"

"There's a couple rooms in there," Mackenzie said defensively. "It's hard to keep them straight."

"One's filled with tack," Joe said. "That's not the feed room. One's got nesting boxes for the chickens in it. Also not the feed room. *One* room is filled with different feeds." He waited for Mackenzie to draw his own conclusions.

"Is there a 'kiss my ass' room? 'Cause I think that's the one we should be heading for."

"I'll kiss your ass in any room you want," Joe promised.

"Except for the bedroom, apparently."

They weren't really squabbling, but there was more of an edge to their teasing than they usually had. Joe wasn't sure whether it was coming from him, from Mackenzie, or from some weird combination of the two. But he knew he didn't like it. So he held out his hand. Mackenzie looked at it doubtfully but then stretched out and wrapped his fingers through Joe's. Joe stepped closer and reached for the other hand, then focused on Mackenzie's face. He'd been away for almost three full days. He'd been working hard, apparently, although Joe still wasn't quite sure what the hell models did all day that could be that tiring. He'd spent one day hungover, one night on a friend's sofa, and then he'd come back to a smelly barn and a grumpy boyfriend. That would suck. Joe kissed him gently. "Let's go to the house," he said. "I can shower off some farm smell, we can go to bed, maybe eat something before I come back out...."

Joe could feel the tension draining out of Mackenzie's body.

"I was kinda looking forward to the feed room," Mackenzie said with a mischievous grin. "But maybe something more than blowjobs?"

"There's no lube up here. And are we still okay for no condoms?"

The stunned look on Mackenzie's face had to be a pretty good mirror of Joe's own expression. He hadn't known he was going to say that. Hadn't even known he was thinking it.

"I mean...," Joe started, and then he stopped. He let go of Mackenzie's hands and took a big step backward. What the hell *did* he mean? "I know we're together. Up here. Just us. But... I don't know; it's different when you're away, maybe. You're back with your old friends, you're in clubs, it's a different vibe. Right? I just...."

"That'd be okay with you?" Mackenzie asked. His tone was unreadable.

"Okay? Not... not *okay*, no. It's not what I want. But if it's what I have to accept, I guess I could. If I have to. But I'd want to know." He frowned, then hastened to add, "Not details! But I'd want to know in general terms. Not just because of diseases or whatever, but because...." Another frown as he tried to figure this out.

"So you could do the same," Mackenzie suggested. He still wasn't giving any clues about his feelings on this topic.

"No," Joe said. He was pretty sure that was true. He didn't want an open relationship, didn't want to fool around with some other guy. He'd been terrified of coming this far in the relationship, but he'd made it and he wasn't interested in taking any steps backward. But if it was what Mackenzie wanted.... "I guess I just wouldn't want to be the stupid one. I'd want to know just... just to know."

Mackenzie's expression was becoming clearer now, and Joe wished it would go back to being unreadable. "I was with Nathan for more than *five years*, and I never cheated on him! I have never given you a single reason not to trust me! You honestly think I'd fuck around just because I was away for a couple nights? You think I'm such a slut that I couldn't control myself if I went to a few clubs?"

"You were so drunk you can't remember how the night ended! You told me that five minutes ago! I mean, if you were so in control of yourself, how'd you end up getting so wrecked the night before a big day of work?"

"You think every time I get drunk I fool around with the first guy I see?"

"Not the *first* one, maybe." Okay, that hadn't come out quite right. "Fuck, Mackenzie, I just *asked*. If you say nothing happened, I believe you. It just seemed like the sort of situation where something *might* have happened, and I wasn't sure we'd ever really had a conversation about it, so... I guess I just wondered. That's all."

"Because we hadn't had a conversation about it?" Mackenzie's outrage seemed to be growing with each attempt Joe made to explain. "You know what? We haven't had conversations about *lots* of things! We've never explicitly said that I shouldn't pour bleach down your throat when you're asleep, but that doesn't mean I'm going to do it!"

"Okay, I think having sex with someone is a *bit* more tempting than killing me with bleach. Jesus, Mackenzie, that was the first thing that popped into your head?"

Mackenzie huffed out an exasperated puff of air. "Okay, yes, that was a strange example. But, seriously? If I'd gone down there and fucked around for two nights and come back up here, that would have been okay with you? I mean...." He looked like he knew he shouldn't say the next part, but then he decided to say it anyway. "Nathan would have kicked me out for even thinking about it. But you're just all casual—"

"No," Joe said quickly. "Not casual. And it wouldn't have been okay. But, I guess... I guess if it came down to having you on those terms or not having you at all, I'd take you on those terms. You know?"

And now Mackenzie's expression was back to being unreadable. Finally, he stepped forward and reached for Joe's hand. "You're an idiot," he said as he tentatively entwined his fingers with Joe's. "And I forget that sometimes. I think that just because I'm crazy about you, and just because I tell everyone I know how crazy I am about you, and just because it's sickeningly obvious to anyone with eyes that I'm completely crazy about you... I think you might actually see that yourself. Silly me."

Joe didn't really want to argue on this one. "Sometimes I need things spelled out for me," he admitted.

Mackenzie nodded, then stretched up to give Joe a gentle kiss. "First letter is I." He stepped back far enough to get a good view of Joe's expression. "Second letter is L." He was still watching Joe closely, as if expecting him to bolt. "Then O," he whispered.

Joe was frozen. Things were happening too fast. Well, not in general. He'd been thinking about saying what he was pretty sure Mackenzie was saying. Thinking about it for a while. But ten seconds ago they'd been fighting, and now this? He was a bit dizzy, but he wasn't sure that was a problem. "V?" he asked.

Mackenzie nodded with a relieved smile. "V," he confirmed. Then, "E," followed by a kiss, and then a grin as he said, "U. Because I don't want to waste any more time spelling when my lips could be used for much better purposes."

And that, at least, was an area where Joe knew what he was doing. It was familiar now, kissing Mackenzie, but still special. The thrill of the unknown had been replaced with the comfort of familiarity: Joe knew how Mackenzie liked to be kissed, knew how to touch him to make his breath catch and his body shudder with pleasure he didn't even try to control. When Joe eased his hand inside Mackenzie's jacket, then under his shirt to find the warm skin beneath, he felt Mackenzie's body tensing in anticipation.

"Maybe I'm not going to," Joe teased. "Maybe this time I won't."

"Right," Mackenzie gasped, his head thrown back to give Joe's lips access to his neck. "You found my on switch. You know you're going to use it."

"It's only *one* of your switches," Joe said with a grin, and he nipped Mackenzie's earlobe, another spot that always got a response.

Mackenzie gasped and dug his fingers into Joe's back. When Joe followed with a hard tweak of Mackenzie's nipple, Mackenzie turned his fingers into claws, both of them dealing pain and pleasure to the other.

The earlier negotiations about location seemed ridiculous now. There was no way they were going to make it down to the house. Even the feed room was too far away. They were already rutting against each other through their jeans, Mackenzie pulling Joe's hips in harder with every stroke. Joe managed to work his hands between them to get both of their flies undone, and Mackenzie wrapped his fingers in Joe's hair, pulling his head in for another long, sloppy kiss. "Fuck me," he whined, his words halfway between an order and a plea.

Fuck, yeah. "Get me wet," Joe said, gently pushing on Mackenzie's shoulders. He felt Mackenzie easing his pants and underwear down, then staggered a little as Mackenzie enveloped his cock with his perfect lips. But instead of one of Mackenzie's traditional and greatly appreciated cock-worshipping sessions, this was quick, almost cursory, clearly more focused on spreading spit than creating pleasure. Which was just fine, because Joe was as eager as Mackenzie to get to the next part of their plans.

Mackenzie shrugged his pants down as he straightened, turning an ass that was already developing goose bumps in Joe's direction. He arched his back, presenting a target he knew was irresistible, and Joe let his hands rest on the two perfect mounds of muscle. Then he dug his thumbs in a little, spreading and massaging and tantalizing himself. Mackenzie looked back over his shoulder, his eyes hungry and demanding, his lips parted in a perfect, perpetual gasp.

Joe leaned forward, easing his cock into the crack of Mackenzie's ass and working it toward its target. He added a little more spit and eased in, watching Mackenzie's face closely. There was no sign of anything but pleasure, and Joe let himself relax, let the glorious pressure and friction register. He bottomed out and kissed Mackenzie, both of them distracted by other stimuli but still connected, still together.

"Fuck me," Mackenzie whispered. "Come on, Joe...."

There were times when Joe liked to hold off as long as he could, teasing and torturing, but this wasn't one of those times. He pulled out, drove in, felt Mackenzie's body reacting and pushing for more. Mackenzie's gasps and words of encouragement were as exciting as the physical sensations, and Joe let himself gorge on them, his endless hunger never sated. By the time Mackenzie stopped using words and was just repeating Joe's name on an endless, beautiful loop, Joe's own body was aching for release. He could feel his climax building but refused to give in. He wanted to come, but not yet, not yet, not yet....

Mackenzie shuddered, his voice became a long, syncopated moan, and Joe let himself go. He kept moving as he came, his cock gliding more smoothly with the extra lubrication, thrusting and filling and laying claim.

They rested together, Joe still inside, kissing lazily over Mackenzie's shoulder.

"I missed you," Mackenzie finally whispered.

"I missed you too." Joe was scared of the next part, but he knew he wanted to say it. "And I love you."

Mackenzie smiled at him. "Damn right you do. I'm awesome."

"Yeah, you're okay," Joe agreed, and they stayed like that until the cold wind reminded them that they needed to get dressed.

Chapter Four

"Where's my daddy?" Austin asked, taking a break from building a tower with his mashed potatoes. He was looking at Joe, of course, his trusted source for all questions, and Joe was staring back at him like a deer in the headlights.

"Who do you mean, buddy?" Joe finally asked, and he'd managed to make his voice level and calm. "You've got a lot of people who kind of split that job up. Can you use a name? Who are you looking for?"

Austin looked impatient. "My *daddy*," he repeated. Then he looked around the table. "Lacey and Vannah's daddy is in heaven. Ally's daddy is in heaven. Where's *my* daddy?"

"Toronto," Joe said simply.

"Practically the same thing, really," Mackenzie suggested, but Joe just made a face at him and then turned back to Austin.

"Like I said, you have lots of people who act like daddies. Lots of people who help take care of you and love you. But technically, Nick's your father."

"Nick?" Austin looked confused. "The one who visits?"

"Yup," Ally said, jumping in happily. "It just shows how *technical* titles aren't really all that important, you know? Technically, Nick's your daddy, but really Joe or Will or even Mackenzie do a lot more to look after you, right?"

Austin nodded.

"Some might say *Griffin* does more to look after you," Ally continued, her tone sweet.

"Ally," Joe warned.

"Griffin saved him from a blue jay this afternoon," Ally responded. "That's more than—"

"Ally!" Joe said. His voice wasn't loud, but there was a tone in it that demanded respect. He waited a moment to be sure she was done, then turned to Austin. "Was a blue jay being mean to you? Do you want to tell us what happened?"

Austin certainly did, with much hand waving and excitement. It was an absolutely epic tale, especially when Savannah joined in with her own version of events. Joe watched the kids, and Mackenzie watched Joe. He was so good with them: patient, affectionate, supportive without being overprotective. He was a perfect father to this brood, only two of whom shared any blood at all with him. It made Mackenzie want to see Joe with a baby, someone of uncomplicated parentage who could just be Joe's kid, not his sister or his nephew or an orphan he was taking care of. Instead of adoption, maybe he and Joe should look for a surrogate. Mackenzie didn't have a strong urge to see his own genes replicated, but Joe's? Yeah, Joe should definitely reproduce.

Possibly Mackenzie was getting a little ahead of himself. But they loved each other. They'd said it, and they'd meant it. It had only been a few days, but things had been perfect since then. Joe was busy, sure, but when he was with Mackenzie he was really *with* him, focused and attentive and loving. It was important not to rush things, especially with someone as skittish as Joe, so Mackenzie would keep his little dreams to himself, at least for a while. It wasn't like he needed something to distract himself from reality, anyway. Reality was pretty damned sweet.

Especially when Joe asked Ally and Lacey what their plans were for the evening. It was Friday night, after all. But they smiled at him, and Ally said, "We're going to stick around here. Cally and Jen might come over to watch movies. Is that okay?"

"No big plans? No parties?"

"Nope," Lacey said. "And we can watch something G-rated until the little guys go to bed."

"Which means you're off duty for the night," Mackenzie said to Joe. It hadn't been hard to persuade Ally and Lacey to babysit, but Mackenzie was still proud of his achievement. "I was thinking we could go out."

"Out?" Joe asked. He sounded genuinely perplexed.

"Out," Mackenzie said in what he hoped was an encouraging tone. "We could have drinks, hear some music... you could catch up with some old friends, if you have any...."

"He doesn't," Ally said. "No friends. Everybody likes Joe, but he hasn't got any friends. It's a paradox."

"Shut up, Ally," Joe said.

"Maybe it's because he's kind of rude," Ally suggested. "Even to those closest to him."

"We could go over to Darton and see a movie, if you don't feel up to conversation. Maybe get dessert afterward." It was a bit sad that this was what passed for a big night out in Mackenzie's new life, but he'd be with Joe, so he'd be happy.

"They're watching movies *here*," Joe said, apparently still resisting the *out* part of Mackenzie's plans. "We have dessert *here*."

"Joe," Mackenzie said with as much calm as he could muster. "I'd like us to go out tonight. Away from the house. Together. Are you really going to turn down a request that reasonable?"

Joe paused as if considering his options, then seemed to accept that he really didn't have any. "No," he said. "I'm not." Another pause, and then he said, "Thank you for thinking of this. I'm sure it'll be fun." He sounded a little robotic, but at least he was making an effort.

"It will be," Mackenzie confirmed. "Now go get pretty and we'll be on our way."

Joe gave him another look, then stretched, his long arms covering almost the entire length of the table, his shirt riding up a little to give just a peek of his washboard stomach, his chest stretching its buttons almost to the popping point. "This is as pretty as I get," he said. "I'm ready to go whenever you are."

Mackenzie's mouth was a little dry. "I should go clean up," he managed to squeak.

"You look good," Joe said firmly.

"I can look better." But he didn't move, frozen by the intensity of Joe's gaze.

"Too much better and I won't be able to stand it," Joe said quietly.

"Stand what?" Austin asked.

Joe grinned at him, then stood and scooped the boy out of his chair. "Stand *up*," he said, and he lifted the boy above his head. "Way up!"

"Ceiling!" Austin crowed, and he stretched up to brush his fingers along the surface.

"Get the cobwebs, buddy. Clean them up!"

Austin squinted around and pointed to a corner. Mackenzie was pretty sure there was nothing there, but Joe played along, carried the boy over, and let him grab at the imaginary filaments.

Then Joe dropped the boy, catching him when he was at about eye level. "Mack and I are going to go out tonight. Do you want Ally to help you with your bath, do you want to have a shower on your own, or do you want to go to bed *dirty*?"

Austin looked thoughtfully in Ally's direction.

"We can play with the zoo," Ally promised.

"Ally!" Austin crowed.

"Easy choice, when there's a zoo involved." Joe rested the boy on his hip and looked at Mackenzie. "Okay, then. You ready?"

"Yeah," Mackenzie said. He stood up and looked at the older girls. "Thanks, guys," he said.

"Have fun," Lacey said. She rested her arm on her sister's shoulders. "My slave and I will take care of the dishes."

"I'm not your slave!" Savannah said fiercely, pushing Lacey's arm off, and Mackenzie watched as Joe resolutely turned his back. The girls squabbled a lot, and Joe seemed to ignore all of it.

Mackenzie had no idea if that was a good plan or not, but he certainly wasn't going to challenge it. So he walked over to Joe's side and kissed Austin on the temple. "Thank you for letting me borrow Joe," he said quietly.

Austin thought for a moment, then said, "'Borrow' means you give him back."

"I could never keep him away," Mackenzie promised. "And I'd never want to."

He was treated to one of Austin's patented 'can I trust you?' stares, followed by a bright grin. "We can share!"

"Fantastic idea," Mackenzie agreed. "That'll make us both happy."

"And make *me* happy," Joe agreed. "Now, we should get out of here before someone develops diabetes."

Austin gave him a curious look. "Diabetes?"

"It's a disease. People get it from...." Joe caught himself and looked almost guiltily in Ally's direction. Her passion for fact-checking generally seemed to focus on Joe's statements. "Well, I guess I don't really *know* why people get it. But we say it's from eating too many sweet things. So when you said something sweet, and Mack said something sweet, and then *I* said something sweet...."

"But we weren't *eating* the sweet things," Austin said, still trying to figure it out.

"I was being silly," Joe replied, and Austin smiled, satisfied with the answer. He was pretty used to Joe being silly.

Griffin disentangled himself from the pack of dogs waiting for table scraps and bounced over to join Mackenzie on whatever adventure he was planning. Joe set Austin down next to him. "Have you thanked Griffin for the blue-jay save?" Joe asked.

Austin threw his arms around the dog's neck, and Joe nudged Mackenzie toward the door. Griffin stared after them longingly but didn't budge, too aware of the fragile human currently attached to him.

"Good dog," Mackenzie said softly.

"See you, Austin," Joe said at almost the same time. Then he raised an arm to the crowd in the kitchen, grabbed his jacket, and was out the door.

Mackenzie followed suit. "I think we got away clean."

"I'll believe you when we're off the property." Joe headed for the truck, but Mackenzie didn't follow him and Joe turned around. "What?"

"*My* car," Mackenzie replied. "This is my night. So I'm driving, and I'm paying."

Joe raised an eyebrow. "Big talk. Do you have any idea how to get anywhere?"

"The role of navigator is an important one," Mackenzie said archly. "It allows the captain of the vessel to focus his attention on the tricky technical requirements." He walked to the secondhand Toyota he'd been driving since Nathan had canceled the lease on his regular car. It wasn't the sort of statement vehicle Mackenzie would have liked to be in, but it ran well, and that had to count for something.

Joe followed him obediently and wedged himself into the passenger seat. Mackenzie glanced at him as they headed down the long driveway. "I don't get it," Mackenzie said. "You aren't that much bigger than me. How do you take up so much space? How can you look so totally cramped when I fit in without any problems?"

Joe wiggled a little. "I'm not cramped. I'm fine."

"It's the shoulders," Mackenzie decided after another quick look. "There's room for your height. But you can't really fit in side-to-side."

"I am usually happiest on a bench seat," Joe confessed. "But this won't kill me. You'll just have to massage out any kinks, okay?"

"Absolutely."

They drove over to Darton and chose a comedy to watch, bought popcorn, and had a normal night out. Sure, Mackenzie's friends in the city would have thought it was hopelessly mundane, but Mackenzie was surprised by how little he cared about that. He didn't need to be unique, didn't need to do special things in order to *be* special. He was with Joe, and that made him as special as he could ever want to be.

They were walking down the sidewalk toward the car, and Mackenzie grabbed Joe's hand and leaned over to give him a quick peck on the cheek. "Thanks for my night out," he said softly.

They both jumped a little when they heard the loud voice from not far behind them. "Fucking faggots," a man said, his disgust clear.

Joe kept looking straight ahead and didn't let go of Mackenzie's hand. Mackenzie followed his lead, resisting the urge to either run or turn around and respond.

"Shouldn't be allowed out in public," a different voice said. Great, there was more than one of them. But the car was just ahead, and Mackenzie and Joe would be safe once they reached it.

Mackenzie forced himself to keep his stride even, but he almost balked when they got a few steps away from the car and Joe quietly said, "Keep going."

What the hell? Why weren't they getting in the car and getting the hell out of there? But this was Joe's environment, and maybe he had a secret plan.

There was an all-night convenience store and gas station on the corner, and Joe led Mackenzie to it. As they crossed the tarmac by the gas pumps, Mackenzie saw the shadows of the men following them, lit from behind by an overhead security light. Four of them. And they took the same turn Joe and Mackenzie had.

And when Joe stopped just under the canopy of the pumps, the shadows stopped as well. Joe turned, his face calm, and Mackenzie found his view of the four men mostly blocked by a pair of broad shoulders. "Call the cops," Joe said quietly over his shoulder. "We're at the corner of Fourth and Dawson."

That was the first sign of sanity Joe had displayed since any of this started, and Mackenzie hurried to comply. But why weren't they hiding inside the store? Mackenzie stared at the men as he waited for the call to connect. They weren't all that big or all that tough-looking, really. Just farm boys looking for a little fun. Mackenzie looked at Joe, then heard the operator's voice and started talking. "We're at Fourth and Dawson in Darton, and some assholes are harassing us. They followed us down the street and now they're staring us down. We need cops, now…. No, I don't want to give you my name. They can hear what I'm saying, and I don't want them to know my name."

"Joe Sutton," Joe said, loud and clear. Jesus, what the hell was Joe doing? He stared at one of the men and said, "You look like a Wallace. Are you Steve Wallace's little brother?"

There was a glimmer of reaction from the man, and Mackenzie started to see some hope. It was all about community in the country: who people knew, the history and the complicated web of relationships. Joe was going to use that to get them out of this mess. But Mackenzie's hope was dashed when Joe added, "Yeah, Steve's an asshole too. He was always too much of a pussy to do anything about it, though. I figure you're the same way."

"Get them here *fast*," Mackenzie yelped into the phone. Joe was trying to get them killed.

"What the fuck?" Steve Wallace's brother said, and Mackenzie had to agree with the sentiment. "Are you calling me out?"

"You swear at us, follow us here, and do your little stand-off bullshit, and you think *I'm* calling *you* out?" Joe shook his head in amazement at the man's idiocy. "The cops are on the way. You can stick around and explain yourselves to them, you can pussy-walk out of here, or you can come at me. I honestly don't see any other options."

"We could all just talk it over," Mackenzie tried, but no one seemed to be paying attention to him.

"You're calling me a pussy?" the brother asked, stepping a little closer.

Joe half turned in Mackenzie's direction, but he didn't take his eyes off the other men. "You should go inside, get them to lock the door."

"No way," Mackenzie said. He'd never been in a fight in his life, but he couldn't just leave Joe alone in his idiocy. "Come with me."

"Four on two," Joe mused, clearly not talking to Mackenzie. "Yeah, that's a pussy move. Someone with some balls would go for a fair fight. You'd still be ignorant bigots, but at least you wouldn't be cowards. But four on two? Four on two is four pussies, for sure."

And that was it for one of the men who hadn't spoken yet. He charged forward, fists raised, and yelled, "Fuck—"

That was as far as he got. Mackenzie wasn't quite sure what happened, but there was a blur of movement, and then Joe's hand was shooting forward into the attacker's jaw, Joe's foot was striking at the man's leg, and as the man crumbled, Joe's knee met his nose with a sickening crunch. Joe danced backward to stand in front of Mackenzie again, and the attacker rolled on the ground, trying to stop the blood gushing from his face.

"Holy fuck!" Steve Wallace's brother yelled. "You fucking psycho!"

"That's right," Joe said, his voice calm. Mackenzie wanted to look at Joe's face but was afraid of what he'd see. Could any sane person act the way Joe was?

Five heads turned a little as the sound of sirens drifted through the crisp air. Joe was the only one who didn't react. "Police will be here soon," Mackenzie said, trying desperately to sound reasonable. "You probably don't want to be around anymore."

The man with the broken nose staggered to his feet. The other three stared at Joe, then one of them broke and stepped backward. "We need to get out of here," he said. He sounded as freaked out as Mackenzie felt.

The others followed his lead, scurrying out of the parking lot like cockroaches fleeing the light. One of them yelled back, "You fucking psycho fag!" And Joe actually laughed.

"What the fuck, Joe?" Mackenzie gasped. "Why did that just happen? Why didn't we get in the fucking car?"

Joe frowned at him as if genuinely confused. "Why should we? Why should *we* run away from *them*?"

"Because there were four of them? Because they might have had weapons? Because they might have all attacked at once, and I'm sorry, Joe, but I am *not* a fighter! I would have helped if I could, but seriously...."

"Then they would have gone to jail," Joe said calmly. He pointed up at the canopy over their heads. "Security camera. Gas stations always record people buying gas at self-serve pumps."

"They would have gone to jail," Mackenzie repeated numbly. "But we would have been in the hospital. Or the morgue!"

"I told you to go inside," Joe said. "I didn't make that decision for you."

"But why did you make it for *you*?" The sirens were loud, now, the police almost there, but Mackenzie wanted this answered before they arrived.

Joe frowned at him. "Because I live here," he said, his quiet voice almost lost in the wail of the sirens. "Because if I ran away from them this time, they'd do it again, and again." He shook his head. "No way. I won't live like that."

Mackenzie wasn't sure whether to admire Joe's courage or be appalled at his recklessness. But not quite reckless... he'd had the presence of mind to walk to the gas bar and stand inside the camera's range.

The police arrived then and were at least some distraction from the questions racing through Mackenzie's mind. He didn't complain when one of the officers led him away from Joe to take his statement, and as he ran through the events for her, he thought about them himself. What would have happened if they'd stopped walking at the car? If they'd gone right inside the store? More chillingly, what would have happened if all four men had attacked at once?

Joe seemed to know the officer taking his statement. Apparently there were different volunteer fire departments for different towns, but just one police detachment for the whole county; Joe must have met most of the cops at different fire or accident scenes over the years. The reminder of Joe's history made things a bit easier to understand, maybe. Joe was used to making fast decisions and behaving calmly in the face of danger.

By the time the police had finished with their questions and collected a copy of the video surveillance, Mackenzie's adrenaline had worn off and he was exhausted. Joe approached him a little warily, but Mackenzie was too tired to worry about any of it. This was Joe. Joe would take care of him. He tucked himself in against Joe's shoulder and started walking toward the car.

"It was my fault," he said when they got there. He walked around to the driver's side, leaving Joe standing on the curb. "Because I kissed you. This never would have happened if I hadn't held your hand and kissed you."

Joe nodded slowly. "Yeah. That's how they get you. It's your fault for doing something simple and natural, not theirs for being violent, bigoted assholes. And if I'd gotten beat up, that would have been my fault for standing up to them, not their fault for being violent, bigoted assholes. You seeing a trend here?"

"They're violent, bigoted assholes," Mackenzie agreed. "But I know people like that are out there. If I don't take steps to protect myself against them, then how can I say it's not my fault if I get picked on?"

"You can fight back," Joe said. He leaned on the roof of the car and stared intently at Mackenzie. "You can make them think twice before they pick on a gay couple again, because maybe it'll be another psycho fag."

Mackenzie sighed. It sounded so reasonable now, but he could still remember the metallic taste of fear, the dizzying panic of not knowing what was going on or who was going to get hurt. "Did you break that guy's nose?"

"Yeah," Joe said simply.

"Have you done that before? I mean, you seemed pretty good at it."

Joe made a face. "Yeah. I don't like to... I'm not a kid anymore, you know? And I hear what you're saying: they *could* have had weapons, or they could have all jumped us at once. I get it. I just hate running away. It's what they expect."

"They'd think you were a pussy," Mackenzie said, and then, despite himself, he giggled. "My God, Joe, I've never heard anyone use that word more often in a row! 'Four on two is four pussies,'" he mimicked. "I'm going to tell Ally you were using that word as an insult. I'm pretty sure it's sexist."

"Don't tell Ally," Joe said seriously. "She'll get upset."

"How much of this stuff do you keep from them? Ally said it tonight... 'everybody likes Joe.' Does she honestly think that's true? Because you don't tell her about stuff like this?"

"I'm not going to tell my baby sister about somebody calling me a fag and wanting to beat me up. No way."

"So it's happened before."

"Jesus, Mackenzie, of course it's happened before. And don't even pretend it hasn't happened to you, because Toronto *isn't* heaven. I've been there, and I know there's just as many assholes down there as up here."

"It's happened," Mackenzie admitted. "But not often." He thought for a moment, then admitted, "I guess I hardly ever left the gay village."

"And I hardly ever leave the farm," Joe said with a smile. "We've both got safe homes."

"We shouldn't have to hide."

"Yeah. That's why I didn't get in the car or go in the store."

"Yeah." Mackenzie frowned thoughtfully. "Yeah. Okay. I get it. Hey, you think you could show me some moves? Make *me* a psycho fag too?"

"You're too pretty," Joe said. "I don't want anyone messing up that face."

"I'll mess *them* up." Possibly Mackenzie was getting a little carried away, but it was fun to play, especially after all the tension.

"Okay, tough guy," Joe said patiently. "Now will you get in the car? We should go home."

"You want to drive? I'm sleepy."

"What happened to your 'my night, my car' rule?" Joe asked, but he was walking around the hood as he talked.

"I got sleepy," Mackenzie said. It was the only explanation he needed, although it probably wasn't the entire reason he wanted Joe to take charge of their travel. He waited until Joe took the keys, then turned to go and found his hand caught by warm, gentle fingers. He turned back slowly.

"I'm sorry your night got wrecked," Joe said.

Mackenzie shook his head. "It wasn't wrecked. A bit more excitement than I expected, but not wrecked."

Joe looked at him for a long moment as if gauging the truthfulness of his words, then said, "I love you, Mackenzie." His kiss was sweet.

"I love you too," Mackenzie said when his lips were free. "Now drive me home so we can go to bed and *sleep*."

"Yes, sir," Joe said.

Mackenzie climbed into the passenger seat and buckled himself in, then turned his head so he was looking at Joe. He felt his eyes drifting shut and let sleep come to him. It had been a strange end to the night, but it was all over now, and he was safe and warm and loved. In the morning, he was probably going to think about the whole thing some more, and maybe he wouldn't like what he came up with. But for the time being, he was content.

CHAPTER FIVE

"THEY FIGHT a lot," Joe admitted. Jean Carpenter, the social worker looking after the Walton girls, nodded sympathetically, but Joe still felt like a complainer. It wasn't like the Suttons were a tension-free family, after all. But at least it seemed like Sutton fights were generally *about* something. And they didn't have the bitter edge that the Waltons had developed. "A lot of name calling. Like, pretty mean names. *Slut*, and *bitch*, and stuff like that."

"And how have you been responding?" Jean rested her elbows on the kitchen table and waited patiently for an answer.

"I tell them to watch their language, especially if Austin's around. That's about it." Damn, that didn't sound like enough. He should have done something more, found some way to make the girls gentler with each other. "I thought if I ignored it, it would go away," he said, but it sounded like a lame justification. "Or that I needed to give them time to adjust to a new way of doing things. I didn't want to slam them with a bunch of new rules when they're still getting used to so many other new things."

Jean smiled at him, and the expression seemed genuine. "Those are great instincts. But you can't forget about taking care of yourself and your family too. Kids who are raised in a household with a lot of anger develop a sort of immunity to it. Like kids of smokers who can't smell the stale smoke in their clothes. You and your family don't have that immunity, and it's probably really stressful for you to be dealing with it."

"They've both been good with us," Joe hastened to add. "It's just with each other that they get mean."

"I'm going to mention it to them on the ride," Jean said, "and I can almost guarantee that they won't have any idea what I'm talking about. For them, it's just how you talk to family. They've learned they can't talk that way to other people—school has socialized them that well, at least. But with each other...." She made a face. "That's the default. Doesn't mean they can't learn to behave differently, but it'll probably take some work, on their part and on yours." Another face before she added, "And I know you've already got a lot on your plate."

"So do they," Joe said. He was torn. If it was just him, he could deal with it. A bit of negativity wasn't the end of the world. But he didn't want Austin growing up around that, didn't want the little man's meanness detectors burnt out the way the girls' had been. "If they could learn to dial it down, at least...."

"They can. And, Joe, don't think that it means they don't love each other. This family... these girls... that's their biggest strength. Lacey's been looking after the little ones her whole life, and they know it. They've been insistent on staying together. One of the most compelling reasons they had for wanting to move back up here was wanting to be near Kami."

Joe tried to control his expression and sound casual as he asked, "And how's she doing?" How was she dealing with the effects of his mistakes? Had the few extra seconds he'd taken to get her out of the house completely destroyed her brain?

"Quite well," Jean said, but Joe knew it was a relative term. "She's settling in to the new facility. Getting a good start on the therapies. And she's always happy to see her sisters. I was hoping to talk to you about getting them over there more than once a week. I know it's a bit of a drive, but I think Lacey's comfortable enough that she could be in charge of things, if you were able to give her access to a vehicle to get there."

"Yeah, for sure," Joe said. "She can take my truck, anytime. I mean, I might need it for the farm, but if she gives me warning I can work around it."

"Excellent," Jean said with a smile. "And there's one more thing. I wouldn't normally ask, but given where you live... I know you care about animals...." She stopped and looked at him as if he was supposed to guess what she was hinting at.

"I'm going to need more words on this one."

"Jasper," she said. "Their dog, from before. Apparently he was living at the vet's for a while, then taken to the shelter when their aunt wouldn't take him. He hasn't been adopted yet, and they're worried about him."

"The dog?" Joe remembered the animal. He'd grabbed it while he was carrying Kami out of the fire. If he hadn't taken that second, maybe she would have inhaled less smoke or gotten oxygen sooner. But that was Joe's fault, not the dog's. "Yeah, of course. He can live here." He tried to remember the animal's size, but the adrenaline that had been coursing through his body at that stage of the fire had made everything seem light and small. "Is he healthy?"

Jean grinned. "Apparently they were a bit concerned about brain damage, and he was acting a bit goofy, but the girls tell me he's always been like that."

"Why wouldn't they have told me this themselves? We've got four dogs on the place already. A fifth isn't going to be a big deal, as long as we can convince Red to let him live. They could have just asked."

"They're pretty aware of everything you're already doing for them," Jean said carefully. "I think they're a little worried about asking for any more favors."

Shit. Another failure on Joe's part. "I need to make them more comfortable. They can talk to me about stuff. They can ask for things!"

"I think they know that, intellectually. They just aren't quite ready for it yet, not with things that feel like luxuries. If you and I keep talking, we can keep each other in the loop. You can tell me if they're having troubles, I can tell you if they need something and are worried about asking. It'll be a good system."

"And you're sticking around? You're going to be on the job for a while?"

"The girls are provincial wards. You're their legal guardian, but the province still has final say. I'll phase myself out once they get established here, but unless you go through the formal adoption process, they'll remain the responsibility of the government and we'll keep checking in on them."

"And if I did adopt them?" It wasn't something Joe had given a lot of thought to, but maybe it was time he started. Lacey was almost an adult, but Savannah was only nine. She deserved a real family, somewhere she knew she belonged.

But Jean didn't look enthusiastic. "I wouldn't advise that you rush that. See how things work for you and the family. Financially, for sure, it makes sense to keep them as foster care. Even for Lacey, the government will pay for her education costs if you can manage to get her into some sort of postsecondary program. We wouldn't do that if she was adopted."

"I'm working hard just to get her to stay in high school," Joe said. It was true. The girl was turning eighteen in a couple months, and once that happened she'd be legally able to drop out and get a full-time job. Joe was pretty sure she was working on her résumé more than her homework.

"I'll try to help with that," Jean said. She pushed her wooden chair back from the table and heaved herself to her feet. "I'm glad the girls are here, Joe. It's the best place for them. And if you can find space for the dog, that'd be even better. Lend the truck to Lacey for visits to Kami, and you qualify for full herohood."

"Let's not get carried away," Joe said.

"You're a good man, Joe Sutton. Sorry if you don't want to hear it, but I'm afraid it's true."

"I'll call the girls," he said, and he headed for the base of the stairs.

Ally and Austin came down with the girls, and after they left with the social worker, Ally stayed in the kitchen, looking at Joe expectantly. He ignored her on principle, saying only, "Can you watch Austin for a couple hours?"

She said, "Oh, are you going out?"

"Thought I might." He considered it. "Actually, Austin can come. You want to go for a car ride, buddy?"

Much to Ally's obvious annoyance, Austin didn't ask where Joe was going, just trotted to the mudroom to start putting his boots on. Joe followed and bent to help him, aware of Ally hovering in the background. Austin was completely ready and Joe was reaching for his own jacket when Ally finally said, "If you happen to be going to the animal shelter... I could come. Make sure you get the right one."

He didn't look at her, annoyed that she knew him so well. And annoyed that she'd known Jean was going to tell him about the abandoned animal but hadn't thought to give him a heads-up herself. "How many dogs named Jasper do you think they have?"

"I don't know. Sure would be funny if there were two."

He stepped to the side, making room for her in the doorway, and she practically sprinted toward him, then skidded to a stop in front of the coatrack. "This is so cool," she said as she tugged the boots on. "It's going to be such an excellent surprise!"

"You know my not so excellent surprise today?" Joe asked, trying to keep his voice mild. "I found out that two kids who've been through a lot wanted to put a bit of their family back together, and I didn't make it happen because I didn't know about it." He stepped around so Ally couldn't get past him and tried to look her in the eye. It wasn't easy when she refused to turn in his direction. Finally, he gave up and spoke to the side of her head. "Why didn't

I know about it?"

She pulled her jacket on. "It's not easy, Joe. If they say they don't want me to tell you something, I'm supposed to respect that, aren't I?"

Good point. "As long as it's not about something that could get someone hurt, yeah, you should respect it. But, damn, Ally, couldn't you have dropped a hint or something? Or couldn't you have convinced them it would be good to tell me themselves?"

"I was *trying* to do that!" Ally grinned at him. "But I knew Jean would tell you, once she got you alone. And this is going to be a good lesson for Lacey and Savannah, probably. They need to start getting trained in how to get you to do what they want. It's not nearly as hard as most of my friends have it. *They* want something, they have to manipulate and connive. Me? I want something? I have to *ask for it*."

"You're not that spoiled," Joe protested.

"Only because I don't want to be," Ally said gleefully. Then she saw his expression. "Oh my God, Joe, are you going to worry about this now? You're not a pushover! We have more chores than almost any of my friends, if that makes you feel better. And our rules are good. I mean, they're a bit vague, maybe, but...."

"What *are* our rules?"

"I don't know. Like... tell people where you're going to be. That's a good one. Help out with the little guys, clean up your own stuff. It's not like it's all written down somewhere...." She raised her head with the sideways tilt it got when she had an idea she really liked. "Some houses are like Canada, or the States, with a written constitution that they all think is really important. And some are like the UK. They don't have a written constitution... did you know that? Not, like, one big document that has all the big rules in it. Just a lot of scraps here and there, and a lot of tradition. That's what we're like. Our rules are mostly tradition, but that doesn't mean they aren't real."

"Are you sure you don't want to be a lawyer?" Joe asked as he stepped aside and let the young ones precede him out of the house. "This whole vet thing might not be your future after all."

"Help us, Ally!" she said in a squeaky, distant voice. "We're waiting! Help us!" She skipped down the walkway, holding Austin's hand. Over her shoulder she said, "That was the animals."

"I thought it might be."

"They still need me."

"I wonder how many of our current animals will still be alive by the time you get out of vet school."

She gave him a dirty look. "The horses still should be, at least."

"I'd say there's a 10 percent chance of me putting a bullet in Misery's head on any given day. The odds of her making it that much longer...."

"There's a zero percent chance of you ever doing that." Ally corrected. She let go of Austin's hand, and he stopped walking as if his off switch had been tripped. Ally stepped back and punched Joe in the shoulder. "You love that horse, and we all know it."

"The feeling is not reciprocal," he said gloomily, and he tried not to let his mind jump to another relationship where Joe's affections may not be returned. Mackenzie was back in the city for another shoot, being reminded of all the things he was missing up in the country. After their previous conversation, Joe's brain seemed to have stopped torturing him with images of cheating, but it still liked to remind him that Mackenzie could call anytime he wanted and say he'd changed his mind and wasn't coming back. That could happen, and Joe wouldn't be able to do a thing about it. So he shouldn't think about it, not if there was any way to avoid it.

"Let's go find a dog," he said, swooping Austin up and giving him an airplane ride to the truck.

Three hours later, they were back at the house with Jasper *and* a young ferret. Joe should have known better. Ally and him in an animal shelter? It was a wonder they hadn't come back with *all* the residents. As it was, they'd both resolutely maintained their focus on the task at hand until Austin had seen a volunteer playing with the rodent and fallen in love.

"It's time he had a pet of his own," Joe rationalized as he unloaded the wire cage they'd bought on the way home.

"It'll help him learn responsibility!" Ally said brightly. She grabbed the tote bag full of ferret supplies, Jasper's leash in her other hand.

"Might be good for the girls too," Joe said. "It'll show them it's not a big deal that they get a pet. We're casual about that around here."

"Excellent point," Ally agreed. She really was a good coconspirator. "It would have been irresponsible to come home *without* a ferret."

"Absolutely," Joe said. "We probably should have gotten two."

"Do you have a plan for introductions to the other dogs?"

"To the ferret? I was planning on keeping them away from each other."

"No, to Jasper. Although I think we could probably introduce them to the ferret too, eventually...."

"Let's focus on Jasper for now." Joe looked down at the scruffy creature. "They've probably already met, in the forest or something. And Jasper's smaller than Red, doesn't seem like he'll want to be dominant. Maybe it'll go just as well as it did with Griffin."

"If Red kills him, we have to tell Lacey and Savannah that he was already adopted when we got to the pound."

"Red's not going to kill him."

"He'd better not," Ally said glumly.

"Let's put the ferret upstairs so the poor thing doesn't have a heart attack, then introduce the dogs outside. Fair?"

Ally nodded.

The farm dogs were still penned up, as they had been since the social worker's visit, and they weren't used to being contained for so long. Joe reconsidered the plan. "Actually, let's take Jasper in with us for a bit, and I'll let the dogs out to run some steam off. Then we can do the introductions one at a time."

"Everything gets complicated, doesn't it?" Ally asked sympathetically.

She was right. Nothing was ever as a simple as Joe wanted it to be. But he was doing the right thing. Finding a way for the girls to have their dog was important. It was worth the hassle. The ferret, on the other hand.... But then he thought of Austin's glee as the little creature had investigated his ears and neck. It was time there was something in the house smaller than Austin, something he could be in charge of. Joe would just have to make sure the creature was cared for properly.

One more responsibility. But it was okay. It was what people needed, so Joe would take care of it. That was what he was there for.

CHAPTER SIX

ONCE AGAIN, Mackenzie's life seemed to be spinning in strange directions. He was pretty sure there was a connection between the feeling of being out of control and the consumption of massive quantities of alcohol, but he was going to have to wait until he sobered up to really puzzle that relationship out. For now, he was just letting things happen.

It had sounded like a good idea when Anton had called to suggest it. A friend had opened a bar and was trying to drum up business; he was offering free drinks to a select group of gorgeous people if they came and had an obvious good time, and Mackenzie and Kristen were good-looking enough to qualify. Mackenzie hadn't seen Anton since the party at the church, but the guy always seemed to have good connections. Good drugs, too, but Mackenzie had resolutely stayed away from those on this occasion. Alcohol was controllable, at least in theory.

Mackenzie leaned back against the leather couch and looked out at the bar. He was pretty sure he still *looked* sober enough. He wasn't tipping over or anything. That was important. And the bartenders seemed to have cut him off, or at least started putting so much mix in the free drinks that there wasn't much chance of getting any drunker, so that was good too. He could manage this night. Another hour or two, maybe, then he'd drag Kristen back to her place and they'd get some sleep. Mackenzie had worked all day, but the next was just bureaucracy—a meeting with his agent, a fitting—nothing he couldn't do hungover. Everything was fine.

He wasn't being irresponsible. He missed Joe, but he was coping with it.

"You look miserable," Kristen said, flopping gracelessly onto the ottoman in front of him. "Why don't you dance?"

"Turns out I don't like dancing unless I'm high," he said sadly.

"So get high." Her expression made it clear she'd found the obvious solution.

"Nah," he said, leaning back into the leather. "Don't feel like it."

"Is this a Joe thing? Does Cowboy Joe disapprove of drug use?"

Mackenzie frowned. Kristen wasn't the first friend who seemed to have gotten a negative impression of Joe, and it was beginning to be annoying. "I don't think so. And he's not here. I can do what I want. I just don't feel like getting fucked up. I'm a bit too old for it, you know?"

"You're two years younger than I am!"

No way was Mackenzie drunk enough to pursue *that* topic. "I'm thinking another hour or two, and then home to bed?" He could tell as soon as he saw her expression that he wasn't going to like her response.

"Actually... I was thinking of bed quite a bit sooner." She grinned and cut her eyes toward a young preppy guy standing by the bar, clearly waiting for her. "But he lives somewhere...." She frowned as she tried to remember the details. "I don't know. Somewhere I can't go. So we need to go to my place."

The effect that would have on Mackenzie was clear, but he tried to delay the discussion of it. "Is it possible he lives *with his parents*? He's just a kid, Kristen!"

She grinned again. "I *know*. He's going to be fun!" And then she got more serious. "But you know how small the apartment is. It's would be a bit... you know. Kind of awkward. If he's in with me and you're out on the couch, hearing everything...." She made a cutesy face that had probably been a lot more effective when she was the age of her prospective fuck. "You can find somewhere else to crash, right? I mean, you know lots of people here tonight…."

Mackenzie did know them. Or at least, he had. But they'd drifted out of his life over the past months, and he hadn't missed them. Kristen was the only friend from the city he'd stayed in touch with, and now she was ditching him for some guy. Which, of course, was completely in keeping with the rules they'd always had for their friendship. It wasn't Kristen's fault that Mackenzie had settled down and gotten boring.

He forced himself to smile at her. "Have fun. I'll find somewhere else, no problem."

His response earned him a quick kiss, and then she was gone, giggling and grabbing the prep's hand. He sighed. He wanted another drink, a real one.

Well, it wasn't *that* cold of a night. He could take the subway back up to where he'd parked the car, sleep in it, and pay a couple dollars for a shower at the community center the next morning. Not his ideal night, but not the end of the world, either. It was a workable plan. He'd wasted too much money the last time he was in town, so there was no way he was paying for a hotel, and he really didn't want to beg a bed from any of the people he saw in the bar.

It all made sense. Which made it that much more confusing when, less than an hour later, he found himself being dragged out of the bar, Anton clenching his hand as if one or both of them were drowning, heading for…. "Where? Where are we going, again?"

"The Blue Room," Anton said. "It's just down the block. Or a few blocks. I don't know, it's in here somewhere."

"And Alexi is there?"

"That's what Casey said. That son of a whore! He said he wanted a quiet night at home! Said he needed some peace!"

Well, that would certainly not be something he'd get hanging out with Anton, Mackenzie mused. He stumbled along behind as Anton continued to rant and rave, managing to wrench his hand free just in time to avoid being run into the sandwich board advertising dinner specials outside a restaurant. He glanced in through the tall glass windows and saw four men, maybe a bit older than him, looking out at him with a mix of horror and amusement.

They weren't envying his youth and beauty, he realized with a start. They weren't wishing they could live a carefree life of adventure and glamor and flirting and late-night fun. They thought he was a mess.

Anton grabbed his hand again and yanked him forward. "Move it, Mackenzie!" he ordered.

Mackenzie let himself be dragged along, but his mind was back with the men in the restaurant. They hadn't looked like tourists, or even suburbanites. They lived in the city, they were part of the community, they were enjoying the cultural offerings on tap... they were just doing it in a different way. A way Joe would have been comfortable with.

It wasn't about city versus country. Mackenzie could feel the truth of that, and he tried to chase down the details. It was just lifestyle choices. There were people getting messed up and doing crazy things out in the country, and there were people having quiet dinners with friends in the city. There had been a time Mackenzie had *wanted* the craziness, but that time was gone. He wasn't living the way he was because he was stuck in the country; he *wanted* a quieter, saner life. *With* Joe, but not *because* of Joe.

He didn't want to be drunk and confused, getting dragged through the streets because Anton was trying to track down some maybe-boyfriend and punish him for some real or imagined slight. Just because work brought him to the city didn't mean it had to bring him to his old lifestyle.

It was a good thing to realize, he was pretty sure, and he tried to run over it in his mind so that at least the major features of the idea would still be there when he sobered up.

"He's in there!" Anton hissed, dragging Mackenzie past the wide window and toward the bar's doorway. "You need to play along, okay?"

"Play along? What are you doing?"

But Anton didn't answer. He was too intent on getting the door open and pulling Mackenzie inside. The place wasn't too crowded, but Mackenzie had no idea what Alexi looked like so he didn't bother looking for him. Anton ordered them shots of something, so that was a silver lining, and then there was a cocktail of some sort to follow, and Mackenzie hadn't paid for any of it. This wasn't too bad.

Anton was talking about something, his face too animated and his voice too loud, but Mackenzie was still able to tune out most of it. And it took him quite a while to notice just how close Anton was standing, and how possessively he had his arm draped around Mackenzie's shoulder. When he finally figured it out, he sighed loudly enough for Anton to give him a dirty look before resuming his monologue.

They were making Alexi jealous. How original. And how productive. This was a scenario designed to produce drama, not to strengthen a relationship. More likely to tear a couple apart, really, but Anton probably didn't care about that. It was his pride that was hurt, not his heart.

Whoever Alexi was, he didn't seem to be taking the bait, and, as Mackenzie should have known he would, Anton upped his game. He leaned in and started whispering in Mackenzie's ear, then nuzzled his neck, leaving a cold trail of alcohol-infused spit behind.

It wasn't a big deal, nothing Mackenzie would have thought twice about back in the day. Nathan's friends used to do this sort of thing all the time, under Nathan's watchful gaze, of course. Sample the merchandise, understand how this was one more of Nathan's top-drawer possessions, but don't go too far. Touch the car's leather, but don't take it for a test drive. Or maybe for a drive, even, but not too far. Down the street and back, not out to the highway. Nathan would ride along, of course, and make sure his property came back to him in pristine condition.

Different now, though. Mackenzie was pretty sure Joe wouldn't be quite so relaxed about it all. He didn't think he owned Mackenzie; no, he seemed convinced that he didn't have any permanent claims at all. He'd take this as one more piece of evidence that Mackenzie wasn't truly committed. And Mackenzie was tired of Joe feeling that way.

So he pushed gently at Anton's chest, bringing the man's face around so he could see and hear Mackenzie. "One more minute," Mackenzie said. "I'm counting to sixty. Then I'm out of here. You can come with me if you want it to look like we're going home together."

Anton looked petulant. "I'll buy you another drink," he suggested.

"Eight," Mackenzie said. When he saw Anton's confusion he added, "I started counting as soon as I told you I was going to count. We're at twelve now...."

"Oh, come on!"

"Fourteen." It was kind of fun. "Fifteen, sixteen, seventeen—"

But it was pretty hard to keep talking with Anton's tongue in his mouth. Not something Mackenzie had ever wanted, but he'd made the deal and he'd do it right. He wasn't kissing Anton, he told himself. He was kissing his old life, all the good times and the bad times and the friends who had faded away when he'd moved, the bright lights and crazy nights. He was kissing it all good-bye, and he'd leave the life with the same enthusiasm with which he'd lived it. So he grabbed Anton's ass and pulled him in tighter, brought a hand up to muss his hair, and kissed his old life for all he was worth. Then he pulled away, ignoring Anton's clinging hands. "Sixty," he said, and he smiled. "I'm out of here."

"I'm coming with you," Anton avowed.

Mackenzie didn't object. He just headed for the door. The cool air helped him clear his head, at least a little, and he took a moment to orient himself before starting down the sidewalk toward the nearest subway stop.

He didn't even realize Anton was beside him until the man said, "Kristen's busy, right? You want to come to my place?"

If Anton had only been offering his sofa, it would have been an easy answer. But things were never that simple, and Mackenzie really didn't want to fight off unwanted advances or deal with a guilt trip. Besides, Anton was from the old life, and Mackenzie had moved on. "No, I'm all set. Thanks, though."

"Your loss," Anton said. "I'm getting a cab—you want me to drop you somewhere?"

"No, I'm okay." Mackenzie stopped walking. "Thanks, though." He'd known Anton a long time, and they'd been through a lot together. "For everything."

Anton shrugged, "It was just a cab ride," he said with a bemused smile. Then he stepped to the curb and raised his arm, his gaze on an upcoming taxi with a lighted roof sign. When the car stopped, Anton opened the door and looked back at Mackenzie. "You sure?"

"Yeah," Mackenzie answered. It was true. He was on the right path, and he had no doubts about it. "Take care of yourself, okay?"

Anton either didn't hear him or didn't think an answer was needed. He just climbed into the cab and waved as it pulled away.

Mackenzie was left alone on the busy sidewalk, and he stood for a moment and looked around. He'd be back. This was still the gay village, still his home turf. But maybe the next time he was there he'd check out one of the finer restaurants, or go to a bookstore or something. Hell, maybe he'd go to a sex shop, but he'd be buying something to bring home to Joe.

That thought was enough to keep him warm as he hurried toward the subway station. Joe might not be too wild socially, but he was completely comfortable with himself, and with Mackenzie, in the bedroom. Or wherever they happened to be. Yeah, they could have some fun with toys. And it would be a novelty for Mackenzie to get to pick them according to his own tastes instead of having to go along with whatever his partner wanted.

He was moving in the right direction. He could feel it. Things were changing, but that was okay. It was good. Things *needed* to change. Mackenzie had a brand-new life, a life with Joe, and a family, and, inexplicably, a farm and an old church being slowly converted to a gay wedding chapel. It wasn't where he'd expected to be, but he wouldn't change it for the world. Not even if he had to spend the night sleeping in his parked car.

CHAPTER SEVEN

JOE TRIED to get comfortable in the old leather armchair. He hardly ever sat in the living room and hadn't really figured out which seat fit him best. Jasper was lying by the fire, as he always seemed to be, and he was staring at Joe like he was an alien invader. The little dog was a bit odd. Joe squirmed a little, then jarred his side and sucked in a pained breath.

Ally, of course, noticed. "You're such a loser," she said with an unsympathetic smile.

"I'm fine. Just a little sore."

"That's not what the doctor said."

"She said I had bruised ribs and a broken wrist. She *didn't* say I'm a loser."

"I think she was hinting at it." Ally stood up and headed for the kitchen. "Do you want more ice?"

"No," Joe said. "It's too cold."

"The ice is too cold," Ally said. "Yeah, that's a common complaint. I could warm it up for you, but...."

"You're not helpful. How long until Austin gets home?"

"You think Austin's going to help you out?"

"I think he's going to be less annoying. Are you sure you don't want to go to school? I hear school is fun."

"I told you, it's a waste of a day. Christmas assembly this

morning, and then everyone skips in the afternoon. I'm more useful here, looking after you."

"You're not actually any use at all. You won't even warm up my ice for me."

"Wrong!" Ally said, her triumph clear as she handed Joe a glass of water. "Look! Warm ice!" She held out her other hand, two white tablets in her palm. "And drugs! I'm like Santa Claus!"

"Santa can't be trusted," Joe mumbled as he held the pills on his tongue and reached for the glass with his good arm.

"I know you think that," Ally said soothingly. "But those are your prescribed painkillers and anti-inflammatories, not a strong sedative that will put you under for three days and allow me to run a drug ring out of the kitchen."

"Your imagination frightens me."

"Better than reality," Ally said darkly. The mudroom door banged shut and she looked over the back of Joe's armchair and loudly said, "Oh, hi, Mackenzie. Joe's just fine. No problems here. Nothing to worry about."

"What?" Mackenzie said. There were muffled noises that Joe was pretty sure meant Mackenzie was taking off his boots and coat, and then soft footsteps. "Why wouldn't he be just fine?"

"Well, hypothetically," Ally said, ignoring Joe's attempts to shush her with vigorous one-armed waving, "Maybe he might have fallen off the top of a truck. Maybe he was trying to attach a cable or something as a way to pry a crumpled-up cab open to get the driver out, and he might have slipped and fallen and hurt himself. But that probably didn't happen."

"Another stupid volunteer fireman call?" Mackenzie asked. The words were hard, but his voice was soft as he fell to his knees in front of Joe. "I hate them." He leaned forward for a soft kiss, and Joe felt himself relaxing. Mackenzie was home. Everything would be okay. "But how far did you fall? A pickup is, like, six feet tall, maybe?"

Mackenzie looked to Ally, who was all too happy to explain. "Not a pickup. A tractor trailer. And it was all kind of buckled up in the air. I drove past it on the way in to the hospital. The top of it was probably twenty feet in the air, at least!"

"It wasn't that high," Joe said, keeping a close eye on Mackenzie's expression. Was this going to be a little problem or a big one?

But Joe's phone rang then, and Ally pulled it off the table and made a face as she saw the name on the call display. Instead of answering, she handed it over to him. He looked at the display and then back at her, then lifted the phone to his ear. "Joe Sutton," he said, trying to sound casual.

"Mr. Sutton. Richard Bowerman here, the principal at the high school. We have a problem."

Joe hoped it was just about Ally's attendance, but he was pretty sure the principal didn't call home about a straight-A student missing a day of classes. "What's up?"

"Miss Walton is in my office right now. I contacted Jean Carpenter, and she referred me to you."

"Okay," Joe said. He wished he hadn't taken the pain pills quite so fast; it was starting to seem like he was going to need his full attention for whatever Bowerman was leading up to. "Why's she in your office?"

"She's drunk," Bowerman said, his voice clipped. "She was seen in the company of several other people, but they left the area and she's refusing to identify them. We believe that the group was responsible for some vandalism and theft in the kitchen storage room, as well."

"What kind of vandalism? What theft?"

"They jimmied the lock on one of the freezers and stole and cooked and ate some french fries."

"Okay," Joe said. French-fry theft. He tried not to wonder whether Lacey had consumed something more than just alcohol.

"What's the next step?"

"Miss Walton needs to give me the names of the other students involved in this incident."

"You said she was refusing to do that, right? So what's the next step *after* that?"

"There *is* no next step after that. Until I have a full list of names, we don't proceed any further."

Joe hadn't fallen on his head, but it was beginning to ache anyway. He glared at Ally. If she'd known about any of this, she was going to have some serious explaining to do. But that was for later; right now, he needed to deal with Bowerman. "Well, obviously the world isn't going to just stop spinning for us to just sit around and wait for Lacey to give you names." He tried to lift his arm to look at his watch, but winced in pain and let it fall back into its sling. "What time is it?"

"Almost three o'clock."

"Okay. She can't take the bus home, right? If she's drunk?"

"And suspended."

"Okay. She's suspended. That's one of those next steps I was wondering about. How long is she suspended for?"

"Mr. Sutton, I'm not sure you're taking this seriously enough."

"I'm trying to, but you're really not making it easy. Is there any chance you could be a bit less of a cartoon villain about all this? I mean, could you just pull the stick out of your ass and then—"

Mackenzie was pretty quick when he wanted to be. He had the phone out of Joe's hand and up to his own ear before Joe had time to register what was happening. "We'll be in to pick her up," he said. "About half an hour, probably. We can talk more then, but I should warn you... Joe was injured earlier today, part of his role as a volunteer fireman. You know how important they are to this community, and the work is *quite* dangerous. Anyway, he was injured during a daring rescue, and he's been prescribed some painkillers. He won't be driving, and I don't think he needs to come inside, either. I'll come in to pick up Lacey, and we can have a meeting about all this after the Christmas break, okay?"

There was a pause while Bowerman said something, and then Mackenzie laughed. He sounded genuine, even as he rolled his eyes in Joe's direction. "Oh, I'm sure it's confusing, absolutely! But you can call Jean and review it with her. My name's Scott Mackenzie. She knows the situation." He made a face while he listened, but made sure he was smiling when he added, "I really want to thank you for all you're doing for Lacey. I'm sure she's a challenging student—so much has happened to her recently, and we think she's doing a great job of coping with it all, but, of course, you must see a different perspective. It's easier for us to be flexible when we only have a few kids in the house, instead of a few hundred!"

Even without hearing Bowerman's side of the conversation, Joe could tell that things were going much better since Mackenzie had taken over. Which only made sense. This was Mackenzie's thing—he was social, good with people. Joe leaned his head back against the leather and wished the armchair was a few inches taller. He also wished Mackenzie was a few inches closer, and it sure would be excellent if they didn't have to drive into town to pick up a drunk teenager who'd been suspended from school.

He opened his eyes as Mackenzie ended the call. "Fuck," Joe said. "What the hell was she thinking?"

"Let's go find out," Mackenzie said softly. "Can I pull you up? And what is that on your wrist? Is that a new kind of cast?"

"It's a splint," Ally said, eager to be part of the conversation. "They can't put the cast on until the swelling goes down. He's supposed to ice it and take the anti-inflammatories, and then we'll take him in tomorrow. Dr. Michaels said I can help put the cast on, if I want. I did a co-op at the hospital last year, and she knows I want to be a vet."

"So this has worked out pretty well for *you*," Joe growled. "But it's going to get a lot less pleasant if I find out you knew Lacey was planning to drink at school today."

Ally frowned, suddenly serious. "I didn't know. Lacey's... she's weird about alcohol. You know, because of her parents. She doesn't usually drink at all. But I've seen her get totally wasted a couple times. I don't know why she'd do it at school, though."

"I don't know why either." Joe heaved himself to his feet, staggered just a little, and headed for the door. "Ally, you stay here."

"But *I'm* coming," Mackenzie said, obviously ready for an argument. "And I'm driving."

"I'm sore all down one side," Joe said. It sounded less like whining if he was sharing the information for a reason. "I don't want to fold myself up in your little car."

"Newsflash," Mackenzie said with a raised eyebrow. "I can drive your truck. You let Lacey drive it, for God's sake. You really won't trust me in it?"

Oh. Well, now that Joe thought about it, there was really no reason they couldn't do things that way. "Okay. You can drive."

They were halfway to town when Mackenzie said, "You're really hurting, huh?"

"What?"

"Usually when I drive, you stare at the road like you think you can control the car telepathically. You keep one hand on the door handle and the other near the parking brake. But today you're just staring at the floor, flinching every time we hit a bump."

"I'm not hurting too much," Joe lied. "I'm just thinking. What am I supposed to do with Lacey?"

"You're the one with all the parenting experience. Lacey's your fourth teenager, isn't she?"

"Sarah and Ally were never any trouble. Not like this. I worried about them... you know, going out to parties or whatever. Worried that they'd get hurt. But they never did stupid stuff like this. This is more of a Nick move."

"So what'd you do with Nick?"

"I yelled at him. Grounded him, and then listened to the whole 'you're not my father, you can't ground me' bullshit. So, first, not pleasant for anyone, and second, it didn't really work. He did stupid stuff all through high school, and he's probably down in the city doing stupid stuff as we speak. It'd be nice if Lacey could actually *change* her behavior, you know?"

"She should be seeing a counselor." There was something about the way Mackenzie spoke the words that made Joe feel like they'd been building for a while. "Jean is great, and you're great, but she needs more than that. *Most* teenagers are a bit fucked up, just from going through too many changes too fast, and then you add in all the extra crap Lacey's had to deal with? She's doing really well, but she could be doing better."

A counselor. Will had insisted that the whole family go to a grief counselor after their parents had died. Joe hadn't had much to say, but he'd tagged along so the other kids would think he approved of the process. But he wasn't sure it had really done any good. Their parents were dead. No amount of counseling was going to change that.

And Lacey's parents were dead. Her sister was brain-damaged. What the hell was anyone going to be able to say that would do her any real good?

"I went to one," Mackenzie said, taking his eyes off the road long enough to judge Joe's reaction. "When I was a teenager."

"What for?"

"I'm not sure. My parents thought it would be a good idea. I guess... maybe it was because they thought I was gay."

"Gay? Really? You?"

"Crazy, I know. They said it was because I seemed unhappy, but I don't really remember feeling that way."

"And how'd it go? Was it useful?"

"I'm not sure."

"You didn't talk about being gay?"

"No."

"Seems like kind of a big thing to leave out."

"It does," Mackenzie agreed. "I can't remember what I was thinking. But for Lacey, it could be better. She's been through way more than I had. Maybe Savannah should go too. Different therapist, maybe. Or some family counseling."

"One kid gets drunk at school and the whole family has to go into therapy?"

"We don't *have* to. But it might not hurt. Just to have someone help us have good conversations."

"We aren't having good conversations?"

"I don't know. Maybe we are. I'm just trying to answer your question. What should we do about Lacey?"

"I think I'll just lock her in her room for a couple months," Joe said, letting his eyes close. "And take away all her Christmas presents. That should take care of things, right?"

"I'm sure Mr. Bowerman would approve of that approach."

Well, that was a pretty clear sign it wasn't the way to go. But Joe couldn't think of any real alternatives, not with his head as foggy as it was. Damn, it wasn't like he was on morphine or something. He'd taken the same pain medication before without feeling like he was shutting off his brain.

"You fell twenty feet?" Mackenzie asked. It felt like he was really far away, and Joe had to fight to make himself answer.

"I don't think it was that far. I slid for a while before I ran out of roof."

"Did you land on your head at all? Did the doctor check for a concussion?"

"I'm fine. It was Dr. Michaels. She checked me over. And, no, I didn't land on my head."

"You were a bit dopey after the Walton fire too," Mackenzie said. It sounded like he was thinking out loud. "But I blamed that on stress or trauma or something. Is this just the way you act when you're hurt?"

Joe didn't really think it was, but he wanted Mackenzie to stop talking, so he nodded. "I guess so."

"So we'll go get Lacey, we'll yell at her until the little guys get home from school, and then we'll have a shower, and I'll put you to bed. We'll stay in there until tomorrow morning and you'll be fine."

"There's one shower for the whole house. You and me aren't sharing it while the place is full of kids."

"We'll send them to town for dinner."

"That's a great punishment for Lacey."

"We'll ground Lacey and tell her she has to stay in her room. No peeking. And we'll send the *other* kids to town for dinner."

"Or we could just skip the shower part," Joe said. "And stay in bed until tomorrow *afternoon*." He just wished he were feeling better so he could take full advantage of the opportunity.

That was when his phone rang again. He winced at the call display. What else was going wrong? "Hi, Joe Sutton," he said cautiously.

"Joe, it's Vicki at the elementary school. Austin didn't get on the bus. He's in the office. He says he has an—" There were vague sounds of commotion, and then the secretary's voice was back. "Well, that clears things up, at least. He definitely has an upset tummy. He just threw up. Marion's with him, but he'd really like his Joe as soon as possible."

But Joe was struggling with his own realization. He wasn't reacting to the drugs, he was sick. His skin was clammy, he felt dizzy... "Feel my forehead," he ordered Mackenzie, who gave him a strange look before complying.

"Oh, shit, you're really hot," Mackenzie said, jerking his hand away as if it had been burned. Or maybe he was just worried about contamination.

Joe groaned into the phone. "I think I have the same bug," he admitted. "We're on our way into town anyway. I'll be there in ten minutes, okay? Tell the little guy to hang in there."

"Thanks, Joe. Terrible way to start the holidays."

He hung up and let his head flop back against the seat. "Austin's sick," he said. "I'm sick. Lacey's drunk. Are *you* feeling okay?"

"I am right now," Mackenzie said, cautiously rolling the window down. "But I'm not looking forward to the drive back out to the ranch."

It turned out to be a quiet trip, at least. Joe curled up in the backseat with Austin, and Lacey sat in front with the window partway down, all of them isolated by their misery. Joe found enough energy to call Dr. Michaels and find out that there absolutely was a stomach bug going around and she'd seen two kindergarteners with it already. She gave him instructions for care and for when to bring Austin in if there was no improvement, and he dutifully repeated them all to Mackenzie so someone with a clear brain would know what was going on.

They got to the house and Joe herded the kids inside. He let Ally carry Austin up to bed and watched as Lacey staggered her way after them up the stairs. He took a moment to take a deep breath, then turned around and headed back out. "Where are you going?" Mackenzie asked. He sounded like he wasn't sure whether to be amused or concerned.

"I'm going to do chores early. Feed the animals now, then go to bed."

"Are you delirious?" Mackenzie was quick again, darting between Joe and the door. "You need to go to bed *now*. Ally and I can deal with the animals."

"Ally and *you*?" Joe leaned his fevered head against the doorjamb. "You're scared of every animal on the place except Griffin and Jasper. You're going to feed them, now? Really?"

"Ally will do the scary parts," Mackenzie said with dignity. "I will do the rest."

God, Joe wanted this. He wanted to crawl into bed, preferably with Austin snuggled up against him, and he wanted to know that the farm was being taken care of. More than that, he wanted to know that *Mackenzie* was the one doing the chores and that he'd found a role for himself on the farm and was becoming part of the life Joe loved. But that should happen because Mackenzie *wanted* it, not because Joe got a little bug and was too pitiful to resist. "I can do it," he said as firmly as he could.

"You're an idiot," Ally said from behind him. She was already back downstairs and brushed past him with a vigor he found completely exhausting. "You were going to have enough trouble just being one-handed and sore. With a stomach bug added in, you're no use at all. Mackenzie and I are probably going to be sick by tomorrow, so we need you focusing on getting better now so you'll be able to take care of us then. If *you're* still sick, we'll have to call Sarah, and *nobody* wants that."

That was true enough. Sarah's response to illness always seemed to involve cooking a huge meal, with lots of banging pans and sickening food odors, even though she knew no one would be able to eat anything. She'd babble about keeping their strength up and then bang some more pans.... "No Sarah," Joe said fervently. "Will would be better."

"He's on a plane," Ally said calmly. "You know this, Joe. Cancun for Christmas? You were making fun of him about it two days ago."

"Santa's never going to find him," Joe muttered. He really was feeling terrible.

"Since you think Santa steals from people, you should be happy for him," Mackenzie said. He gently prodded Joe to turn around and head for the stairs.

"I'm jealous," Joe said. "Santa's going to rob us blind."

"I really wish I could blame your insanity on the fever," Ally said. "But that's not the main thing right now. Mackenzie and I have things under control. Savannah will help when she gets home. You need to go get some sleep."

"Just a nap, maybe," Joe said. If he could just lie down for a bit, let the fever do its work, he'd be fine in no time. "I can still do tonight's feeding."

"Joe, I've done evening chores alone plenty of times," Ally said tiredly. "You're not magic—other people can do the same stuff you do, and we do it almost as well. You need to let us."

"Mackenzie's afraid of cattle," Joe half whispered. He was at the bottom of the stairs now, and he was pretty sure he'd rather lie down on them and sleep right there rather than force his drained body to climb all those steps.

"I'm *nervous*, not afraid. Now, go! One step up." Joe could feel Mackenzie right behind him, nudging him forward but ready to catch him if he fell. Joe took the step. "Keep going," Mackenzie urged. "We're almost there."

"We're on the second step from the bottom," Joe complained.

"Oh. I thought maybe you were too out of it to notice that. But, yeah, okay, we're *not* almost there, but we're on our way. We've made a good start!"

Joe didn't have the energy to resist. He wasn't the cowboy; he was the cow. He let himself be herded up the stairs and down the hall to be penned into the bedroom. Ally'd had the decency to head to the barn on her own, at least, so only Mackenzie saw Joe's weakness as he sank onto the mattress and groaned.

"I'll bring you a puke bucket," Mackenzie promised, "in case you can't make the bathroom." He was untying Joe's boots as he spoke. They should have been taken off downstairs, but apparently Joe had missed that step. "And maybe some soup or something?"

"I'm not hungry," Joe said. He tried to help as Mackenzie dragged his jeans down and replaced them with a cozy pair of sweatpants. Even the brief exposure to the air of the bedroom had Joe shivering, and he burrowed under the covers as soon as Mackenzie let him go.

"I'll bring you aspirin in a bit," Mackenzie promised, "Once the painkillers from before are worn off better. Okay?"

Joe was pretty busy just trying to control his body's shaking, but he managed to say, "Thank you," before his chattering teeth got in the way.

Mackenzie's hand was cool and smooth on his forehead. "Get better, Joe." A gentle kiss on his temple, then, "I love you. And I want you to stop falling off trucks and getting the flu. Okay?"

"I'll try," Joe promised. He was still shivering, and he didn't want Mackenzie to leave. And somehow, even without words Mackenzie seemed to realize that. He moved away for only a moment, long enough to shed a layer of clothes, and then he burrowed under the covers behind Joe and spooned up behind him, providing another level of warmth and comfort. It was stupid, of course. Mackenzie shouldn't be taking the chance of getting infected; Joe wasn't a little kid who needed to be babied through his weakness. Austin was in his room all alone, for God's sake, and *Joe* needed a living teddy bear? It was pathetic, and Joe shouldn't let himself be so weak.

So he gathered his strength... and used it to grip Mackenzie's arm and pull it more snugly around his shoulder. He was weak: he'd take comfort while he could and deal with the consequences when he had to.

CHAPTER EIGHT

MACKENZIE ENDED up being the only one in the house who didn't catch whatever it was. Well, it wasn't totally clear whether Lacey had the bug or just a wicked hangover, but she did her time hanging over the toilet one way or another.

"I wouldn't mind the hay if it wasn't so scratchy," Mackenzie said as he heaved a few dry flakes into Misery's stall. She pinned her ears at his voice and edged her ass in his direction, threatening to kick, and he got out fast. Joe had told him the warning signs of equine aggression but had also said the first sign that Misery was about to attack was that she was breathing. After four days of helping with chores, she was the only animal on the farm that still scared Mackenzie, and he was pretty sure his apprehension was just good sense.

"Sorry," Joe said. He wasn't at full strength, between his newly casted arm and his recent illness, but he was still getting twice as many animals fed as Mackenzie. "I'll try to find some less scratchy stuff."

"That'd be nice."

By the time Mackenzie finished doling out horse hay, Joe was taking a breather, leaning against one of the rough barn beams and watching Mackenzie through lazy, predatory eyes. Like a lion that wasn't actually hungry but was still watching the antelope. Weakened Joe was strangely sexy. Strong Joe was sexy too, of course. Mackenzie hadn't really found a flavor of Joe that *wasn't* sexy, now that he thought about it. Well, puking Joe hadn't been too hot, but after he'd brushed his teeth, when he was sitting in the shower because he wanted to clean off the fever sweat but had been too weak to stand up... that had been kind of appealing.

"I like you when you're weak," Mackenzie said out loud. Probably a mistake, judging by the way Joe's eyes flew open.

"I'm not weak," he protested, pushing away from the support beam. "I was just waiting for you to finish!"

Mackenzie rolled his eyes. "You're not weak as a rule. And you're not weak now, by ordinary standards. You're just a little less superpowered than usual. You're in Clark Kent mode, how 'bout that?"

Joe looked slightly mollified and reached out to pull Mackenzie closer, then wrapped his good arm around Mackenzie's waist. "You my Lois Lane?"

"Jimmy Olsen," Mackenzie said. He let his lower body lean against Joe's but kept his shoulders and head pulled away. "I'm the young ingénue, eager to learn the ways of the workplace. Please, Clark, tell me more about haylage."

"You're not ready for that knowledge, Jimmy. You need to work up to it." Joe's lips were soft and warm as Mackenzie kissed him. They stayed like that for a while, their jackets open in front to share their heat as the cold air of the barn made their personal cocoon cozier and more intimate. "Ally will be here soon," Joe warned as Mackenzie slipped his gloves off and eased his hands inside Joe's shirt.

"I'm just warming my fingers," Mackenzie protested.

"You're warming more than that," Joe said with a grin. Between absence and illness, it had been a while since they'd done more than snuggle, and it was gratifying to realize that Joe had felt the lack. Mackenzie liked being the one to initiate things, but he liked it even more when Joe tightened his arm around Mackenzie's waist and spun them, eased Mackenzie against the beam, and pressed in for a hard, deep, full-body kiss.

Neither one of them was happy when the barn door creaked open. Joe pulled away and tugged his clothes straight, and Mackenzie followed suit. It was frustrating to be interrupted but hard to resent the cause, and they both turned to watch as the parade came in from outside. Ally and Lacey, Savannah and Austin, all bundled up against the cold and carrying the wicker baskets that had been used for this since the tradition began. The dogs trailed behind with Christmas bows around their necks, although Red stopped just inside the doorway and pawed his off, then picked it up and carried it to Joe as if he'd killed a new and exotic animal and wanted approval. Red had spent the night on the bed with Joe the night before—their Christmas Eve tradition—but apparently it hadn't really gotten him in the holiday spirit. Griffin seemed quite pleased with his bow, trotting over to greet the men and show off his gay apparel.

"Is it time?" Austin asked seriously. He claimed to remember the custom from the year before, but he'd needed some extensive prompting to recall the details.

"I think so," Joe said. "The feast is ready?"

Savannah held out her basket for inspection, and Austin followed suit. "It looks delicious," Mackenzie said. It was almost true. The kids had made a sort of oatmeal, full of dried fruit and bits of grain and applesauce and whatever else they figured the animals would enjoy. Joe and Mackenzie had brought up a few extra buckets' worth when they'd come to the barn, enough for all the cattle to get at least a taste, but the kids' smaller containers were for the special animals, the ones they'd made into pets.

Joe and Mackenzie stepped back and watched as the older girls helped the youngsters with the feeding. Angel and Devil, the sweet, placid horses for the farm's beginner riders, got heaping servings. The chickens squawked and pecked at their scattered offering, and Flower and her calf, Blossom, the milk cows slurped up as much as Ally would give them. She spent a moment with

Trout, her quarter horse, and Lacey helped the younger kids give treats to the other horses as well.

"Nothing for Misery?" Mackenzie asked Joe. They were still snuggled together, Joe's arm a welcome weight on Mackenzie's shoulders, and he could feel the man's chuckle through his chest.

"Crazy bitch would probably be happiest if she got one of my fingers for a snack."

"Well, it is the Christmas season. A time for giving. But you're already down one arm. I think we should hang on to your fingers."

"I'll let her lick out the buckets after the cows are fed," Joe said, and he heaved himself away from Mackenzie. "And the sooner we get to that, the sooner we can get back to the house for presents."

So they fed the cattle, then trooped back to the house for breakfast and stockings and gifts. A year before, Mackenzie had spent his Christmas in Nathan's glamorous, sterile condo overlooking the water in downtown Toronto. Now, he was in a century-old farmhouse, with shabby wallpaper and ancient furniture and warmth and love and family. He absolutely knew which place he preferred, and he leaned back against Joe's chest, ignoring the sofa spring digging into his ass.

"They're happy," Joe said, sounding relieved. He and Mackenzie were perched above the scene, looking down at the kids like they were puppies. Even Ally and Lacey had dropped their teenage dignity and were sitting cross-legged on the floor, comparing gifts and giggling.

Austin had opened one present, a plastic airport with planes and helicopters, and refused to take interest in anything else. Joe said he'd done the same thing last year, and they'd just stretched Christmas out for him, opening a present a day until it was over. "Maybe he's destined to be Jewish, and he's trying to start a Chanukah tradition," Mackenzie had suggested, and it earned him a smile and a kiss to the temple.

Savannah was looking through her pile of gifts with a strangely mixed expression, and when Lacey finally noticed her, she said, "What's up, Vannah? You didn't get what you wanted?"

"There's stuff from Santa," Savannah said bemusedly. "I thought...." She cast a quick look in Austin's direction, then said, "You know. Mom and Dad. I thought...."

"Whoever cares about you," Joe said quickly, easing down to the floor near the girl and keeping his voice low enough that Austin couldn't hear. "Santa can be anyone who cares about you, not just moms and dads."

Savannah squinted at him, then whispered, "You?"

Joe smiled gently. "With help," he said, nodding in Lacey's direction.

"Lace?" Savannah said incredulously. When her sister nodded, Savannah sprang to her feet and launched herself into Lacey's arms. She didn't say anything, just burrowed in and hung on, her face hidden from view, while Lacey's own face crumpled into smiling tears. Austin buzzed around them with a little red airplane until Ally tackled him and rolled him over for tickles.

"You didn't tell her about Santa being a thief," Mackenzie said quietly when Joe returned to the couch.

"He stole a lot out of my wallet," Joe muttered. "That should count."

"Do you want your present from me?" Mackenzie asked.

"I already know what it is," Joe said. "And if I have the option of not accepting it...."

"You don't." Mackenzie said it quickly, lightly, and tried not to look hurt. It wasn't like he hadn't known it was a bad gift. Giving a shirt and tie and dress pants to someone like Joe... it wasn't a gift at all, really, not when the only reason Joe needed the clothes was so he could dress the way Mackenzie's parents would expect when they met each other.

"Hey," Joe said. He waited until Mackenzie turned to look at him. "I want it." He shrugged. "It's good for me, right? I'm not a little kid. I should have real clothes. And I want your parents to like me."

"It doesn't matter what they think," Mackenzie said, maybe a bit too loudly. Two teenage faces turned to look at him, then went back to their Christmas activities with a little too much casual disregard. Their eyes might not be directed toward the sofa, but Mackenzie was pretty sure their ears were. But that was how conversations tended to happen in this family. The bedroom was safe, as long as they kept their voices down, but everything else was pretty public. Mackenzie shrugged and spoke more quietly. "It doesn't matter. They live three hours from here, and this is the first time I'll be seeing them since I met you. That tells you everything you need to know about what a close family we are. It really, really doesn't matter whether they like you."

"And it wouldn't bother *you*?" Joe looked at the chaos on the living-room floor, then back to Mackenzie. "Or maybe *this* bothers you. I mean, it's a lot, I know. It's a lot for *me*, and I'm used to a big family."

"I like it," Mackenzie said. He leaned in harder—enough pressure that if he'd been on Joe's bruised side there probably would have been pain. "It doesn't bother me. This is what Christmas *should* be."

"Without all the puking," Joe said, wrapping his arm tight around Mackenzie's shoulders.

"Yeah, less puke would have been nice. But that just means we have room for improvement. Next year, all the family fun, less vomit. Let's see if we can do it."

Joe nodded in agreement, then pulled a slightly crumpled envelope out from somewhere in the seat cushions. "Yours," he said like a bashful kid. Actually, Austin's presentation of flowers and leaves was quite a bit more sophisticated than Joe's delivery.

"You can exchange them if you want. I made sure."

Mackenzie wasn't sure what to expect, but he opened the envelope with a smile. It was the thought that counted. Then he saw the tickets, and his smile got a little more real. "*Les Misérables*? In Toronto?"

"You liked the movie," Joe said quickly. "But you've already seen it, so I wasn't sure if you'd really want to see the play too...."

"Of course I want to see the play," Mackenzie said quickly. "I *love* it. I love theater, I love live music! I love this gift!"

"You get to see *Les Mis*?" Ally said enviously. "You know, Mackenzie, those are *your* tickets. One of them doesn't have to be for Joe. You can take anyone you want. Gifts don't come with strings attached. You could take someone who might appreciate the show a bit more...." She smiled winningly.

"I watched the movie," Joe protested.

"You watched Hugh Jackman!" Ally shot back.

"Not true. I'm not saying I was totally caught up in the singing, but not Hugh Jackman."

"The other one," Mackenzie said sagely. "The young one, with the lips."

Joe shot him a look, then shrugged casually. "Yeah, more him." He nodded at the tickets. "But you can change them if you want. See something else, or get a refund...."

"Joe." Mackenzie put his hand on Joe's arm and waited until he had his full attention. "I want to see this show. I love this gift. And the best part? Now you have *two* places to wear your new clothes!"

Joe nodded. "That had occurred to me," he admitted. "I didn't want to be all dressed up with nowhere to go."

Mackenzie snuggled back into his Joe nest and smiled in satisfaction. The tickets were perfect, an excellent way to begin his new way of experiencing the city. Nathan hadn't liked theater much, so Mackenzie had never really gone, not since his mom had dragged him to things when he was a kid. But now he was an adult. He and Joe would drive down to the city a couple times a year, catch a show, maybe stay in a boutique hotel. A different one each time, until they found their favorite, and then they'd become regulars. They'd eat at a different restaurant each time, though, because they didn't get to eat out enough to crave familiarity. They'd make friends with other people who liked the theater, and they'd go for drinks after a performance, probably scotch or something like that, and they'd discuss what they'd seen and debate the relative merits. It was new, but it would be excellent.

The happy glow lasted all through the afternoon and evening. They played with the new toys, and Austin even got around to opening a second gift. They cooked together—each person in charge of his or her own side dish while Joe concentrated on the turkey—and they set the big table in the dining room and ate until they were ready to burst.

The holiday spirit was dampened a little when Joe and Ally had to go to the barn for evening chores, but Austin insisted on going with them, and then Savannah thought she should go to, and finally Mackenzie and Lacey gave in and started bundling up, so the family unity was maintained.

"That was a good day," Mackenzie said quietly as he lay next to Joe in bed. Their hands were roaming, casually exploring and appreciating each other's bodies, but their heads stayed close together, their conversation gentle and easy.

"It was," Joe agreed, and he kissed Mackenzie's cheek, then down to his lips. "Thank you."

"Thank *me*? Thank *you*. You did most of the work."

"Nah," Joe said. "Team effort, as usual." He was getting a bit bolder now, less exploring and more claiming territory. "But if you think differently, maybe it's time *you* did a bit more work." He rolled over onto his back and tugged gently on Mackenzie's hip, making it clear what he had in mind.

Mackenzie had no intention of arguing. He threw a leg over Joe's hips then leaned over to the bedside table for lube. As his chest brushed past Joe's face, Joe caught his nipple between his strong lips, sucking and nipping until Mackenzie's whole body arched and twitched in pleasure. Joe wrapped his hand around Mackenzie's cock and jacked it in time with his tongue. No matter what position they tried, it always ended up like this, Joe taking charge and giving pleasure, Mackenzie receiving.

"What if I wanted to fuck you sometime?" Mackenzie asked, trying to cling to a coherent train of thought through the waves of sensation.

That got easier when Joe released his nipple and stared up at him. "You can," he finally said. "If you want. We'd have to go slow, though. I haven't done that in a long time."

"Do you like it?" Mackenzie had no idea why he was pushing this.

Joe shrugged. "Sure, I guess. It's not my favorite, maybe, but we can mix it up."

"I don't want to," Mackenzie said. It was the truth, but Joe's expression didn't seem appreciative of that fact.

"So why are you asking about it?"

"I just wanted to know. You know, some tops are all macho about it, like it makes you less of a man if you can take a dick up your ass."

"I don't think you're less of a man, Mack."

"But you're always in charge. I mean, I could bottom and still take charge of things. If I wanted."

"*Do* you want?"

"Not really," Mackenzie admitted.

"We could be fucking, but instead we're having this conversation," Joe mused. "I really don't understand why that's happening."

"If I bought something... toys, or something. Could I use them on you?"

Joe squinted at him. "Depends what they are, I guess."

"Butt plug?" Mackenzie hadn't known he was thinking about that, but once he'd said it out loud, he liked the idea. A lot. "Not a big one, maybe. But with ribs, or something." He sat back up and squirted lube into his hand, then slowly set the bottle on the bed beside him and lined their cocks up together, running his lubed fingers along their matched shafts. "Something I could use to make you squirm. Play with you, tease you. Then maybe I'd fuck you, maybe I wouldn't." Joe's cock was hardening, but that could just be because it was getting a massage. Hard to be sure what messages Joe's brain was sending it. "Could we do that?"

"Yeah," Joe said. His arm with the broken wrist was out to the side, out of the way, but his other hand was strong and comfortable on Mackenzie's hip. "Sure."

"Do you *want* to do that?" They were both hard now, and Mackenzie shifted up onto his knees, guided Joe's cock to his opening, and teased them both by gliding it just past his hole, letting it catch a little, then pulling it away. "Or are you just willing to make me happy?"

"I want to make you happy," Joe said. "Mostly. But maybe I'd like it more once we got started."

Not the most enthusiastic response ever, but at least it was an honest answer. And as long as they were being honest... "And maybe I won't like it at all," Mackenzie admitted. "Maybe it's one of those things that seems good in my mind but ends up being gross or too much trouble or something, in reality."

"Be kind of ironic if I ended up loving it and you didn't like it at all," Joe said with a grin. "You might regret having started this." His smile shifted into something different as Mackenzie sank down, letting Joe's cock stretch him and slide inside. Joe's head flopped back as he closed his eyes. "God, you feel good," he said, running his hand over Mackenzie's stomach and chest before sliding it down to wrap around his cock.

Mackenzie couldn't talk, not while they were like this. The sensations were too intense, and it took all of his mental energy to just keep himself moving in something approaching a rhythmic manner. His cock and his ass were joined in a glowing orb of pleasure, and nothing else mattered, nothing except the friction and the movement and the glorious pressure. He leaned back enough that Joe's cock was hitting his prostate dead-on; almost too much but not quite. As long as he was in control, he could handle it, taking himself right to the edge of overstimulation and then easing away. He could hear his breathing, the soft whining sounds that came unbidden when he was driving right into his prostate, the grunting moans that escaped his lips as he changed the angle enough to give himself a break. If he got too loud, Joe would shush him, but that hadn't happened lately; he was getting used to having sex in a house full of kids. So he was free to let himself go, let the sensations wash over him.

His orgasm caught him almost by surprise, and it wasn't completely welcome. He'd been enjoying the buildup so much, and he'd thought he'd found a plateau where he could stay forever, basking in the pleasure and warmth. But one thrust too many against his prostate and he was off, his body shaking as he spurted over Joe's hand, his stomach, his chest. As always Joe seemed to be able to time things perfectly, gripping Mackenzie's hip and thrusting up a few extra times before his own body arched and he gasped in perfect completion.

Joe was in charge of cleanup, and Mackenzie let himself be rolled around and then bundled under the covers, Joe's long, strong body curled around him. "We can do anything you want," Joe promised, kissing the back of Mackenzie's neck.

"I just want more of that," Mackenzie replied.

"Good," Joe said, and his chuckle resonated through Mackenzie's body, rocking him easily to sleep.

Chapter Nine

THE HOUSE was almost exactly as Joe had pictured it in his mind: red brick, white pillars out in front, a house designed to make a statement of stability and solid upper-middle-class wealth. This was where Mackenzie had grown up, where his parents still lived. It was the place he only visited once a year, even though he lived just a few hours away.

"Karen's already here," Mackenzie said, nodding toward a BMW in the driveway. "Her husband is Lionel, their daughter is Peyton. Make sure you pronounce the T properly; if it slides into any other consonant you *will* be corrected."

Joe nodded. "Karen, Lionel, Pey-Ton. Karen's a teacher because she loves kids, not because she couldn't do better. Lionel's a corporate lawyer."

"Very good. And my brother?"

"Colin is in banking. He's bringing a new girlfriend today. I'm hoping she's black or blind or something, so the focus won't be on me."

"She'll be blonde and able-bodied," Mackenzie said with certainty. "You're the designated freak of the day. Sorry."

"At least I'm a sharp-dressed freak," Joe said. He was wearing a pair of Will's shoes, but the rest of him was brand new and Mackenzie-approved, so he assumed he was at least somewhat stylish. Not altogether comfortable, but it only made sense for his physical state to match his emotional one.

They stopped at the front door, and Joe said, "This isn't going to be any fun at all, is it?"

"This is a festive family dinner, Joe. It's not about fun—it's about reestablishing and reinforcing the hierarchy. And you and I will be at the bottom of that, in case you were wondering."

"I wasn't wondering."

Joe tried to let go of Mackenzie's hand as they waited for their knock to be answered, but Mackenzie gripped his fingers tightly. "I might not have come out until university, but I *did* come out. I'm gay. They know it."

"Yeah, but they don't know *I'm* gay," Joe said. "Maybe you and me are just friends...."

Then the door opened, and they were still holding hands, so that plan went out the window.

"Scott," a silver-haired man said with a smile and an extended hand. "Good to see you, son." Then he turned to Joe and waited.

"Dad, this is Joe Sutton," Mackenzie said dutifully. "Joe, this is my father, Michael Mackenzie."

"Sir," Joe said, extracting his good hand from Mackenzie's grip and extending it for shaking. "It's good to meet you."

"And you," Michael said. "Come on in. Let me take your coats."

It was a bit more formal than the mudroom entrances Joe was used to, but Mackenzie's father seemed friendly enough. And when an older woman came bustling out from somewhere in the back of the house, wearing an apron over her ivory lace dress, she was smiling as well.

"Scott," she said, reaching up to pull her son down for a kiss on the cheek. "And...."

"Mom, this is Joe Sutton," Mackenzie said. He was sounding a bit bored, and Joe frowned at him. Maybe it was a stupid ritual, but it didn't hurt to do it properly. "Joe, this is my mom, Carol

Mackenzie."

"Ma'am," Joe said.

"Joe? Or Joseph?"

"Just Joe, actually. That's what it says on my birth certificate. My brother's Will, not William. I guess with surprise twins, my parents wanted to keep things as simple as they could."

She laughed, a little too loud and a little too shrill, and Joe was startled to realize she was nervous. He smiled at her and glanced at her husband. If Michael Mackenzie had been a steer, he'd be the one Joe expected to bolt out of the herd, his eyes too wide and flickering around too much to be calm. This wasn't the placid, self-satisfied family Mackenzie had led Joe to expect.

"Thank you for having me here today," Joe said, trying to find the words that would make these people calm down. "I know it's a time for family, and I'm really glad you're letting me push in a little."

"We're pleased to have you," Carol said, and she sounded like she meant it. Then she turned her focus back to her son, and her voice was more formal, almost careful. "You're looking well, Scott. I guess life in the country is agreeing with you?"

"Life with Joe is agreeing with me," Mackenzie said, and it sounded like a dare. Kind of sad that no one in the room seemed interested in taking him up on it.

"That's good, then," Michael said, and he clapped Joe on the shoulder.

"Careful, Dad!" Mackenzie said. "He's got a sore side!"

"My ribs are sore, Mack. My shoulder's fine." Jesus, Joe had no idea why Mackenzie was wound so tight. "Everything's fine."

"What happened?" Carol asked, her eyes wide as she looked at the cast on Joe's wrist.

"Just a stupid accident. I fell down."

"He fell off the roof of a tractor-trailer," Mackenzie said as if it made Joe sound like *less* of a loser. "He's a volunteer firefighter. He saves lives."

"On a good day we save lives," Joe said. "On a bad day I just contribute to the skyrocketing costs of health care in this country." He held up his cast as evidence.

"Well, what's the point of living in such a wealthy land if we can't take care of our heroes?" Carol asked sweetly. "Now, come into the living room, both of you. Karen and Lionel are here, and Scott, you won't *believe* how much Peyton has grown."

The T *was* a bit overemphasized, but it wasn't enough to earn the eye roll Mackenzie sent Joe's way as they trailed behind his parents into the living room. "Be cool," Joe whispered, but Mackenzie either couldn't hear or pretended he couldn't.

The well-dressed couple sitting on the sofa with glasses of wine looked up as Joe and Mackenzie came in, but only the man stood. The little girl playing on the floor at their feet didn't even glance in the direction of the newcomers.

"Lionel Katz," the man said, extending his hand to Joe while simultaneously nodding in Mackenzie's direction. "Good to see you, Scott."

"Nice of you to drop by," the woman agreed icily. So there was the first hint of tension that wasn't coming from Mackenzie, but really, it wasn't too surprising that she might resent her brother's long absence and prodigal reappearance.

Joe wished he were better at small talk. There was probably something light and easy he could say just then that would help everyone get past the initial tension, but he had no idea what it might be. Mackenzie could have thought of something good, but he was pretty obviously not interested in lessening the tension in the room. In fact, he seemed determined to wallow in it.

So they sat where they were directed, on opposite sides of the room, and Mackenzie's dad brought them drinks while his mother bustled back to the kitchen. Joe earned a smile when he offered to help her, but she turned him down. Which was too damn bad, because that left him stuck in the living room with the squabbling siblings. Then he remembered some of the scenes Mackenzie had been part of between Joe and Nick, and he forced himself to relax a little. Families fought. It didn't have to be a huge deal.

Lionel and Michael returned to a conversation that had apparently been interrupted when Joe and Mackenzie arrived, something about a big corporate merger that might or might not be happening after the holidays, and they tried to get Mackenzie involved in it. Joe sat on the sofa next to Karen, both of them carefully squished to their respective ends, and forced himself to sip his beer slowly instead of gulping it. When the little girl finally deigned to notice the new arrivals, he hoped she might be a source of entertainment, but as he watched her meticulously straighten the folds of her white dress, his hopes lessened.

Still, at least she was talking to him. "Who are you?" she demanded.

"Joe. I came with Mack—Scott."

"MacScott?" she said. It could have been playful, but there was a sneer in her voice, an eagerness to find a weakness. It would have been unpleasant in an adult, but in a child it seemed especially ugly.

But Joe smiled anyway. "Scott. I usually call him Mackenzie, but that doesn't make much sense here, with so many Mackenzies."

"Why do you call him that? His name is *Scott*."

"It's how he introduced himself to me. I guess people get to call themselves what they want."

"People should call themselves their real names."

"Even if they don't like their real names?"

"They should just *like* their real names."

"Okay. Interesting perspective. You want to play with your

doll some more?" *Or do anything else, really.* Joe had never met a kid he couldn't get along with, but he had a feeling this one might be his Waterloo.

"No. I want to talk to you. Do you know my name?" There was a light in her eye, a quick glance toward her mother that made Joe feel as if he was being invited into a trap.

"I do," he said.

"What is it, then?"

Joe knew the mature response. Say her name, overpronounce the 'T,' carry on with his life. But there was just something irritating about the little brat. "Play Town," he said.

"What? No, that's not even a name. Do you know my name or not?"

"Play dough?"

"*Play dough?* No! That's not a real name either!"

"Wait. I almost have it. Is it PoTaTo?" he asked, emphasizing the Ts for all he was worth.

"Mommy!" she screamed. Joe winced. He'd taken it a bit too far, apparently.

"Peyton, sweetie, what's wrong?"

"He said my name is Potato!"

The men looked over at the commotion, and Mackenzie twitched his lips in amusement. He was clearly pleased Joe was joining him in subversion, but Joe wasn't sure if that was a good thing. "I was joking," he said to the girl's mother.

"Oh, really? You don't *actually* think my daughter's name is Potato?" Another line that could have been delivered with humor but was instead dripping with acid.

The girl's head was buried in her mother's lap, and her shoulders were shaking with sobs, but when she glanced in Joe's direction, her face was dry. Joe just smiled at her. Fuck it—they weren't *his* family. "Nope. Just thought she might find it amusing."

"I don't think she did," Karen said archly.

"Doesn't seem like it." But Joe was done with that, and if Karen was waiting for an apology, she'd better get comfortable. So he smiled again and said, "Mackenzie says you're a teacher? What grade?"

But Peyton increased the volume of her wails to a level that made conversation impossible. Carol came in from the kitchen, looking not exactly alarmed, but certainly not pleased by the commotion. "Karen, Peyton," she said, loudly enough to be heard. "Would you like to come make the table beautiful? Peyton, you're so good at that!"

"Let's go help Grandma," Karen said, shooting a dirty look in Joe's direction. "She needs you to use your designer's eye! Can you show her how to make the table pretty?"

Peyton was obviously torn between the chance to show off and the opportunity to milk the potato incident for a little more sympathy. Joe focused on his beer bottle and resisted the urge to make a face at the little girl. He was there to help Mackenzie, not to make things worse by taunting a child.

There was noise from the front of the house then, and two new faces appeared in the living room door, their cheeks rosy from the cold as they shed outdoor clothing.

"Uncle Colin! Aunt Moira!" Peyton screamed, and she launched herself toward them. "The mean man said I look like a potato!"

"What?" The new woman said, lifting the girl into her arms. "Who would say such a horrible thing?"

Peyton was all too ready to point out the transgressor, of course, and that was how Joe was introduced to Mackenzie's brother and his girlfriend, who was, indeed, blonde and fit. He didn't even try to defend himself, just shook hands as required and retreated back to his seat and his rapidly warming beer.

The rest of the afternoon went about the same way. Only

Karen and Peyton were actively unpleasant, but they had a way of dominating the conversation to make it feel as if everyone was being negative and unfriendly. Peyton seemed to make it her mission to torment Joe. He knew how long that behavior would have lasted if it had been coming from one of the kids under his authority, but Karen either didn't notice or didn't care, and no one else dared to challenge her.

After dinner, Mackenzie's mom finally took pity on Joe and let him help her in the kitchen. They filled the dishwasher together and put the leftover food away, then started on the pots and pans too big for the dishwasher. "You're doing pretty well with that broken wrist," Carol said. "And you obviously know your way around the kitchen. Do you do a lot of cooking?"

"I guess, yeah. Nothing too fancy, though. We raise beef, so I can do a lot with red meat. Potatoes and frozen vegetables with it. I guess I kind of cook like I'm living in the seventies."

"It wasn't a bad decade," she said with a smile. "And Scott? He helps you cook?"

"Sometimes. He usually helps with cleanup."

She nodded in apparent approval. "Division of labor. It's an important part of a good partnership." They worked quietly for a while, and then she asked, "Is he happy?" She sounded almost desperate, and she tempered her expression as soon as she heard herself, laughing self-consciously. "A mother always worries. And we don't see him all that often."

"I worry too," Joe admitted. "About everybody. About Mackenzie. I think... yeah, I think he's happy. It's not perfect. He misses the city, I guess. The glamor and everything. The money."

"He never brought Nathan to meet us," she said softly. "We went into the city a couple times and met them at restaurants, but Nathan never came through the doors of this house." She handed him the washed roasting pan and said, "That must mean something."

"Means Nathan wouldn't come, probably." Joe focused on drying the pan, trying to find a way to hold it that didn't put strain on his wrist. "I don't think he had a lot of time for sentimental stuff."

"But you do?"

"I have time for Mackenzie. I try to do what he wants, and he wanted to come here today."

"Did he?" She sounded grateful. "He wasn't just guilted into it?"

Well, that was a tricky question. Mackenzie hadn't exactly been enthusiastic about the visit, but he hadn't tried to get out of it, either. "He wanted to come. But I guess he was maybe a bit worried about it too."

"We haven't always been what he needed." She pulled the plug in the sink and started wiping the counter with fierce efficiency. "It took me a long time to realize that. But sometimes... sometimes we were just trying to keep him from making mistakes. Trying to get him to *be* something, to *do* something. He thinks we wanted him to be an achiever, but it was never about that. He was always different, always on his own path. We just wanted... we hoped he'd find something meaningful, not just spend his time at the gym and in clubs."

"Has he told you about the church?" Joe asked. "There's not much action right now, in the winter, but he's got quite a few things booked for the spring and summer. It's a beautiful building, and he's making a lot of people happy with it."

"I'd like to see it," she said wistfully.

"You should come up sometime." He was probably crossing a line, but he didn't care. Mackenzie's mom should get to see at least a little of the life he was building for himself. "I'd invite you to stay at the farm, but we'd have a hard time making you comfortable. The house is pretty full. But there's a B&B in town, or you could just make it a day trip—it's not all that far."

"I'd like that," she said. "If it'd be okay with Scott...."

"I'll talk to him about it," Joe said. "Maybe we could set something up for the spring. The church has really nice gardens, and he's worked hard on them."

They rejoined the rest of the group then and listened to a bit more of Karen explaining how wonderful Peyton was, and then Mackenzie looked at his watch and raised his eyebrows at Joe. Joe nodded back at him. Time to make their escape.

The good-byes were friendly but cool, at least by Sutton-family standards. Peyton stuck her tongue out at Joe, and he smiled back at her and said, "See ya, Pop-Tart." He made sure the T was clearly pronounced.

"Nice to see you making friends," Mackenzie said as they retreated down the driveway, Peyton's outraged wails fading into the distance.

"She's not my favorite kid," Joe admitted. "And her mom's wound a little tight. The rest of them seem okay, though."

"You and my mom seemed to get along pretty well. Too well for my comfort, to be honest. I think she wants to have your babies."

They stopped at the truck, and Joe fumbled for his keys. "Maybe she's hoping the next batch of kids will come around a bit more often. Seriously, Mack, I think she really misses you."

Mackenzie didn't have a reply to that. They were out of the subdivision on their way to the highway before Joe said, "I'm sure there's a history and everything. Families are complicated. I get it. But right now? I think your parents are both really trying to make things right. I think they want to be in your life."

"Yeah, so they can tell me how to run it to their satisfaction."

"Maybe a bit. That's kind of a parent thing, isn't it?"

"You should have heard them when I came out, Joe. They were *not* as cool about it as they seem to be now."

"Yeah, okay, but what parents are? My dad threw my ass out of the house when I told him I was gay. We got over it."

Mackenzie shook his head. "Well, maybe you shouldn't have! You practically dare a bunch of homophobes to come at you when you meet them on the street, but you let your own dad get away with treating you that way? Maybe you should have stood up for yourself!"

"You think so?" It probably wasn't fair to get mad at Mackenzie for judging Joe's family decisions, not when Joe was in the middle of judging Mackenzie's, so he tried to keep his tone moderate. "You think it'd be better for anyone involved if my dad had gone to the grave with him and me still mad at each other? If my mom had spent her last years torn between her husband and her son? You think that would have been a better solution?"

Mackenzie was quiet for a while, then said, "Well, the dead-parent argument kind of trumps anything I was going to come up with. I guess you win." He didn't sound angry, exactly, but he wasn't too pleased either.

"It's not about winning," Joe said tiredly. "They're your family; it's your call. I can't tell you what's right for you, or right for them. I just... yeah, I guess the dead-parent thing *does* give a bit of a different perspective. It doesn't make me regret every single fight I had with them, but it sure makes me wish I could take *some* of them back."

They were on the highway by the time Mackenzie said, "And what about 'Potato'? Do you wish you could take *that* back?"

Joe smirked and looked over to see a matching expression on Mackenzie's face. "Nope. I kinda wish I'd figured out a way to talk about getting her mashed that didn't sound like I was advocating child abuse. Other than that, I'm satisfied with the situation."

"I'm satisfied with it too," Mackenzie said. And at least in that one small area, Joe believed he was.

CHAPTER TEN

MACKENZIE DOZED most of the way home and was still so sleepy when he arrived that he was tempted to lift up his arms in the same pose Austin used to get Joe to carry him into the house. If Joe had two good arms it might have been worth trying, but as it was, Mackenzie hauled himself out of the truck and trailed along behind Joe as they made their way into the house. Neither of them was expecting to see Ally and Lacey sitting at the kitchen table, clearly waiting for them.

Well, waiting for Joe. Mackenzie needed to keep reminding himself of that. This was Joe's ship, and Mackenzie was just one more homeless waif taking shelter on its decks. So he hung in the background as Joe stepped into the kitchen, still with his outdoor clothes on, and stared at the girls.

"Do I want to know what's going on?"

"It was my idea," Ally said quickly. "And I think you'll agree it was a good one, at least once you hear the whole story. Or, maybe not a good *idea*, exactly, but a good reaction. Making the most of a bad situation, that's what you'll think it was."

Joe sighed as if he'd already had the weight of the world on his shoulders and he saw someone coming at him about to add the moon. He shrugged out of his coat and draped it on the back of a chair, then sat down. "Okay, hit me with it."

Ally took a deep breath, looked at Lacey for support, then said, "Kami's asleep upstairs."

"Kami." Joe looked from Ally to Lacey. Kami was *her* sister, after all. "Why?"

"You should have seen it, Joe!" Ally's eyes were filling with tears at the memory, and unlike Peyton's, these tears were real. "We went to see her—you knew we were going to do that. And it was a *good* visit. She was talking, and laughing, and she unwrapped her presents all by herself, and she was playing with them. She's doing really well."

"She's doing well because she's in a facility that offers her extensive rehab. A place with people specially trained to give her what she needs and help her figure out how to function again."

"What she needs?" Lacey spoke for the first time, her voice bitter. Mackenzie edged a little closer, compelled by the rawness of the girl's expression. "She needs to be *loved*. She needs people who care about her and treat her right!"

"They wanted to put her in a straitjacket, Joe!" Ally's tears were loose, now, streaming down her cheeks, but her voice was still strong. "They called it *restraints*, but it was a straitjacket! We had that great visit, and then she got upset when we were trying to leave!"

"We were *all* upset," Lacey said. "So it was our fault, really, me and Savannah. We set her off. She wanted to come with us, and we had to leave her behind, and she tried to come with us and they stopped her, and she fought them. She was scared, and she didn't understand, and she's only *eleven*! She weighs less than a hundred pounds! It's not like she was going to *hurt* them or something."

"So they tried to put her in restraints," Joe said. He still sounded pretty calm, but Mackenzie could feel the tension beneath the surface. "Then what?"

"Then we said they shouldn't," Lacey said. "And they said we should mind our own business, and we said she's our sister, so she *is* our business, and they said if we wanted her, we could have her."

"So we took her," Ally said. Her tears had stopped.

"Because the staff at the rehab facility *dared* you to?" Joe asked. He was starting to lose his cool.

"Because we couldn't leave her there with them," Ally said pleadingly. She looked at her big brother like he was a hero, someone who had her absolute trust, and it occurred to Mackenzie for the first time how oppressive that kind of respect must be. "She's *family*, Joe." It was the magic word, of course, and Ally knew it. Mackenzie was almost disappointed in her for using it. She knew how to get Joe to do what she wanted, but usually she didn't take advantage of the fact. He supposed that was her side of the oppressive balance with Joe. She worshipped him, but she also protected him. Usually.

"She's family," Joe repeated dully, and he didn't point out that Kami wasn't *his* family, wasn't Ally's sister. Instead he leaned back in his chair and softly said, "Fuck."

The kitchen was silent as he stewed. Finally, he pushed away from the table and stood up. "Do you have her medications? She must be on some. Where's she sleeping? What happens if she gets up in the night and doesn't know where she is and wanders outside? How long's she going to last out there in this weather?" He paused for a breath, but obviously wasn't out of questions. "Have you told anyone where she is? Does Jean know about any of this? Shit, do the *cops* know? Because I don't care what the idiots at the rehab center said, you can't just take her home because she's *family*. She's a ward of the state. They could call this kidnapping if they felt like it." He looked at his chair as if thinking about sitting down, then crossed to the sink instead, leaned against its cool porcelain, and stared out through the window into the night. "Is there a plan?" he asked, more quietly now. "We take her back tomorrow, right? We talk to them about restraints, we come up with a system for leaving, so it's less traumatic. If they don't cooperate, we make a complaint, we get Jean involved, we call whoever we have to call." He turned around. "I'm not saying it was a good situation. I can see why you did what you did, but that doesn't mean it was what you *should* have done."

"We should have left her there?" Ally said. She started crying again.

"You should have called me," he said dully. "But I left my phone in the truck so it wouldn't go off during dinner. And if you'd gotten hold of me, I would have been three hours away, too far to really do anything."

Mackenzie's lips twitched in a bitter smile, but no one was looking in his direction. Of course this had turned out to be Joe's fault.

"The plan is for her to live with me," Lacey said into the silence. Ally looked as stunned as Joe, but Lacey focused her energy on the older Sutton; she knew who she needed to convince. "I'm eighteen in three weeks. If they don't kick me out of school for the drinking thing, I'll quit as soon as I'm old enough. I'll get a job and find somewhere to live, and I'll look after her. That's what *you* did, Joe, so don't tell me I shouldn't do the same."

Joe stared out the window at the darkness for too long, then turned and walked to the fridge. He pulled out three beers, then pulled out a fourth and looked at Mackenzie questioningly. He wasn't asking for Mackenzie's opinion about the wisdom of giving alcohol to two underage girls, one of whom had recently displayed behavior that suggested a problem with the substance; he was just checking whether Mackenzie wanted a drink. So Mackenzie sighed and nodded. He wanted something a lot stronger than a beer, but he'd take what he could get.

Joe twisted the caps off for all of them, distributed the bottles, and sat down at the table. He took a long pull before he said, "It's not the same, Lacey. Not even close." He held up his hands to silence her when she started to protest. "It's not. I was older than you are. I was done with any school I ever had any plans of doing. I had Will to help me out, and the kids we were looking after were older. None of them had special needs. And I didn't have to find a job *or* a place to live. We even had insurance money to help us with expenses. That's a lot of stuff that made things way easier for me and Will. And, Lacey...." He leaned forward and waited until she met his eyes. "It was still really, really hard. Two of us, done with school, taking on older kids, no special needs, and enough money to be safe, and I wasn't always sure we were going to make it. You've got one person, younger siblings, one with special needs, and no money whatsoever." He leaned back in his chair and sighed. "I understand the instinct. I mean, *obviously* I understand, right? But it's not the same situation. Not at all."

"It's my call," Lacey said stubbornly.

"Probably not," Joe replied. "You'd have to get approval from the government, and I doubt they'd give it to you. But even if they did, this isn't about you. It's about Kami. What's best for her? Growing up in total poverty, with a sister who's working too hard and is too stressed to give her any attention? 'Cause assuming you get a job, it's going to be minimum wage. Maybe you'd get some money for fostering her, but maybe not because you're related. And even if you do get it, it's not a lot. You've seen the bank accounts I set up for you and Savannah, where I put all the foster-care money. Maybe it looks like a lot when it's just sitting there, but you take rent for a two-bedroom apartment out of it and you're done. Food, transportation, clothes... there goes your paycheck. Maybe you can use the school as a day care, at least ten months a year, but where does Kami go over summer vacation? What about March break and Christmas, or if your work hours aren't exactly the same as her school hours? What if she gets sick and can't go to school? You take enough time off work to take care of her and you're going to get fired. And sure, there's day programs where Kami could get some more rehab, but how does she get to them? You take more time off work and drive her there in a car you don't own, with gas you can't pay for."

"So what would you do?" Lacey asked quietly. "If you were me. What would you do?" There was an intensity to the question that suggested it wasn't rhetorical. Lacey really wanted to follow Joe's example.

But he just snorted. "Not a good standard, Lacey." He held up his wrist and displayed the cast. "I'd probably do something stupid, 'cause that's what I do. I'd probably get stubborn and refuse to take anybody's help or advice, 'cause that's another thing I do." He smiled gently. "I'm asking you to do something *better* than what I'd do. Just because I don't use my head doesn't mean you can't use yours."

"She's my *sister*," Lacey said. She wasn't crying, but somehow that made her heartbreak even more poignant. "I should have gotten her the hell out of that house before the fire. The social workers kept asking if things were okay, and I kept lying and saying they were." Her brow was furrowed as if she couldn't understand her own decisions. "Kami shouldn't have had to live like that for as long as she did. None of us should have, but now things are better for Savannah and me, but not for Kami." She looked pleadingly at Joe. "Does that seem fair? Is it right? She lives the first eleven years of her life in a house like that, and then she's going to live the rest of it in an institution, somewhere that people want to strap her down when she gets upset about her sisters leaving her?" Her voice was shaking as she whispered, "It's not right. It's not fair."

Mackenzie's beer bottle trembled as he raised it to his lips, and he wished again that it was something strong. These little girls were being asked to bear things most adults wouldn't be able to stand.

Joe was staring at the wood of the kitchen table as if it had the secrets of the universe written on it, but when he raised his eyes, it was clear he hadn't been able to read any of the answers. "Okay," he said quietly. "I hear you. I understand. It wasn't your fault, though. Not at all. You're...." He grinned, but it faded quickly. "I know you feel like an adult, but you're still a kid. Any decisions you made? You made them as a kid. The whole point of being a kid is that you don't have good judgment yet. That's why adults are supposed to look after kids. Not just your parents, but the social workers, the cops... your neighbors. *We're* the ones who fucked up, not you. And you paid for it, and Kami paid more."

Joe leaned back from the table and looked over at Mackenzie. Again it was clear that he wasn't looking for advice or consultation. Instead, his expression was apologetic. Mackenzie tried to send a reassuring message back, but he wasn't sure it was received. Instead, Joe turned back to Lacey and said, "I'll figure something out. *We* will. You and me. You can't get your own place. You have to see that won't work. But we'll find other options. Okay?"

"Like what?" she asked, and now that Joe was letting her be a kid again, the tears were coming.

"I don't know," he said flatly. Then he smiled. "But we'll figure it out. Okay?"

Lacey gave him a long, searching look before she nodded. Another disciple for the cult of Saint Joe, Mackenzie thought wryly.

"Go to bed, for now," Joe said. "We'll sort it out tomorrow."

Ally squinted at him and asked, "What about that stuff you were asking about? Her meds, and if she wanders outside? All that?"

"I'm going to make some calls about the meds, see what I can find out at this time of night." He looked at Lacey and asked, "I don't suppose you know what she was taking? I might be able to Google for some info, at least."

But Lacey shook her head apologetically. "There were pills. But I don't know what they were."

Joe didn't seem surprised. "Okay. Go to sleep."

Ally looked like she was thinking about arguing a little more, but Joe pointed his chin in Lacey's direction and the instruction was clear: *take care of your friend.* Ally did as she was told, guiding Lacey out of the kitchen and toward the stairs.

Joe stood up and found another beer in the fridge, then finally looked in Mackenzie's direction. His expression was still apologetic, and he stood there like a little kid waiting for a scolding he knew was well deserved.

"You're going to take her in, aren't you?" Mackenzie asked quietly.

Joe refused to meet his gaze. "I hope not. Maybe there's another facility somewhere, or maybe there was just a big misunderstanding at this one and really Kami's happy there and Lacey's just overreacting. Maybe."

"But if it comes down to it." Mackenzie wasn't sure why he was pushing this, but he felt like he needed to hear the words. "Running a ranch and raising a five-year-old, that's not quite enough for you. So you added an extra teenager to the mix. Can I remind you that you still haven't talked to Lacey about being drunk at school? You still don't know what the hell the school is planning to do about that or about the vandalism stuff. Add in a nine-year-old who's pretty much destined to have some behavior issues of her own, considering her background. But that's not enough." Mackenzie could hear his voice getting louder, but he didn't think he was going to try to control it. It made sense to keep the kids from hearing them having sex, but damn it, maybe the kids needed to know about it when they had fights. "Now you're going to take on an eleven-year-old with brain damage. And don't say Lacey's going to take care of her, because I'm not sure Lacey can even take care of herself. You're going to end up looking after the little girl. That's what's happening here." He set his beer bottle down on the counter. "How much time and energy is left, Joe? Is there *any* left for you and me?"

Mackenzie turned abruptly and stared out the window. "I hate it that I have to ask that. I feel like a shallow, selfish asshole, just because I want to have a life, want to spend some time with the man I love. And then I get mad at you because you're the one who's *making* me feel selfish. I mean, it's not unreasonable, is it?" Mackenzie turned back and stared at Joe. "For me to want to have a life *with* you? 'Cause if I don't have any of your time, what the hell am I doing up here? I have friends in the city, a life I left behind."

Joe's smile was quick and sharp. "Yeah. The city." He made a face as if trying to frighten his anger out of his body, and when he spoke again he was calmer. "Today was about you. Going to see your family. Christmas was good. You said you liked being around the kids. The rest of it?" He raised his eyes in supplication, looking as if he hoped Mackenzie might have all the answers for the questions he was asking himself. "I don't know. What else can I do?"

And that was the question. What else *could* he do? One of the reasons Mackenzie loved Joe was because of his caring, his responsibility. For Joe to walk away from someone in need? It would mean Joe wasn't Joe anymore. But what about Mackenzie being who *he* was? The dream he'd had about them going to the city and seeing plays and finding friends to have dinner and drink scotch with? That dream didn't fit with someone trying to run a ranch and raise three little kids. Sure, it had just been a fleeting thought, not something Mackenzie had been working toward his entire life, but he knew he wanted *something* like that. Social interaction, with adults, surely wasn't too much for a person to want. Joe seemed willing to spend his life exclusively with animals and children.

Ally was some help, but she would be leaving soon, and it felt like Joe was barely keeping it together even *with* her help and even *without* Kami living with them. This wasn't a temporary problem, not by a long shot. "I don't know what to do," Mackenzie whispered. "I wish I did."

Joe nodded slowly, as if Mackenzie had given him the only answer that made sense. "Maybe it'll work out," he said, but he didn't sound like he believed it any more than Mackenzie did.

"I'm going to bed," Mackenzie replied. "You're not coming, right? You have to make phone calls."

"Bad things can happen if you stop taking some medications," Joe said. "I mean, worse than if you'd never started taking them at all. And I need to check in with the cops and with Jean. Even if I just leave messages, at least I can show that we weren't trying to kidnap her or something."

Mackenzie nodded. Joe was taking care of things. That was what he did. "Okay," he said tiredly. It wasn't like he could argue with any of it. He headed for the stairs and only then realized that Griffin hadn't greeted them at the door. When he got to the upstairs hall he found the dog curled up in the hallway, wagging his tail with a gentle thud against the floor when he saw his owner.

"You abandoning me, Griffin?"

The dog stood to greet him, but didn't follow him to the bedroom, lying back down in the hallway instead. It was one rejection too many. "*Griffin, here!*" Mackenzie hissed, and the dog stood reluctantly and came to the foot of the bed. Mackenzie peeled off most of his clothes and climbed into bed, then patted the comforter. "Here, Griffin," he said, and the dog obediently hopped up beside him. "Good dog." It was good to have a warm body next to him, and Mackenzie let himself relax. He was tired. It would all seem better in the morning.

He almost believed it, but then he felt the mattress shift and heard a soft thud followed by the click of claws on hardwood. Griffin was leaving. Mackenzie wasn't even the number-one priority of his own dog. He closed his eyes tighter and willed himself to sleep. He didn't want to be awake anymore, not until his life got a lot easier to handle.

CHAPTER ELEVEN

JOE SPENT the night on the living-room sofa so he could monitor traffic on the stairs. As long as Kami stayed upstairs, she should be okay, but if she wandered down, there was the danger of the kitchen, the even greater danger of the outdoors. Far too many places where a little girl could get hurt, and Joe wouldn't be able to live with himself if she suffered *again* on his watch.

And it wasn't like he'd been going to get much sleep, no matter where he lay down. He'd gotten hold of a night nurse at the residence who'd refused to give out any information on Kami's medications, so then he'd had to call Jean, but she wasn't answering her phone, which made sense, since it was two in the morning on the day after Christmas. He'd left a message and sent her a text and e-mail, but she still hadn't responded. He'd called Andy Stark, who was an OPP officer but also a family friend, and left a message on his machine as well. Joe knew he needed to do something more, but he wasn't sure what. So he'd lain down with the house phone and his cell beside him and tried to get at least a little sleep.

He woke from a light doze when he heard feet on the stairs. He recognized the tread and sat up to see Austin poking his blond head cautiously around the corner.

"Red?" the boy whispered. Joe hadn't realized the dog was sleeping just inside the living-room door, but he heard the heavy thud of his tail hitting the floor.

"Hey, Austin," Joe said quietly, and Austin's head swiveled in his direction.

"Joe?" he said, obviously as confused by his uncle's location as he'd been by the dog's.

"Hey, buddy."

Austin padded over cautiously, peered at Joe's face as if to confirm his identity, then climbed laboriously onto the couch. Joe rolled onto his side, leaving room for Austin to snuggle in next to him. "Blanket," Austin said. It wasn't an order or even a request. More like the verbalization of a wish. Austin wanted to be under the blanket, and if he said this out loud, someone might help him out.

It was so simple, Joe thought, and he squirmed around until there was extra afghan for him to share. Austin snuggled in and pillowed his head on his soft little arm, and Joe felt a wave of love so strong it was almost a physical reaction. This little person trusted Joe and wanted to cuddle with him as they woke up. In a little while he'd realize he was hungry, and it would be up to Joe to take care of that. He'd need help with countless other things through the day, and Joe would be there for him. Joe would *always* be there for him, and it wasn't a burden, it was a gift.

Austin squirmed, and Joe tucked his arm around him to make sure he didn't fall off the couch. A gift, but a heavy one. Maybe that was the way to look at it. Joe had too many gifts, and he had to carry them all. He didn't have Santa's magic sack, so he felt all the weight. And if he was carrying too much, maybe something would get dropped.

That couldn't be Austin. It was impossible to figure out all the different rankings and valuations, but according to any formula Joe could think of, Austin had to be his number-one priority. The rest of it? A blurring combination of needs and wants and wishes. Joe couldn't think about all that and lie still enough to keep Austin happy, so he tried to clear his mind. He breathed in the faint scent of Austin's hair and let himself enjoy the way his warm little body snuggled into Joe's.

"What're we doing today, Joe?" Austin asked. He still sounded a little sleepy, but that was normal. Austin generally took a while to wake up. It didn't mean he was interested in going back to sleep, though.

"I don't know. I need to look after the animals. You going to help with that?"

"Is it cold?"

"It's winter. It's always going to be cold, so we have to wear our warm clothes."

"Are the animals cold?"

"They have warm clothes of their own—their fur and feathers. And they're mostly in the barn, so there's no wind." Usually Joe would prompt Austin to answer these questions himself, but not when Austin was still sleepy. At this time of day Austin didn't need his brain stimulated, he just needed the comfort of familiar things.

"What else are we doing today?"

Returning an innocent girl to an institution she hates? Taking on a new, crushingly heavy responsibility that would inevitably cut away from the attention Austin got from his uncle? "I don't know, buddy. What do you want to do?"

Austin didn't answer. He lay quietly for another few minutes and then squirmed out of Joe's embrace. He padded across the floor to the Christmas tree and squatted to inspect the remaining presents. "For me?"

"Mostly. You can read the tags, okay? Look for your name. Don't open the ones for Will or Lindsey or Sarah or Dave or Nick. Just the ones for Austin."

Austin spent some more time looking at the boxes, then selected a small silver one and carried it over to Joe. "Austin?" he said, pointing at the card.

Joe propped himself up on his elbow, ignoring the protests of a body made creaky by a night on a too-small sofa. "Is there an *A*?"

Austin inspected the card again, then nodded.

"What's the next letter?"

"You!" Austin said with a jaunty finger-point in Joe's direction. The little man was waking up.

"And what's next?"

"Sssssssssss," Austin hissed.

"After that?"

Austin stood straight and put his hands out to his sides to be a T.

"And then?"

Austin stayed straight, brought his hands over his head in a little circle, and waited for approval.

"If the next letter is what I think it is, you're in luck. What's the next letter?"

"N-ytime, N-ywhere!" Austin said happily. Joe wasn't really sure he liked that little memory trick, but Ally had come up with it, and it certainly seemed to work.

"A-U-S-T-I-N spells Austin, all right," Joe said. Then he squinted at the package. "Let me see for a second?" Austin reluctantly handed the box to his uncle. "Uh, buddy?" Joe said after a quick look. "What's this letter here? The very first letter?"

Austin refused to look at the card. "A?" he said hopefully.

"It doesn't look like an A, buddy. Look at it, all sssnakey and ssslippery. What's that letter?"

"A. For Austin."

"You like this one because it's shiny, right? But you probably won't like what's inside. And it might make someone else sad if you opened their present. Who would be sad if this present was opened before she got it? Whose name starts with S?"

Austin pouted, but finally, reluctantly admitted, "Sarah."

"Yeah. I think you're right; I think this present is for Sarah. I don't think you want to make Sarah sad, right? How 'bout you find one that's for you, okay?"

Austin's longing look suggested that he might not be all that worried about making Sarah sad, but he seemed to realize the present was out of reach and wandered back over to the tree for another selection. Joe pushed himself the rest of the way up on the couch, ready to intercept if Austin tried any more gift theft, and that was when he saw Mackenzie watching him from just around the corner.

Mackenzie's smile wasn't bright, but he came into the room and sat down on the couch next to Joe. "You're thinking you should have bought him a present with shiny wrapping paper, right? You're blaming yourself for ruining his Christmas or something equally insane, just because his gifts were wrapped in paper with puppies and bears and toys instead of shiny silver. Right?"

"I didn't ruin his Christmas," Joe said. "But, seriously, I *know* he likes shiny stuff. Would it have killed me to have put a bit more thought into the wrapping?"

"You're unbelievable," Mackenzie said. It wasn't entirely clear how he felt about his observation. "*Everybody* likes shiny stuff. But we like puppies and bears and toys too. Also, we know we can't always have every single thing our own way all the time." He pointed his chin toward Austin, who was trying to drag a particularly large box out from behind the tree. "He doesn't seem too upset about it. Which is good. Not because him being upset would mean you'd made the wrong wrapping choice, but because it would mean he was a spoiled brat. As someone who's met Peyton, I think you can appreciate how unpleasant it would be if Austin was spoiled that way. But he's not. You've done a good job, despite your instincts."

It was hard to decide whether that little speech was mostly complimentary or mostly insulting, so Joe decided not to try to make the judgment. Better to focus on the practical. "You want breakfast?"

"You have to go to the barn soon, right? I can make breakfast for Austin, if you want."

But Mackenzie was already mad that Joe was thinking about taking on more responsibility. It wouldn't be fair to ask him to assume Joe's existing jobs. "I can do it," he said quickly. "Little man, do you want pancakes or waffles?"

Austin looked up from the half-opened gift. "What *is* this?" he asked with dawning excitement. "I think there's animals!"

"That one's from me," Mackenzie said. He scooted off of the couch onto the floor and reached for the box. "See? It's a farm. Do you want to take the rest of the wrapping off to see the picture, or should we try to open the box right now?"

A choice like that required Austin's full attention, so Joe stood up and headed for the kitchen. Pancakes were marginally easier, so that was what he'd make.

He had the batter mixed and had given Austin his five-minute warning when he heard voices on the staircase. "It's okay, Kami," Ally was saying. "You can hold on to the railing if you want to, but I'm right here. You won't fall."

Joe felt an inexplicable urge to press his palm against the hot skillet. Maybe some part of his brain wanted him to be distracted from what was coming next, but the larger part of his conscience refused to allow him that escape. He'd messed up. He'd been slow, and now Kami was... well, he wasn't quite sure *what* she was. He'd done his best to avoid finding out too many details. But apparently she was afraid to go down stairs. The laughing little girl who'd climbed to the top of the hayloft without a moment's hesitation couldn't handle a set of stairs without help. All because Joe hadn't gotten to her in time.

"NO," he heard, and the voice was a strange mix of familiar and new. "No. No stairs. No."

"You came *up* the stairs," Ally said. "Yesterday, remember? You came up to go to bed. Now it's time to go down and get some breakfast."

"No." Kami's voice was getting louder, with a mix of fear and aggression. "No! No! No!"

Joe turned the heat under the griddle off, then stepped to the bottom of the stairs and looked into the living room. Austin's head was up, and he was listening in confusion and maybe a little bit of alarm. Goddammit. Joe needed to do something before this got more out of control. Of course, he didn't really know what *to* do.

He walked up a few steps until Kami could see him. Which, of course, meant he could see her. If he hadn't known her before, he might not have noticed how thin she seemed, her formerly strong body now frail. She was braced at the top of the stairs, gripping the wall, ready to fight to stay away from what she obviously thought was danger.

"Hey, Kami," Joe made himself say. He wouldn't insult her by talking about the past and trying to apologize for the unforgivable, so he might as well focus on the current issue. "You don't want to take the stairs today, huh? Would it be okay if I carried you down?"

"That's Joe," Ally said quietly. "Do you remember Joe? He's my brother. He's safe. Can he carry you down the stairs?"

Kami looked doubtful, but she didn't try to run away.

"I can carry you," Joe said again. He wasn't really sure she understood his words. Griffin was there at the top of the stairs, watching the whole scene with canine concern, and Joe climbed the stairs to stand next to them all. "Like this," he said, and he gently lifted Griffin up. The dog put his head on Joe's shoulder as if he'd been *waiting* for someone to realize he deserved to be carried everywhere, and he snuggled in as Joe made his way down the staircase. "See?" Joe asked. "I can carry you." He set the dog down gently, and Griffin immediately raced to the top of the stairs. It wasn't clear whether he was hoping for another ride or just wanted to get back to the place he'd been before the random trip downstairs, but he certainly didn't seem upset about anything.

Kami was clearly fascinated by the whole process, staring at Joe, then the dog, then back at Joe. "Again?" she said. Her voice was a little slurred, but still clear.

This wasn't exactly how Joe had planned to spend his morning, but he obligingly climbed back up the stairs and scooped Griffin into his arms. "Picking up," Joe said. He turned and started down the stairs. "Carrying." When he got to the bottom he set the dog down and said, "Griffin, stay." Then he looked up the stairs and held his arms out. "See? Safe. Do you want a ride? Do you want to come down and see Griffin?"

Kami was watching him closely, but again he wasn't sure she really understood what he'd said. "Carry?" he asked, and he held his arms out to show what he meant.

She stared at him as he cautiously approached. When he was close enough to touch, she raised her arms a little. Not a lot, but enough that he was pretty sure she was consenting. He still moved slowly, though, eased toward her and lifted her gently, letting her find her balance as they moved.

When he made it to the bottom of the stairs, Griffin greeted them with as much celebration as if they'd been separated for years. Joe set Kami down with the same care he'd used to pick her up, but she squirmed at the last minute, clearly eager to get her feet back on the ground, and he had to catch her before she fell. "Steady, there," he said, but she didn't even look at him, just crouched to wrap her arms around Griffin's fuzzy neck.

"She went *up* the stairs okay," Ally said, her voice a mix of apology and defensiveness.

"Down is scarier," Joe said. "You have to kind of hang there for a bit when you're putting your foot down a level." It was probably an opportunity to point out that this was just one of the many challenges of bringing someone with special needs into the household, but he was too tired to lecture. "One of us needs to go to the barn, so the other should make breakfast. Which do you want?"

"Whichever you don't," Ally said. "Either's fine."

"You're on breakfast, then. Batter's mixed, griddle was hot a minute ago. There's fruit in the fridge."

Ally nodded, half of her attention still on Kami. Joe grabbed an apple on the way to the mudroom. Not a real breakfast for him, but the animals had waited long enough. He bundled up and headed for the barn, Red at his heels. It was comforting to be around the animals and to follow the familiar routines: feed them all, turn out those who could handle the cold, collect the eggs, milk the cow. Flower still had a calf taking a bit of her milk, so it wasn't too unpleasant for her to have a slightly irregular milking schedule, but Joe still cringed as he felt her udder. It wasn't full enough to be sore, but it was close. The animals were yet another responsibility he wasn't meeting properly.

He stopped and pressed his cheek against Flower's warm golden side. The animals. The farm in general. It was important to him. He loved the lifestyle and the satisfaction of providing food for his family and the wider world, but maybe the farm was what had to go. If Kami stayed, *something* would have to give. He looked around the barn. The beef cattle were how he made his living. They should stay. But the chickens, the milk cattle, the vegetable garden and fruit trees in the summer—that was all optional. He could buy all those things at the store, and maybe they wouldn't taste quite as good, but he wasn't in a position to be too picky.

The horses.... He looked over at Misery as she grumpily chewed her hay, waiting to be put outside. Joe liked working from horseback, but lots of guys used ATVs and did okay. Misery was well trained and had great instincts. She'd be a valuable animal, if he could find the right buyer for her. And the other horses were just pets, really. Ally had her quarter horse, but she'd been talking about selling him when she went away to school anyway. Will or Sarah might go for a ride a few times year, but that was about it. Joe had put Austin on Devil's back once or twice, but the kid wasn't too interested in sitting still when there was running around to do, and his legs were still too short for much active riding. The horses were pets that took a lot of time to take care of, and time was something Joe didn't have.

Damn it. He didn't want to sell the horses. But he couldn't be selfish about it, couldn't send a girl back to an unhappy life just because he wanted his ponies.

It wasn't the solution he wanted, but at least it was *a* solution. Better to have an unattractive plan than to be faced with something that seemed completely impossible.

So he should have been happier as he walked down to the house after finishing in the barn. He saw Jean's car parked beside his truck and made himself walk a little faster. Maybe there was some medical reason Kami *couldn't* be in a private home. He felt selfish for wishing for it, but it sure would solve a lot of problems.

"Joe," Jean said with a gentle smile when he opened the mudroom door. She was sitting at the kitchen table with a cup of tea, surrounded by all the kids. Kami was beside her, playing with a collection of beads on a string. "Thanks for calling me."

"Sorry to interrupt your vacation."

She shrugged. "I got two days off; that's more than I usually manage. Christmas is a stressful time for a lot of people." Another smile as she said, "Including you, I imagine."

"Is Kami okay without her meds?" Maybe he should have made small talk a little longer, but there was no point pretending this was a social call.

"She only takes them once a day," Jean said calmly. "I stopped by the facility and picked them up, and she's taken them now. So it was really only a few hours late—that shouldn't be a problem."

Well, that was something at least. Joe's stomach reminded him that he'd missed breakfast, but he needed to get some things straightened out before he ate. "And the staff at the facility—the people who wanted to put her in restraints—has that been sorted out?"

"Sorted out? Well, they confirmed that it's their policy to use restraints whenever a staff member feels that the patient's actions are a risk to the patient or to others." Jean frowned gently in Kami's direction. "Apparently there have been a few incidents in the past when she got upset and tried to hurt herself, then lashed out at others when they intervened." She leaned over and patted the table in front of Kami, trying to get her attention. "That's what they say, Kami. Does that sound right?"

Kami didn't respond, or show any signs that she'd heard Jean at all.

Lacey was ready, though. "But did they say *why* she got upset in the first place? I mean, she gets frustrated. I can see why. Maybe if they were better at giving her what she needs, she wouldn't get upset!"

"Maybe," Jean said noncommittally. Then she looked across the table at Joe. "Last time I was here you said there was a spot with a nice view of the lake, not far from the house. I wore my warm boots—any chance we could go for a little walk?"

"Oh, the *grown-ups* are going to go talk in private?" Lacey asked bitterly.

"Yes," Jean said calmly as she stood up. "I'll come back and talk to you privately too. But I've already heard quite a bit from your perspective today, so I'd like a chance to talk to Joe for a while."

It was hard for Lacey to argue with such a reasonable answer, and impossible for Joe to ignore Jean's request. So he turned back toward the door, but stopped when he heard Mackenzie say, "Joe."

He turned, and Mackenzie quickly stood up from the table.

"While Jean's getting her coat and boots on...," he said, and he gestured toward the oven. "Your breakfast."

"I can wait," Jean said, but Joe shook his head. He wanted to get this over with. He'd been wearing gloves in the barn, so his hands weren't too dirty. He pulled the oven door open and reached inside to snag one fluffy pancake. Two bites and it was gone.

"You are not a gentleman," Mackenzie scolded. He pulled a silver travel mug out of the cupboard, then headed for the coffeepot. A bit of sugar, a dollop of milk, and then steaming coffee—just what Joe needed.

He smiled as Mackenzie handed the mug to him. "Thanks for looking after me."

"Take another pancake for the road." Mackenzie pulled the oven open, and Joe obediently reached inside and snagged a pancake.

"Breakfast of champions," he said as he and Jean headed out the door.

"Breakfast of busy parents," she countered. They walked in silence for a while after that, Red scouting the path ahead of them, until Jean said, "I'd thought about asking you to take Kami. But I'd decided against it. Not because I took pity on you, but because I didn't think it would be best for her."

There was a little bit of hurt pride, maybe. Jean didn't think Joe could take good care of Kami? That was insulting. But mostly he felt relief. This would be the easiest solution—freedom without guilt, if he wasn't *allowed* to bring Kami into the family. But he needed to be cautious. "That's still how you feel?"

Jean sighed. "I'm not sure. I'll tell you the facts, Joe." She waited as if expecting him to argue, then said, "Physically, Kami has some challenges, but not enough to keep her from living in a family setting. Mentally, more challenges, but again, nothing that many families aren't dealing with. Emotionally? Well, that's a whole other set of challenges. She's lost a lot of her ability to control her impulses. Her emotions are pure, and she acts on them. But again, there are lots of kids living in families while dealing with that sort of thing. If Kami'd had a family and home to go to, she would have been released from the treatment facility some time ago."

"There are foster families that take on special needs kids, aren't there?"

"There are some," Jean admitted, "but not many. And we were trying to keep the girls close enough that they could stay in contact with each other, so that cut down the options some more. I couldn't find anyone I thought would be a good match for Kami."

"Including me," Joe said, and again he felt that little niggle of injured pride.

Jean smiled. "Including you. Not because of anything innate, just because you had too much on your plate. For a special-needs child, we usually try to find a foster home with two parents in a settled, long-term relationship. We hope that one of the parents doesn't work outside the home, and we look for a home without many other children in it. Does any of that sound like you'd be a good fit?"

Joe thought about arguing that Mackenzie was only marginally employed, but he shouldn't be dragging the guy into any of this. And their relationship certainly wasn't long-term, and probably wasn't all that settled, really. "Technically, you could say that the whole farm is my home, so that'd mean I don't work outside it."

"You weren't a good fit," Jean said firmly.

"You're using the past tense for all this," Joe said. He didn't want to ask but knew that he had to. "Has something changed?"

"Not really. I've just gotten a little more desperate." They reached the top of the hill then, and took a moment to look out over the icy scene, white snow drifted across smooth ice, dark pine trees framing the brightness. "There's no one better. And

Kami's not doing too well in the rehab center. It's a sign of her improvement, really. She's getting more confident, expressing her needs more clearly. No one was really sure what to expect from her. Brain injuries are tricky at the best of times, and especially with children, recovery can be unpredictable. When Kami entered the institution we thought she might be there for life. But now, we think she'd do better elsewhere."

Joe stared at the snow, the reflected sunlight glaring deep into his head. "Lacey was talking about getting her own place and trying to make that work."

"We both know that'd be a disaster," Jean said. "For Kami *and* for Lacey."

And if she came to the farm, it would just be a disaster for Joe. The math was simple, really: two disasters against one. He tried to smile. "There's no third door? No hidden solution you've got worked out?"

"I'm hoping you'll say no," Jean admitted with a strange smile. "My duty is to Kami, so I need to do what's best for her. I need to try to find her a home. But I'll feel really guilty if you take this on. So if you say no, I can know that by asking, I did what I needed to do for Kami, but not feel guilty for having added another responsibility to a young man who already has too many."

Joe looked at her in surprise. "I was hoping *you'd* say no," he confessed. "So I wouldn't have to do it, but wouldn't have to feel bad about turning you down." He waited for a moment. "Don't suppose you could do that, could you?"

She shook her head sadly. "I'm sorry, Joe. I think you're the best person for the job, considering that I haven't been able to find anyone else. I think Kami would be better off in a slightly unstable environment with an overworked but incredibly conscientious caregiver than she'd be in an institution."

Joe turned back to the scene in front of him. So calm and peaceful. As a boy he'd been almost hypnotized by winter. He'd find a soft snowbank and flop down on his back, the snow puffing up around him to provide a windbreak, the weak sunlight giving him at least some warmth as he stared at the sky. The light blue of the sky and the bright white of the snow made the horizon indistinct, so heaven and earth blurred together into one endless circle of nothingness. It had been fascinating, then, but now Joe saw his future the same way, and it was oppressive. He was a caregiver. No beginning, no end. Ally was almost grown. Savannah and Austin would mature eventually. But Kami? Kami was forever.

As she should be, he reminded himself. It was his fault she'd been hurt. Kami was blameless in all of this. She'd gone to bed one night, her dog beside her, her parents drinking downstairs, and she'd woken up to pain and fear and confusion that never seemed to end. If Joe had just... if he'd just been *better*.

He shook his head, trying to dispel the useless thoughts. "Okay," he made himself say. "I'll need information, I guess. She should still get some sort of rehab, right? Some of that can go through the school? Is there somewhere else I'll need to take her? And the medications, and whatever medical stuff there is. I need to know about that." He should probably stop talking, but then he'd have to think, and he didn't want that to happen. "I think she shared a bedroom with Savannah last night. The queen bed in my old room, I guess. We'll maybe need to get two twins." What else, what else? "I need to talk to the kids. And maybe get some counseling for Savannah. She's *acting* fine, and maybe she really is, but it'd be good for someone to check in on her, right? And Austin seems okay, but this is a lot of changes for the little guy. Is there a test? Like, a way to tell whether a five-year-old is stressed?"

"What about Mackenzie?" Jean asked gently.

But Joe shook his head. *Mackenzie* was what he wasn't letting himself think about. "Lacey wants to quit school. I think she was almost using Kami as an excuse. I need to figure out a way to keep her there, at least until the end of the year. If she can just graduate, she'll have a better chance of—" Of having a life. Of course, Joe had graduated high school, and look what had happened to him.

Fuck, he needed to get himself under control.

"Red!" he called, and the dog looked up from the tree he'd been sniffing and came bounding through the snow toward his master. Joe crouched down and let Red lean into him. He reached down and found a handful of snow, hoping Jean didn't notice as he rubbed it over his face. The cold helped him regroup, and his voice was controlled as he said, "New family member, Red. No biting, okay?"

Red wagged his tail in agreement, and Joe gave himself a moment to bury his face in the dog's warm fur. He needed to not think. As long as he didn't start thinking, he'd be able to make it through.

He stood up and dusted off his pants. "We should get back to the house," he said to Jean. "Start figuring things out."

She didn't argue, and they started back down the hill together. It felt like Joe was walking to his appointment with the gallows.

CHAPTER TWELVE

MACKENZIE HAD never really believed in destiny. Never given it much thought, really. But insofar as he'd considered it at all, he'd generally thought of it as a force for good. Karma, or whatever. People got what they deserved because the universe had a plan for everyone. Not his philosophy, really, but at least he could understand it.

But when things started happening with Kami, his vague ideas went straight out the window. Everything was happening as if it was meant to be, that was for sure. He wasn't doing anything to guide events, and he really wasn't seeing Joe doing much, either, but somehow, it all just kept coming at them. Doctors, psychologists, physical therapists, occupational therapists, social workers. A dizzying array of well-intentioned professionals, all with their own understanding smiles and practiced optimism, telling Joe what he should and shouldn't do, making schedules Joe needed to follow, setting routines and expectations and goals and contingency plans. It was exhausting for Mackenzie, and he was safely on the sidelines. He watched Joe working through it all, his smile becoming more forced, more robotic with every meeting, and he felt himself being pushed even further away from it all.

Joe had a new challenge. Raise his family? Pretty well finished and started on the second generation. Tame and captivate the feisty city boy? Done. Not even that difficult, to be honest. The new assignment, though... that would take all of Joe's energy and attention. No time to rest on his laurels or fortify territory he'd already captured. He was pressing on, conquering new ground. Rescuing new souls and leaving the old ones to fend for themselves.

Mackenzie shook his head and scrubbed harder at the roasting pan. Ally had made dinner; Mackenzie had offered to help, but she'd widened her eyes and said Joe would skin her alive if he found out she was ditching her chores after promising to help out even more once Kami arrived. But she'd let him clean up; he was allowed to do that when Joe was home, so apparently he was allowed to do that when Joe was away too.

"It's not his fault, exactly," Mackenzie said to Griffin, who was lying annoyingly close to Mackenzie's feet. "It's how people *react* to him, not anything he actually does. He's not like Red," he said quickly, and both he and Griffin cast quick, defensive glances toward the old dog dozing by the outside door. "He doesn't *insist* on being in charge. He doesn't beat people up if they don't go along with him." He crouched down and took Griffin's muzzle between his soapy hands. "But he's pretty hard to argue with, isn't he?"

Griffin panted agreeably. *Yup, that Joe's a character, all right,* Mackenzie imagined him saying. *I like him, but I wouldn't mess with him. No way. He might not beat me up, but he'd guilt me until I cried.* Then the dog lay down on his side and started licking his genitals, and Mackenzie stopped trying to put words in his head.

The outside mudroom door opened, and for a moment Mackenzie thought Joe was home early. The general shape was right, but then the new arrival turned and displayed his face, tanned and relaxed, and the genetic connection wasn't enough for anyone to confuse this man with his twin brother.

"Hey, Mackenzie," Will said, shaking the snow off his coat. "Joe still not home?"

"He called. The weather's slowing everything down. The meeting at the occupational-therapy place started late, and now the traffic's bad."

"Great," Will said. "One more thing to worry about."

"Bad weather? Not even a blip on the radar compared to the rest of it." Mackenzie smiled tiredly. "On the plus side, he said they were going to get dinner from a drive-through, so there's an extra plate in the fridge if you're hungry."

"Nice," Will said. Like Joe, he was *always* hungry.

Once the food was in the microwave, Will turned to look at Mackenzie speculatively. "I was coming out to talk to Joe, but maybe it's just as well he's not here yet. Where are the kids?"

"Austin's in bed; Ally's at the barn; Savannah's reading in her room; Lacey went with Joe and Kami."

"And things are going well there? With Kami?"

Mackenzie sighed. It had been two weeks. Two chaotic, stressful weeks. "She's a sweet kid." He rinsed the last dish and dried his hands. "But she's like a little baby, you know? I mean, she's not, but in terms of the amount of care she takes…. But at least with a baby you'd just sit back and *let* her act that way. Tantrums, panic attacks, weird fears, crying at nothing real. With Kami, we have to try to *fix* her. It's exhausting." Then he felt guilty. "Not so much for me. Joe… well, you know Joe. He takes it all on himself. And Lacey's been good. Her being suspended from school was kind of a blessing, really. I'm not sure how it's going to go next week when she's back in class."

"But Kami's going to school too, right? So at least during the day things should be okay."

"She went in yesterday for a visit. All the kids who'd known her before, crowding around her… Joe said she totally freaked out, started screaming and swinging at the kids…." Mackenzie shook his head. "If he hadn't been there, somebody could have gotten really hurt. She can't go back until they have an assistant set up for her. You know, someone to be with her all the time, at least until she gets used to it."

"She used to be really brave," Will said softly. "Of all three of them, she was the one we always had to keep an eye on, or else she'd get into trouble."

"She's still brave," Mackenzie said. He was surprised by his own vehemence. "Her memory's shot, so she doesn't always know where she is or what she's doing there or who people are. Her processing is all messed up. They say she can either understand what she sees or understand what she hears, but not both at once. If she's got something to look at it's like she's deaf, and if we play music she likes she just stares into space, doesn't see us if we're right in front of her. So she gets surprised a lot. Startled. Everything must seem so confusing to her, so random. But she still gets up and does her best, every day." He stopped. "Sorry. Probably more of a speech than you needed to hear."

Will nodded. "No, it's good. Sorry." He scooped a knife and fork off the dish rack and dried them on his shirttail, then pulled the plate out of the microwave.

"Is that what you came out to talk about?" Mackenzie asked. He followed Will over to the table, and they sat on opposite sides.

"No," Will admitted. He looked unsure, then shrugged and confessed, "Lindsey's pregnant. Hit the second trimester while we were in Mexico. We told her family yesterday, and I wanted to come out and let everyone here know about it too."

"Wow. Congratulations."

"Yeah, thanks." Will poked at the roasted potatoes on his plate. "It wasn't really planned. And it's not a great time. You know, for the family. Lots going on already."

"Is there ever a time when there *isn't* lots going on with this family?" Mackenzie was tired, but he smiled anyway. "If you waited until there was a gap and got pregnant then, by the time the baby was born the chaos would probably have already started again."

"Might have been nice not to get pregnant at all," Will said sourly. "If taking a pill every day was such a nuisance, she should have told me, and we could have used something else." Then he caught himself. "That's the kind of shit I need to not say around anyone else. There's going to be a kid. *My* kid. I shouldn't be saying anything that will make people think I don't want it. In a town this small, that'd get back to the kid someday."

It was a bit more information than Mackenzie really wanted. He and Will were friendly, but not exactly confidants. Maybe Will could talk like this because he didn't think Mackenzie was really part of the community. Maybe he didn't think Mackenzie would be around long enough to spread hateful words to the unborn child. Or maybe he just trusted Mackenzie to keep his mouth shut. "That's one thing me and Joe don't have to worry about, at least."

Will grinned at him and took a mouthful of potatoes. He ate in silence for a while, then said, "Joe likes babies."

"You'd better not be planning on adding a body to the orphanage," Mackenzie warned.

"No. I'll take care of this one. I just... things are turning out kind of strange, you know? There used to be a sort of plan. Before our parents died. Workwise, we're still on about the same track, I guess. Joe's always loved the farm, and I've always liked the contracting business. Made sense for things to get divided up that way. But all the rest of this? Joe looking after all these kids, me having one of my own with a woman I don't—" He caught himself again. "It's all good. I just feel like we used to be driving the car, and now we're out there in traffic, on foot, dodging and weaving and just trying to stay alive."

"I don't think I ever drove," Mackenzie said musingly. "So maybe this doesn't feel as strange to me. But I don't think... I don't think I'm out in traffic, either. I guess I'm kind of in the passenger seat."

"Which is good, as long as you trust the driver," Will said.

"But you're right. I don't think Joe *is* driving, not anymore. Maybe nobody's driving. Maybe I'm sitting over there in the passenger seat and thinking everything is okay, and then I look over and the driver's seat is *empty*." It was almost chilling, but Mackenzie forced himself to laugh. "You and Joe, with your analogies. I always get carried away with them."

But Will wasn't laughing. "You guys are okay? I mean, it's none of my business, but—you make him happy. I like that."

"I don't think I'm making him happy lately," Mackenzie countered. "I don't think I'm making him *anything*. We barely see each other. And when we do, the kids are around. The only time we're alone is in bed, and he's snoring before I have my shirt off." There had been no real sex since Kami's arrival; Joe had given Mackenzie two blowjobs and declined the opportunity to be repaid, preferring sleep to orgasms. That was it.

"It's a rough patch," Will said slowly. "But you'll get through it."

"Will we?" It felt wrong to say the words out loud, but now that he'd started Mackenzie wasn't sure he could stop if he tried. "When? Kami's going to get better, maybe, but she's always going to need extra help. And things are going to get *worse*, not better, when Ally leaves. She's the only one Joe trusts to help him with the animals. And Lacey's a loose cannon. Her heart's in the right place, but her judgment?" Mackenzie shook his head. "Savannah's been no trouble, but Joe got a call from her teacher yesterday worried that maybe she's *too* good. Apparently before the fire she was more social, and now she's withdrawn. So *that* could flare up into something that needs attention too." He stopped and took a deep breath. "I feel like an asshole for complaining. None if this is anyone's fault. But a rough patch?" He shook his head. "The scary thing is, I think this might be the *smooth* patch, before things get really bad."

Will stared at him for a moment, then gloomily smashed a potato with his fork and pushed it over toward his peas. "Maybe not," he tried, but he didn't seem to have anything to back the statement up.

They both sat in silence for a while, and both jumped almost guiltily when they heard the mudroom door opening. It was still a bit early to be Joe, so it was probably just Ally coming back from the barn, and she wouldn't judge them for the conversation they were having. But the face that appeared in the kitchen doorway wasn't Ally's.

"Nick," Will said in surprise. "Hey. What's up?" He looked a little more closely at his brother. "You okay?"

It was a valid question. Nick had the same coloring as the rest of the family, dark hair with light but easily tanned skin, but his features were a bit more delicate than his brothers'. At his best, he looked almost exotic, but he was far from his best right then. He was too thin, and his pallor seemed like it might be coming from something other than lack of sunshine.

Nick's usually easy smile seemed forced, but he said, "I'm good. Just thought I'd come check in on everybody. See how Austin's doing."

"Well, he's asleep right now," Will said carefully. "But I'm sure he'll be glad to see you in the morning."

Nick looked at his watch in surprise. "Shit, is it late?"

"Not for adults," Will said, still speaking cautiously. Mackenzie could understand why; Nick was talking like he'd never lived in the house and had no idea how to raise a child. It was peculiar at best. "But Austin goes to bed pretty early."

"Right," Nick said. He looked around the kitchen, then said, "Joe's not here?"

"He's at a meeting," Mackenzie said.

Nick looked at him like they'd never met. "A meeting?" he asked. "For what? The gay cattlemen's association?"

"Something like that," Mackenzie said. He didn't think he was going to waste a lot of time sharing information with someone that dismissive of Joe.

Nick looked at his watch for the second time since they'd started talking, but Mackenzie bet the guy still wouldn't know what time it was if he were asked. "You want to lie down?" he said, trying to make it sound like a normal thing to do. "You look like you've been up for a while."

Nick's eyes widened as if Mackenzie had accused him of a crime, then narrowed defensively. "I don't know what you mean."

"He means you seem tired," Will said soothingly. "You're staying the night, right? It's a bit of a full house. You can share with Austin, or if you want, you can come stay with me and Lindsey."

"I'm not going to just show up on your doorstep like that," Nick retorted. He was obviously okay showing up on Joe's doorstep, but that was easier, since Nick was a part-owner of the house. "Why do I have to share with Austin? Who's in the other rooms?"

Will squinted at his brother. "We've talked about this, Nick. The Waltons are living here, remember? Lacey's sharing with Ally. Savannah and Kami are in my and Joe's old room. A room for Austin, and a room for Joe and Mackenzie. If you don't want to share with Austin, you could try the couch, or come to my place."

Nick's face was a strange mix of disgust and confusion. "What is going *on* around here?" he asked, but he didn't seem to expect an answer. "Austin still has the bunk beds, right? Maybe I will lie down for a bit."

He stumbled off toward the stairs, leaving Mackenzie and Will alone in the kitchen. They didn't say anything for a while. Then Will broke the silence. "That was a bit weird, right?"

Fair question, but Mackenzie didn't think he wanted to be the one to voice the first explanation that had popped into his head. "Maybe he's got the flu?"

Will squinted at him. "Maybe? But I don't know about anything harder than pot. But he's more into that stuff than I am. Maybe he got in too deep."

Yup, there it was. Mackenzie shrugged to show that he wasn't sure but said, "Might just be coming down off something. If he's been clubbing for a couple days. It doesn't *feel* like sleep deprivation, but that's what it is. With a few extra chemical effects."

"Is this...?" Will made a face. "I don't want to sound like a prude, but is this something I should be worrying about? I mean, he didn't look too good."

"Maybe wait and see?" Mackenzie suggested. "If he looks better in the morning, maybe you don't need to worry too much? It's just kind of like a hangover, you know? But if he doesn't get better soon, then maybe he's been using it too much. Or, you know, maybe it *is* just the flu."

Will looked like he had something to say to that, but then the mudroom door banged open and Kami came inside, looking almost as tired and pale as Nick had. Lacey was right behind her, and Joe brought up the rear. Will glanced in Mackenzie's direction, then smiled brightly.

"Hey, guys, welcome home! And, hey! Good news! Nick's here!"

Joe looked from Will to Mackenzie, then back to Will. "Nick?" he asked faintly. Then, almost to himself, as if he were confirming some inner belief, he said, "Nick. Yeah."

There was a moment when Mackenzie really believed Joe was going to turn around and head back out the door. He almost wished it would happen, because then he could *follow*, and they'd go somewhere together, just the two of them, somewhere with no pressure and no responsibility and no damn family.

Mackenzie would be perfectly fine with that approach. But he knew Joe wouldn't be, so he stood up and stepped cautiously toward him. "We'll figure it out," he said.

Joe stared at him for a long moment. Then he took a deep breath and turned toward the girls. "Lacey, you can help Kami get ready for bed, right?"

Lacey nodded wordlessly, her wide eyes making it clear she knew there was something extra going on in the house. She took Kami's hand and led her through the kitchen, leaving Mackenzie, Will, and Joe staring at each other.

"Nick," Joe finally said. He looked at Will, their shared history clear as he added, "Excellent."

"He might be in trouble," Will said cautiously.

Joe just smiled, his teeth showing too bright and sharp. "Yup, that sounds right. Where is he?"

"In bed. He wasn't feeling well." Will's voice was too careful, and Joe stared at him.

"Do I want to know?"

"There's nothing *to* know," Mackenzie interjected. "Not until tomorrow. Tomorrow, we'll see what's going on and figure something out. Tonight? Go to bed, Joe. Get some sleep."

But Joe, of course, shook his head. "There's paperwork, from the meeting. It seemed like a really good place, and Kami liked it. They say they can take her for occupational therapy once a week, but they need a bunch of forms filled out and stuff put together. Information about her medications, and they want a couple of her toys to work with."

"But it doesn't have to happen tonight, does it?" Mackenzie wasn't sure whether he was more angry or sad. Maybe just tired of it all.

And Joe's mood seemed about the same. "If not tonight, when?" he asked. He waited a moment for an answer he knew Mackenzie couldn't give him, then turned and started for the basement. He had a little office down there where he kept the paperwork from the farm, and it was where he went when he needed somewhere quiet to focus on reading and writing. Neither skill came naturally to him, but he wouldn't take Mackenzie's help, preferring to fight through it all himself.

When he was gone, Mackenzie turned to Will. "You didn't tell him about the baby," he realized.

"Didn't really seem like the right time." Will sighed. "He's not doing too well, huh?"

"He's tired. Nothing a week on the beach wouldn't fix."

"Joe doesn't like the beach. Maybe a week in the mountains."

Joe didn't like the beach. It was stupid for *that* to be the thing that caught in Mackenzie's throat. All the other challenges, all the different ways their lives didn't fit together, and it was preferred vacation spots that Mackenzie was focused on. It all just seemed too ridiculous. They couldn't find any time to be together in their ordinary lives, and then they would have to *vacation* in separate places too? Everything was just too difficult. But it was Joe; he was worth fighting for. If only Mackenzie could figure out who or what to fight *against.*

"Okay," he said tiredly. "The mountains." It wasn't like they had time to go on vacation anyway.

Will stood up and carried his plate to the sink, then turned around and smiled. "Hang in there."

"I'm trying," Mackenzie said. It was true. He *was* trying. But it didn't seem to be doing him any good, and he wasn't sure how much longer he could keep hanging on.

CHAPTER THIRTEEN

JOE HAD always been an early riser. In the summer, it just made sense; there was so much to do on the farm, and he needed every daylight hour to get it all done. And the habit just sort of carried over into the wintertime. So it wasn't that unusual for him to be in the barn well before dawn and well after dark, especially on the shortest days of the year. What was unusual was for him to feel like he was *hiding* in the barn.

"It's a sad day when I'm coming to *you* for comfort," he told Misery as he picked the dirty bedding out of her pen. It was still dark outside, so he wasn't going to put her out yet, so she saw no reason for his presence and just glared at him. "Fine, not comfort. Company?" She still looked offended. "Yeah, you're right," he finally agreed. "If we're not going for a ride, I won't come to you for *anything*."

The other animals might be friendlier, but they were no more likely to help him with his current struggles. He looked at his watch. Almost seven. Austin would be awake soon, if he wasn't already. He was getting pretty good at quietly playing with his toys until someone else woke up, but it wasn't really safe for him to be roaming around the house on his own. Ally would get up with him, but she slept like the dead. If Austin went looking for someone, he'd look for Joe, and that would mean he'd wake Mackenzie up.

Joe dropped his pitchfork off at the tool rack as he headed for the door. Mackenzie was pretty clearly running out of patience with the whole setup, and being woken by a feisty five-year-old wouldn't make him any happier. It wasn't a comfortable feeling, watching the straws piling up on Mackenzie's back, waiting to see which one finally broke it. Joe knew he needed to do something more, but it felt like he was pulling straws off one at a time while they were being dropped down by the armful. Living in the country... slam! Big pile of straw. Joe pulled one or two off with tickets to a show. A crowded house full of annoying family members... slam! Another big pile. Joe could try to keep them away from Mackenzie, but they snuck through. Hardly any privacy... slam! A boyfriend too busy and tired to be entertaining... slam! Not even any sex... slam! An occasional blowjob was *not* going to be enough, and Joe knew it. He needed to find the time. The energy.

Or maybe he needed to give up. He plowed through the snow that had drifted over the path to the house. Maybe he needed to stop trying to pretend he could make this work, stop acting as if he had a prayer of making Mackenzie happy. Even before the extra challenges, he'd known there was a "best before" date for their relationship. He hadn't known exactly what the date was, but he'd felt it there, dancing behind every moment of peace and happiness that they'd found. And maybe it hadn't been a date at all, maybe more of a state: *Best Before Reality Sets In.* Maybe that was what he'd been trying so hard to ignore.

He pushed the mudroom door open and let Red precede him into the warmth of the house. There'd been a time when the dog would curl up in a snowbank and stay outside all day, but now his old bones seemed to prefer the warmth of the rug in front of the fire. Joe couldn't argue with Red's preferences. He shook the snow off his jacket and hung it on the hook, then went into the kitchen and stopped short when he saw Nick sitting at the table. Fuck, he'd actually forgotten about *that* pile of straw.

"You're up early," he said carefully. He headed toward the

coffeepot and was surprised to find it empty. Nick was usually a big fan of caffeine.

"Couldn't sleep," Nick grunted. "Austin kept moving around."

"He's up?"

"What? No. In his bed. He was moving around in the bed."

"You were in bed with him?"

"I was in the *room* with him. That was enough."

"Oh. I didn't know you were such a light sleeper. That sucks." Joe felt like he'd done his duty on the sympathy front, but he pushed himself to go above and beyond. "He should be up pretty soon. You can go back and try again. Or if you're up for good, do you want coffee?"

Nick's voice was explosively loud. "I want some fucking *sleep!*"

Well, Nick was always an asshole, but he wasn't usually quite so obvious about it. But Joe didn't have the strength to get into it with him. Nick could be Will's problem, or Sarah's, or even Ally's, although she'd probably be even less patient than Joe.

But that wasn't anything Joe was going to worry about. He washed his hands while the coffee brewed, fixed himself a mug, and started a pot of oatmeal. Then he went to the mudroom and put in a load of laundry. He returned to the kitchen and stirred the oatmeal. He thought about going upstairs and waking Austin up, but resisted the urge. Finally, he gave up and sank into the chair opposite his younger brother.

"You don't look so good," he said quietly.

Nick snorted derisively. "No shit."

"I don't remember you having trouble sleeping."

"Well, things change, Joe." Nick's voice was bitingly sardonic, and Joe had to force himself not to react. It wasn't like he hadn't known what he was getting into, and he'd sat down anyway, so he needed to keep his cool.

"Did you come up here for help or just somewhere to rest up?"

Nick raised an eyebrow at the idea that he could be weak enough to need either. "I came up here for *money*."

"You burned through it all? What about the bar?"

"It's *for* the bar. We were undercapitalized." Nick looked at Joe as if expecting him to be impressed by the jargon and keen analysis of the situation.

"Yeah? What's that looking like right now?"

"It's looking like us being unable to pay our fucking *bills*, Joe!" Nick laid his hands out flat on the table as if trying to steady himself. "Our revenue isn't meeting our expenses," he said in a calmer tone. "We haven't found our clientele yet, but we have to be open in order *to* find them. So we have to keep spending money, so we need more." He nodded as if satisfied that he'd explained the economic theory in terms simple enough for Joe to understand. "Undercapitalized."

"What's the difference between *undercapitalized* and *going under*?"

"That's really fucking supportive, Joe."

"It's a straightforward question. At what point do you decide that investing more would be throwing good money after bad?"

"At the point that I no longer believe we have an attractive business that will eventually prosper." Nick stood up abruptly. "I'll talk to Will. Sarah and Ally too. You aren't the only source of funds in this family, you know."

"I'm not a source of funds at all. Neither is Will. We're both sinking everything we've got into buying the businesses, and if a third of that money isn't enough for you, we can't help you out." He frowned, then said, "And you can forget Ally too. Number one, she's not going to want to give you anything. But even if she did, she's still a minor and there's no way I'm signing off on her risking her cash on this."

Nick stared at him. "Sarah, then," he said with false bravado.

"Give it a try," Joe invited. "But she's always been pretty tight with her money. You know that." He was tempted to walk away, but Nick *was* his brother, so he added, "You should talk to a bank. They'll have experts on staff, people who can look at your financials and your business plan and figure out if you've got a good chance of making it work. If they think you're good, they'll loan you the money. If they think you aren't, maybe you need to listen to them, Nick."

Another bitter look. "I already *talked* to the banks," Nick sneered. "You think I came here *first*? You think I *enjoy* being patronized and lectured to? Trust me, Joe, you are my absolute last option."

"I'm sorry to hear that," Joe said. He truly was. Not only because he wanted his brother to be successful and happy, but also because he wanted his brother to stay in the goddamned city and out of Joe's hair. He stood up and headed for the stove. He stirred the simmering oats and asked, "Do you want breakfast?"

"Fuck you, Joe." The words were quiet, almost casual, and somehow that made them hit even harder.

Joe didn't turn around. He pulled the dried apples and berries down from the tin above the stove and shook a few handfuls into the oatmeal. He and Ally had harvested the fruit the last summer and fall, Austin helping in his own way. Joe wondered if they'd be able to do that again, or if they'd be too busy. Ally would be away at school for apple season, and Joe had barely been able to find time for berry picking *this* year, with all the other summer work on the farm. He picked a chunk of apple out of the oatmeal and chewed on it gently. Everything was changing. It was falling apart. He'd kept it together for as long as he could, but now it was broken.

He reached up and turned the heat off on the oatmeal, then put a lid on the pot. The family would find it when they woke up. And if Austin got up first and woke up Mackenzie? Well, maybe it was time for that final straw to land. Joe didn't think he could stand waiting for it any longer.

CHAPTER FOURTEEN

"YOU NEED to make Joe give me money." Nick seemed serious.

Mackenzie just stared at him. "*Me*? You think I can get Joe to do a damn thing he doesn't want to? Give me a break."

"You can," Nick insisted. "He's crazy about you. Make it an ultimatum or something. Tell him you'll leave if he doesn't give me the money. He says he doesn't have any, but he's got loads of equity. He could get a mortgage easy, pay off the farm all at once and then pay back the bank instead of paying the family slow."

They were sitting in the living room. Austin was on the floor, playing a game that seemed to involve the animals from his farm set living at his airport. There was a black-and-white cow piloting the plane in Austin's hand. Lacey and Ally had Kami in the mudroom, trying to teach her how to do laundry. It was all such a mundane scene, made surreal by the nonsense coming out of Nick's mouth.

"Why on earth would I try to convince Joe to do that?" Mackenzie was genuinely curious. "I mean, I wouldn't leave him, obviously, but why would I even threaten to? Why would I risk this relationship in order to get you some money? I like you, Nick, but my first loyalty is to Joe."

"Well, maybe not *loyalty*," Nick said. His tone was oily, his meaning obscure.

Mackenzie wasn't sure he had the mental energy for this

conversation, but it was probably best to push on and get it over with. "What are you talking about?"

"The bar's been short on cash for a while. There wasn't enough business to need two bartenders, so I started picking up shifts at a couple other places. Used it as a way to talk up our place."

"Okay?"

"One of the places I worked was the Blue Room," Nick said as if that should mean something to Mackenzie.

"Okay...."

"That doesn't seem significant to you?" Nick waited for Mackenzie to catch up, then added, "A few weeks ago? You were there, with some guy in a shiny green shirt?"

Mackenzie frowned at him. "Oh, yeah, okay. Anton. Yeah, we were there."

"You were making out with him! You went home with him!"

"What?" Mackenzie looked wildly in Austin's direction, and seeing him preoccupied with trying to fit a sheep into a helicopter, swiveled to look toward the mudroom. No sign that the girls had heard Nick's accusation. "Jesus, Nick," Mackenzie almost whispered. "That's not what happened! I let him kiss me because he was trying to make some guy jealous! I gave him *sixty seconds*. That's it! And I did *not* go home with him. He just left at the same time as me."

"That's not what it looked like," Nick said firmly. "He was buying you drinks, and he was all over you, for *way* more than sixty seconds." He leaned back in his chair. "I like you too, Mackenzie. I don't want to see you get caught up in all this. But I need your help. And you need mine."

"Are you kidding me?"

"If I can get the money, I can go back to the city, and we can forget about all this," Nick said soothingly. "It was a mistake you made, that's all."

"Ally!" Mackenzie yelled. His heart was pounding, his blood pressing against his eardrums so hard he barely heard her when she answered his call. "I need you to look after Austin for a bit. I need to go talk to Joe."

"What?" Nick stood up. "Slow down, Mackenzie. You need to play this right. You can't just go charging out there and demand cash. You need to, you know, seduce him into it."

Oh for goodness sake. "You. Get your coat on," Mackenzie ordered. Ally came into the living room now, looking at him quizzically. "Do you know where Joe is?"

"He was checking the cattle in the near pasture," she said, clearly unsure whether this was a situation that called for alarm or amusement. "He would have ridden, but you can walk if you want. Go to the left of the barn and follow the tree line."

"Good. Thanks." Mackenzie strode purposefully toward the back door, Nick following more slowly in his wake.

"This isn't the way to do it," Nick tried.

"Shut up. Get your coat on." Mackenzie was already tugging at his boots.

His adrenaline kept him charging through the snow all the way up past the barn and toward the field Ally had mentioned. Mackenzie saw Joe on horseback and waved; Joe saw him and directed the horse toward them.

"You're playing this all wrong," Nick protested. "Come on, Mackenzie, this is not a good plan."

"This is the only plan you left me," Mackenzie responded. He was nervous, but he knew what he had to do.

Joe got closer. "Something wrong?" he asked, alarm in his voice.

"No," Mackenzie said quickly. He waited until Joe brought the horse to a stop. "But I need to tell you something." He didn't let himself think about it, just charged ahead. "A few weeks ago, when I was in the city, I went out with a friend, and he was trying to make his boyfriend jealous. He was really handsy with me, bought me drinks, and I let him kiss me for sixty seconds. I would have told you about it, but when I got back you were hurt and Lacey got kicked out of school and things since then have just been crazy. It wasn't a big deal, but I can see how it might have looked bad to someone who didn't know what was going on."

Joe swung down off the horse, his expression unreadable. "And you had to come way out here in the middle of the day to tell me about it? How come?"

Mackenzie didn't want to make things worse between the brothers. "Nick saw me. He was there. He asked for clarification, and it occurred to me that it could have been misinterpreted. I wanted to talk to you before that happened."

Joe's squint was pretty powerful. He was obviously trying to burn a hole right through Mackenzie's skull so he could read what was going on in his brain, and Mackenzie was pretty sure he could actually feel a spot starting to steam on his forehead. When Joe turned his gaze toward Nick, Mackenzie's face cooled. Then his whole body chilled when he heard Joe's tone.

"You asked for clarification." Joe stared at his brother, then slowly, almost sadly, shook his head. "That doesn't sound right."

"I was trying to look out for you," Nick said defensively. He looked like he had more to say, but Joe cut him off.

"Bullshit. If you'd been looking out for me, you would have called me the day after it happened. You were looking out for the same person you always look out for—yourself." Joe stepped closer. "Were you trying to *blackmail* him? That's what this is, right?" He looked at Mackenzie for confirmation that Mackenzie didn't want to give, but apparently whatever Joe saw in his face was enough. "What the hell? You haven't got any money, Mack. What did he want you to do?"

Mackenzie didn't want to drive a wedge between the brothers, but he wasn't going to flat-out lie to Joe, either. "He was hoping I'd help persuade you to loan him money." He said it in the most favorable terms he could think of, but it still came out sounding pretty bad.

Joe didn't seem all that angry, though. Instead, he pinched the bridge of his nose as if he was trying to fight off a headache. When he finally spoke, he sounded ancient and weary. "It has to stop, Nick. We love you, and we try to forgive your mistakes, but you are making way too many. If you want to be part of this family, you need to start putting it first, at least some of the time." Joe looked at his brother. "This kind of thing? Nick, it *has to stop*."

Mackenzie saw the words register, but then Nick's stubborn bravado resurfaced. "Or else what? You're going to kick me out of the family? Yeah, like you haven't already *done* that!"

"You're not kicked out, Nick."

"So where was my invitation to Christmas?" Nick jutted his jaw forward, and for the first time Mackenzie saw the similarity between Nick and his son.

Joe snorted. "An invitation? Seriously? If I'd *invited* you into the house you would have freaked out and given me a big speech about how you don't need an invitation to a house you own 20 percent of, and how you'll come home anytime you damn well want—"

"And where would I have slept, Joe? Where's my bedroom? Filled up with random orphans *you* decided to bring into the family."

Apparently that was the sensitive spot that made Joe's temper flare. "Your *son* is in your bedroom, asshole. The kid *you* decided to bring in to the family. Well, except *decided* is a bit generous for being too stupid to use a condom, isn't it? So I guess you're right. Austin *is* a kid Will and I decided to bring into the family, when we tried to clean up after one more of your endless fucking mistakes. And if you're too much of a princess to share a bedroom with him, I guess maybe there *isn't* room for you in the house." Joe stared at his brother, and Mackenzie wondered if he needed to get between them. He was pretty sure Joe wouldn't take the first swing, but Nick looked mad enough to start something, and Joe probably wouldn't have a problem with finishing it.

"This is how you want it?" Nick asked, his voice dangerously quiet. "You drawing lines, Joe?"

Joe's squint was back, and it was good to see. If he was being cynical and trying to figure Nick out, he was using his brain, and surely that would be enough to keep him out of a fight. Then Mackenzie remembered the night at the gas station and how calm Joe had been through it all. He stepped a little closer. If Joe started calling Nick a pussy, Mackenzie would be ready to intervene.

But Joe didn't throw any insults. He just shook his head. "What line? Am I saying you need to stop trying to blackmail my boyfriend? I really didn't think that was something we'd need spelled out, but, yeah, I guess if you need it: you should stop trying to blackmail my boyfriend." He sighed, as if the fight was draining out of him and leaving him exhausted. "The rest of it? You look like shit, Nicky. I don't know what you've been doing to yourself, but you need to stop. Maybe you should stay here, maybe you should go stay at Will or Sarah's. Maybe you should go back to the city. You know the situation. It's your call. But I'm tired, Nick. I can't take care of you, not anymore."

"If you'll just lend me some money—" Nick started, but he stopped when Joe turned away. "Fuck!" he said. "Fine, I'll talk to Sarah. Or Will. Jesus, Joe, do you think I *wanted* it to come to this?"

Joe almost smiled then, although he was still turned half-away so only Mackenzie could see his expression. "You still think people end up getting what they want?" he asked quietly. Then he started walking, the mare trailing behind him as he headed away from Mackenzie and Nick.

"Go back to the house," Mackenzie said. "I need to talk to him."

"This is all your fault—" Nick started, but Mackenzie ignored him. He was too busy jogging after Joe.

"Hey," he said, and Joe obediently stopped walking, although he didn't turn all the way around. Mackenzie caught up and then wasn't sure what it was he wanted to say. "We're okay? It really wasn't a big deal. I would have told you about it, but like I said, we really haven't had a chance to talk. It's been pretty busy."

Joe nodded, but there was no eye contact, no smile. "Did it work?" he asked. "Did the other guy get jealous?"

"I actually have no idea. I haven't talked to Anton since that night."

"Am *I* supposed to get jealous? I don't... I don't know this game, Mack. I asked if you fooled around when you were in town and you got mad at me, then I find out you *were* messing around a bit, and somehow that's not a big deal. I don't get it."

Mackenzie didn't have any words. He wanted to kiss Joe, wanted to *show* him what he couldn't say, but he was pretty sure if he moved forward, Joe would pull away. And Joe had pulled too far away from him already.

And with no answer to his question, Joe was turning away anyway. Mackenzie reached out desperately and grabbed his shoulder. "It's not a big deal! It isn't. It was stupid, I guess, since I know you're not feeling too secure about it all. I get that. I screwed up. But it was a *little* screwup. This is *not* a big deal."

Joe was looking at a tiny tear on the corner of his glove as if it held the answers to every question in the universe. "Okay," he said quietly. "Not a big deal. Okay."

"Jesus, Joe!" Mackenzie wasn't sure whether to get angry or start laughing. If Joe would just look at him, they could laugh together, but with the absence of eye contact, the anger was starting to win. "You're going to act like a wronged princess? Seriously? I kissed an old friend. Not because I wanted to, but because I wanted to help him out. *You*, though? You've turned our lives upside down. I fooled around with a guy for sixty seconds, but you've made a long-term commitment to a whole other family, something that's going to last... I don't know, maybe last *forever*... and you think you have the right to act like *I'm* the one who screwed up? Go fuck yourself, Joe. *You're* the one messing this up!"

The glove was still fascinating, apparently, but Joe managed to at least nod. "So we're admitting it's messed up?"

And suddenly Mackenzie wasn't angry anymore, but he sure didn't feel like laughing, either. "It's... it's a rough patch," he said, and the words sounded as empty coming out of his mouth as they'd sounded when Will had said them the night before.

"I can't give you what you want, Mack." Joe said it softly, like an apology. "It's not that I don't want to, but there's just too much else. The kids *need* me. You know."

"What I want? I want *you*, Joe. The big, glamorous city life? I can do without that. I'm not sure I even *want* it anymore. *You're* what I want."

Joe nodded. "Yeah. But there's not much of me left. I don't know if there's enough for... enough to give you what you deserve."

"You don't get to make that decision. No way." Mackenzie could hear the desperation in his own voice, but it didn't seem to register on Joe. "We'll figure this out. We'll rearrange things, get into a routine. All the stuff we're supposed to be doing, we'll do it. It'll work."

For a minute it seemed like Joe was going to argue, but instead he turned quickly and climbed back onto the horse. "I have to get stuff done," he said. "You should get back to the house before you freeze to death."

Well, Joe was still concerned for his health, at least. That was the only consolation Mackenzie had as he watched his cowboy ride away from him.

CHAPTER FIFTEEN

NICK WAS gone by the time Joe got back to the house that afternoon. Not surprising, of course. Not only had he used up his last chance of getting any money out of Joe, but the place was in chaos. Mackenzie was out, and Joe refused to let himself think about where he was; Griffin was still there, so Mackenzie wasn't gone for good. The bandage was still being ripped off slowly. So Ally and Lacey were in charge of the house, and that was the problem, really. They could handle Austin and Savannah, *or* they could handle Kami, but all three were simply too much for two teenagers.

It was too much for Joe too, but at least he'd had his vacation of shoveling shit and riding around in the freezing cold. Now, he was back, and it was time to deal with a five-year-old boy *and* an eleven-year-old girl, both in tears, while the nine-year-old girl was curled up on the couch with her hands over her ears. "Why don't you take the little guys out to play in the snow?" Joe suggested to Ally. "Bundle them up, though, 'cause there's a nasty wind."

Ally was only too happy to accept the idea, and Lacey didn't even give her token protest about leaving Kami. That was a bright side, Joe reminded himself. Lacey was still talking about maybe getting her own place and moving Kami into it. The more difficult Kami was here, the more clear it would be to Lacey that she couldn't look after the girl on her own.

"You just making a point, Kami?" Joe asked after the other

kids had left. Kami was slumped in a corner of the living room, clutching one of Austin's dolls, with tears running down her cheeks. Joe hadn't asked for details, but he figured the doll was the source of the conflict. Fighting over toys, in a house that was full of them. "You trying to let Lacey know you want to stay here in the land of peace and joy?"

Or, it occurred to Joe, maybe Lacey would think this was evidence that Kami should be living in a home without other kids, if she was fighting with Austin here. So there went his silver lining. He started tidying up the mess in the living room, keeping half an eye on Kami but not giving her any direct attention.

He tried to ignore the voice telling him to let Lacey go. If she and Kami were gone, even if they left Savannah behind, Joe's life would go back to almost normal. Without Kami, Joe would have some energy for the things *he* wanted. Without Kami, maybe he'd have a chance of fixing things with Mackenzie. He'd have to work his ass off, of course, because he'd absolutely screwed things up on that front, but at least he'd have a prayer. Except for the part where he'd be doomed to a lifetime of guilt and worry, a man forced to admit he hadn't learned from his first or second mistakes with Kami. He'd left her in an abusive home, he'd taken too long to get her out of the fire, and if he let Lacey take her, he'd be letting this poor, innocent girl suffer for the third time around.

"Motherfucker," Kami said. Her voice wasn't all that loud, but the word was clear. It was pretty much what Joe had been thinking, but it was weird to hear it come out of Kami's mouth. "Whore. Fucking faggot. Hell. Fuck you, cocksucker."

Excellent. Now the girl was possessed.

"Kami?" Joe said cautiously. "Those aren't good words."

"Shit."

Well, they could agree on that one, at least. But Kami didn't seem angry. "Bitch. Goddamn cunt."

Joe was actually curious to hear what she came up with next.

He was pretty sure she'd run through the whole list of really bad words.

And maybe she agreed, because her voice was a little quieter when she said, "Asshole."

Joe needed a strategy. He needed to know why this was happening and whether it was likely to happen again. At school, around Austin... hell, even around Mackenzie would be bad. Lacey and Savannah would probably think it was funny. Joe hoped they hadn't trained Kami like a parrot.

"Fuck you, cocksucker," she said, looking straight at Joe.

Good, she was starting to repeat herself. Maybe she was winding down, albeit on a particularly unpleasant note. Had she picked that particular insult on purpose, or was it just chance?

"Fucking faggot," she said.

Nice. She *was* possessed, and the demon was homophobic. Joe dumped his armful of toys into the storage box and picked up the afghan Savannah had been hiding under. If Kami was looking for attention, he needed to not give it to her. If this was something else? He had no idea what to do if this was something else.

"Fucking cocksucker needs to mind his own goddamn business, not go poking around in other people's families."

It was the longest sentence Joe had heard from Kami since the fire. And it didn't sound like something she'd have come up with herself. He turned to look at her. Her eyes weren't focused anymore. She looked the way she did when she was listening to something, but there was nothing for her to hear. At least not in the room Joe was in.

"If you go running over there one more fucking time, I will beat the shit out of you, you fucking cunt. I'll teach you who's in charge around here. I'll go over to the fucking Sutton *ranch*, and I'll burn the goddamn farmhouse to the ground. You hear me, bitch?"

Joe couldn't move. Kami was reciting from her memory, and it was pretty clear who had spoken the words the first time around.

Joe was hearing a dead man's words. He was a witness to the life the Walton girls had lived before the fire, the anger and fear they'd had to deal with. Kami was eleven, and she'd heard these words. Hell, Lacey was only seventeen, and he was pretty sure they'd been *directed* at her. Joe had known something was wrong, but he hadn't done anything about it. He'd left the girls in that hell.

He still had the afghan in his hands, and he moved slowly toward Kami. He didn't care if she hit *him*, but when she was upset she sometimes hit *herself*, and he needed to be sure that didn't happen. "Kami," he said gently, although he was pretty sure she was too far away to hear him. "It's okay, Kami. That's over. That's never going to happen again. Okay?" He touched her shoulder, just the faintest whisper of fingertips at first, then a little more as she didn't respond. "You're safe here, sweetie." He eased around behind her and wrapped the afghan over her thin shoulders. He was probably acting more to comfort himself than to help her, but she didn't object when he slowly, carefully picked her up and carried her over to the couch.

Thin as she was, she was still bigger than Austin, and it took some arranging to find a way for her to be in a position he assumed she'd find comfortable. Finally, he managed it, his hands locked together to form a sort of basket for her to sit in, his cast hopefully not digging into her anywhere. Her muscles weren't rigid, exactly, but she wasn't relaxed, either. She'd allowed him to arrange her limbs, but she hadn't surrendered all control over them. Fair enough: a little control was probably a precious commodity in this girl's world.

They sat like that for a long time, no more words, and finally Kami sighed, and her whole body just melted, sagging down as she relaxed. She shifted a little, snuggling in like a kitten, and let her head fall onto Joe's shoulder.

She fell asleep, eventually, snoring softly into his neck, and Joe let himself relax, easing back against the couch cushions and slowly unlocking his hands so she was leaning on his body and the end of the couch instead of relying on his arms. His broken wrist was complaining about the abuse, but he ignored it. He was pretty sure he hadn't done any actual damage, hadn't shifted the healing bones out of alignment or anything, so it was nothing he needed to deal with.

When he heard the outside door open he thought about carrying Kami upstairs, away from the racket of incoming kids, but he figured the jostling was more likely to disturb her than the sound was. And for some reason, the sound didn't come.

He cautiously turned his head and leaned back a little, enough that he could see through the living-room doorway to the hall and a bit of the kitchen. Mackenzie was at the counter, unloading something from fabric bags. He didn't know he was being watched, and Joe took advantage of the opportunity to feed his starving eyes. The way Mackenzie looked, the way he moved, the fact that he was right there, in Joe's kitchen, cruising around like he *belonged* there... it just felt *right*. But how could it last? And how was Joe going to make himself function when Mackenzie was gone?

When Mackenzie finally looked over and saw Joe, he looked startled, and maybe not entirely pleased. He set down whatever he was working on and almost reluctantly walked to the living-room door. His expression softened when he saw Kami curled up on Joe's lap. "She okay?" he whispered. "The kids were outside, and they said she was upset."

"Are they staying out there to hide? I don't want them to freeze to death."

"They were heading for the hayloft, going to hang out in Savannah's fort. It gets pretty warm in there."

"Hay's a good insulator."

"And Kami?" Mackenzie asked again. "Is she okay?"

Joe sighed. Not an easy question. "I think I need to find her another psychologist. She's got the one for her brain... like, the educational stuff, helping her learn, whatever. But she's remembering stuff from before the fire. Nasty stuff. The dad was...." Joe huffed out a breath and tried to make his shoulders relax, but his muscles didn't cooperate. "I should have gotten them out of there," he said. "They shouldn't have had to live like that."

Mackenzie sighed and sank down on the arm of the couch. "How many times are we going to talk about this, Joe? The *neighbor* thing is nice and everything, but you guys did what you were supposed to, right? You called the cops, you called the social workers, you gave the kids a safe place to stay when they needed it. What else were you going to do, storm over there and kidnap the kids? End up in jail? The system failed, yeah, but you aren't the system." Mackenzie shook his head. "You need to let it go."

Joe nodded. He couldn't stop feeling guilty, but at least he could stop boring Mackenzie with endless conversations about it. "I'll try to find a counselor," he said instead. "Someone with experience in trauma, or recovered memories, or... I don't know. Somebody who can help her."

Mackenzie had looked startled for a moment, then smiled sadly. "I thought maybe you meant a counselor for *you*. For the guilt. I thought maybe that'd be a good idea."

"Maybe I'll get some of that ex-gay treatment at the same time. I mean, if I'm working on denying reality and hiding from the truth, I might as well go all the way, right?"

Mackenzie didn't answer. He just stood up and said, "I bought stuff for dinner. You didn't have anything planned, did you?"

Joe tried to get his mind on the new topic of conversation. "There's thawed ground beef. I was thinking meatloaf. But it'll keep, if you want to do something else."

"Nothing fancy, but I thought we could mix it up a little. I bought some salmon."

Flown in from the ocean, because Mackenzie was tired of red

meat all the time. Tired of Joe's beef. There was an obvious pun in there, but Joe was too tired to make it. He just leaned his head back against the sofa. He'd been operating on too little sleep for too long. It would feel so good to let his eyelids fall. But not exactly polite to let a houseguest cook dinner without assistance. "I can help," he said. He looked down at the sleeping girl in his arms. "I think she's right out. I can probably move her without waking her up. Or maybe I *should* wake her up, so she'll sleep tonight." One more decision, and his brain was too fried to make it easily.

But Mackenzie held his hands up. "No, don't worry about it. Like I said, it's simple. I'm fine."

Mackenzie didn't need Joe's help. It was sad but true. Mackenzie was the other adult in the house, the only person who didn't rely on Joe. And because of that, he was the one Joe was neglecting.

It was easy to see it, easy to understand what was happening, but much harder to do anything about it. But Joe needed to try. He moved slowly, gently shifting Kami out of his lap. She stirred, muttered something, then snuggled down into the sofa cushions just as peacefully as she'd been while Joe was holding her.

He walked quietly to the kitchen. "Let me do something," he said. Cooking together—that was probably a good bonding activity. "A salad?"

"Joe," Mackenzie said, and in that one word his voice made it clear that this was *not* going to be the happily shared time Joe had been hoping for. "I'm not completely incompetent. I can make *dinner*. You don't need to supervise me."

"I wasn't going to supervise. I thought I could help."

"Even though I said I didn't *need* any help."

Yeah, things had definitely gone way off course somewhere. "Okay," Joe said tiredly. "Sorry. I'll do laundry."

"Or you could sit back down and rest for a few minutes."

Joe ignored that suggestion and headed for the stairs. The kids would need clean clothes for the next day, and he should probably change the sheets on the beds too. He wasn't sure when he'd last done that, but it was probably too long.

"Joe," Mackenzie said when Joe was at the foot of the stairs. "My agent called. He's got a week's work for me. A catalogue. They had somebody, but he broke his ankle, and they want continuity, so... yeah. A full week. They want me there tomorrow, first thing."

And there was the bandage getting pulled off another tiny bit. "You driving down tonight or getting up early tomorrow morning?"

Mackenzie looked frustrated, but Joe had no idea why. "I guess tonight," he finally said. "They're talking about some weather maybe blowing in by morning."

"Do you want me to wash anything for you?"

"That's all you have to say?"

"What do you want me to say?"

"I want you to say you'll miss me!" Mackenzie's voice was loud, but he glanced toward the living room and continued more quietly. "I want you to give a goddamn that I'm about to go away for longer than we've been apart since we started!"

"I'll miss you," Joe said flatly. He'd miss Mackenzie this time, and he'd miss him when he was gone for good.

But Mackenzie just snorted. "Yeah, I can feel the love."

Joe bit back an angry retort. He stood quietly for a moment, then stepped back into the kitchen. "I love you," he said. "I'm sorry you don't feel it."

Mackenzie looked disoriented; he'd clearly been expecting something else. "But you're okay if I go to the city? I mean, after last time? Kissing somebody else?"

"I don't own you. If you want to go, you'll go."

"Yeah, Joe, I *will* go if I want to. What I'm asking is, how do you feel about the idea?"

"Why? I mean, what's the point in me telling you how I feel about something you're going to do anyway?"

"Because maybe I could do something to make you feel better about it?"

"Like what? You could give me a big lecture about how you're not a slut and you don't fool around with people just because you're drunk? Nah, I don't think I need to hear that again. Really not going to have the same impact this time around, you know?"

"I can't figure out if you actually think what I did was cheating, or if you're just picking a fight because you're... I don't know... because you're pissed at the way your life is going and you need someone to blame."

"I don't blame you for anything." That was true, at least.

"No, of course not. Nobody else on the *planet* can take the blame for anything. You need to keep all the guilt for yourself."

"I don't blame myself for you kissing somebody else. No, that wasn't my fault. Wasn't yours either, I guess. It was just the way things went." The way they were meant to be.

"Come down with me," Mackenzie said. He looked surprised by his own words, but continued anyway. "Take a vacation. Sarah said she'd babysit whenever you needed. Ally and Lacey can take some time off school to help out. You and me, Joe. We could reconnect, figure things out, remind ourselves of all the stuff we like about each other. All the stuff we love."

Joe wanted to say yes. It was a stupid, irresponsible suggestion, but he wanted to go along with it. Instead, he said, "Ally and Lacey have two weeks before exams; they need to be in school. And Kami's not going to have much fun stuck on the second floor all week, just 'cause Sarah isn't strong enough to carry her downstairs safely. And we're still figuring out her meds, and I have appointments with a bunch of different people, and I need to get that therapist figured out, and the school said she can probably start school on Wednesday, but they wanted me to be nearby in case it doesn't work and she needs to get picked up, and the animals can't just be boxed up and put in the warehouse, and—"

Mackenzie raised his hand, silencing Joe. "Okay," he said quietly. "I get it. You can't come."

"I really can't."

"Ever?" Mackenzie said quietly, as if he was just now realizing the magnitude of it all.

"I don't know," Joe said. He was pretty sure Mackenzie knew he was lying.

"That's not...." Mackenzie stopped as if he was reconsidering his words, then continued anyway. "It's not what I expected when this started."

"Not what you signed up for," Joe said. He could tell where the conversation was going, and in a way it was almost a relief.

"I love you," Mackenzie said desperately. "I really do. I just...."

"I know."

It was probably good that the mudroom door banged open then, Austin standing in the doorway with a red, tear-covered face, his legs extended awkwardly to the sides. Griffin was there, trying to lick his cheeks. Ally stood behind them looking guilty.

"Hey, buddy," Joe said, forcing his voice to be light. He made himself walk away from Mackenzie and refused to take the cheap comfort of brushing against the man as he passed. "What's wrong?"

"I p-peed," Austin sobbed.

It had been a long time since Austin'd had an accident, and Joe felt a lurch of familiar guilt in his gut. Of course a five-year-old couldn't be bundled into his snowsuit without taking a trip to the bathroom first, couldn't play outside for hours without a break, and of course Joe should have reminded Ally of that. "That sucks, little man. It must be really cold, right?" Joe bent down and pulled off Austin's mitts, then unzipped his jacket. "But the best thing about having the laundry in the mudroom? Easy-peasy to clean up!" He looked up toward his sister. "In or out, Ally. I want the door shut when I strip him down."

She stepped the rest of the way inside and closed the door behind her, but kept her hat and mitts on. "I should go back and get Lacey and Savannah, if... you know, if things are calm in here."

Joe had been thinking about napping on the couch while four kids were huddled outside afraid to reenter the house. Excellent. "Yeah, go get them," he said as he kept stripping Austin down. "We'll make hot chocolate or something. In the future, though, don't freeze yourselves to death. We're going to have to get used to outbursts, I think."

"We weren't freezing, were we, Austin?"

Austin looked up at his sister. "We were h-having fun," he hiccupped. Then he looked at Joe, allowing himself to be lifted clear of his wet snow pants, pants, and underwear. "In the fort."

"Sounds good," Joe said absently. Austin's thighs were red and chapped where they'd been wet. Where was the diaper cream? Had Joe been naïve enough to get rid of the last tub? Probably. He picked the boy up for a quick hug, brushing the remaining tears off his cheeks. "You good being naked for a bit, little man? We'll leave your shirt on so you don't freeze, but you can be bare on the bottom? It'd be good to air things out a little."

Austin's eyes widened. "There's *girls!*" he said in a hushed, scandalized voice.

"What? You've been naked around girls before. Ally's a girl, buddy. So's Sarah."

Austin cast a dubious look at his young aunt. "*Real* girls," he whispered. "Lacey and Vannah and Kami."

Annoying time for the kid to get modest. "Okay, go upstairs and find some clothes, okay? Something soft—maybe your green sweatpants? We could wash you, but I think the water would sting right now. You can have a bath after dinner."

Austin obediently scampered for the hall, his nudity concerns apparently forgotten as he lifted his shirt over his head and waved it around in the air. Joe wasn't sure what that was about, and habit made him look over to share his amusement with Mackenzie. But Mack wasn't smiling. He was watching Austin, sure, but he looked like he wanted to cry.

Thinking about saying good-bye, Joe realized. Austin was a loveable kid. He might be a nuisance, might get in the way of Mackenzie's dream life, but that didn't mean Mackenzie didn't like the little guy. There *had* been some good memories in the house, after all. Mack was going to miss some of what he left behind.

But he'd have lots to distract himself with. Once he got back to the city, life on the farm would fade away like a distant memory.

Joe heard stirring in the living room. Kami was awake, and she tended to be just as disoriented as Austin on first waking. But where Austin was generally sulky, Kami tended to get scared. So Joe lifted Austin's soggy clothes into the washing machine and gave his hands a quick rinse in the laundry sink, then headed toward the living room. He didn't look at Mackenzie as he passed. There was no point torturing himself, coveting things he couldn't have.

Chapter Sixteen

Mackenzie rested the phone against his temple. He wished the technology worked that way. If he could just beam his *thoughts* to Joe instead of having to figure out the words, he had a feeling everything would go more smoothly. Even better if he could bypass the thoughts and send the pure emotions. Sure, there'd be frustration and anxiety and fear, but there'd be love, too, so much love that even someone as stubborn as Joe would have to admit it was real, and important.

But the technology hadn't been invented yet, so Mackenzie pulled the phone away from his head, selected Joe's number, and braced himself.

"Hi," Joe said over the phone. He sounded exhausted, as usual.

"Hi," Mackenzie replied. Yeah, telepathic phones would be *way* better than this. "How're things going?"

"I'm on my way to a meeting with the principal. Lacey's in trouble again."

"Drinking?"

"Failing all her classes, he says. I don't know." Joe sighed, and Mackenzie could picture him, the way he'd be slouched in the truck, talking to the point on his steering wheel where he'd decided his hands-free mike was hidden. Mackenzie was sure that the mike was somewhere higher, maybe in the rearview mirror, and they'd play-fought about it one afternoon driving back from the grocery store. If Mackenzie tried to argue about it now, Joe would probably hang up on him. "How're things with you?" Joe asked. "The shoot going well?"

"Yeah." Mackenzie took a deep breath, then said, "They want me to stay for another week, do some work for their American line. It's a really good opportunity. I mean, good money, but exposure too."

There was barely even any hesitation. "Sounds great. Congratulations."

"Did you know that Kristen thinks you're controlling and possessive?" Not really the approach Mackenzie had planned to take, but apparently his mouth was operating independently from his brain.

"What?" Joe sounded about as surprised as Mackenzie.

"Yeah. She thinks I don't do drugs because you don't approve. She thinks you control me just like Nathan did."

"Is this... are you going somewhere with this? Are you trying to make a point? Or just start a fight?"

"A fight? No, we wouldn't have a fight. A fight would take too much energy. A fight would mean you noticed that I existed and cared about what I was doing or saying or thinking. No, we're not going to have a fight."

"What the fuck, Mackenzie? What are you mad about?"

"I tell you I'm going to be away for another week, and you tell me, 'Sounds great, congratulations'? Seriously? That's how much you care?"

"What? Something good happened for you, so I'm happy. And you think that means I don't care. You're not making any sense, and I'm not going to be an asshole just to prove some point to you. I'm not Nathan, Mackenzie. I'm not playing that game."

"You can be an asshole in more ways than one. Yeah, he tried to control me. But he didn't *ignore* me."

"Are you hearing yourself? This is the conversation you want us to be having?"

Jesus. No. This wasn't what Mackenzie wanted. He wanted Joe, warm and relaxed and happy. But apparently he couldn't have that, so he'd decided to settle for any attention he could get, even if he turned himself into a harpy in order to get it. "No," he admitted. "This isn't the conversation I want us to be having. I want us to be talking about pleasant things and exciting plans. I want us to be joking and laughing and acting like we're in love. That's what I want, Joe."

There was a long pause. "Yeah," Joe finally said. "That'd be nice." Another pause, then he said, "I'm at the school, and I'm already running a little late. I need to go in and get this sorted out. But I'll call you tonight, okay? After the kids are asleep."

"After the kids are asleep, *you'll* want to be asleep."

"No, I'll want to be talking to you."

"And you'll yawn, and I'll feel guilty for keeping you up. Damn, this guilt thing is contagious."

Joe took a long time to reply, and when he did, he sounded even more tired than he had when the conversation started. "Do you want me to not call? I don't...." Yet another pause. "Are you trying to break up with me? Trying to push me to break up with you? Is that what this is about?"

No! Mackenzie's mind screamed at him. It was impossible, unimaginable. Living without Joe? Walking away from him now? It couldn't happen. Mackenzie would have to be crazy to even consider it. "I don't know," he whispered. "*Something* has to change."

"Well, maybe you could get back to me when you have something a little more definite," Joe said. He didn't sound hurt, exactly. It almost like he was satisfied his predictions had finally come true. "I need to go. You can call me tonight if that's what you want, or not call me if you don't want. Whatever. But it'd be nice if you didn't leave me hanging for too long."

And that was it. Joe ended the call, and Mackenzie stared at the handset. Joe was accusing *Mackenzie* of leaving him hanging? After all the passive-aggressive, mind-controlling bullshit of the past weeks, Joe thought *Mackenzie* was dragging things out and not being decisive? It was truly mind-boggling.

"We're ready for you, Mackenzie," the photographer's assistant said politely, and he tried to get his mind back on the job.

When the shoot was finally over, he stumbled outside into the cold evening air and let himself actually think about it. Was this the way things were going to end? Not with a bang, but a whimper?

Life without Joe. The problem was, Mackenzie felt like he was *already* living without him. Sure, he still *saw* Joe, but that was just tantalizing reminders of how things used to be. They weren't *together*, not the way Mackenzie wanted them to be. So what was his choice, really? He had to decide whether it was better to be with Joe as he was or leave him entirely, giving up the hope that things might get better.

Hope. It was powerful, but it couldn't conquer everything.

Mackenzie was still working through it all when he reached his destination and pushed the restaurant door open. It was a café, trendy but casual, and Mackenzie didn't have to wait for a maître d' to show him to the table. He just cast his gaze over the room, found his agent's smiling face, and headed in the right direction.

"Hi, Carson," he said, and they shook hands and settled into their seats.

"You're eating light, right?" Carson asked. He'd clearly already looked at the menu. "They have a seared trout that would be good, or an herbed chicken breast."

But apparently Mackenzie was feeling a bit contrary. "I was actually thinking in terms of red meat. Steak and potatoes, if they've got something along those lines." He picked up his own menu and found what he was looking for. When the server came over for drink orders, Mackenzie asked for a beer.

Carson looked like he wasn't sure whether to be amused or alarmed. "Comfort food?" he asked gently.

Mackenzie decided to tackle it head-on. "This next shoot. A whole week. Is there any way to shorten that? Or get some time off before it starts?"

Carson looked surprised, then shook his head. "You're hardly at the level where you can start making demands like that, dear. You're doing well—developing a reputation for being professional and easy to work with. You lose that and you're just one more overaged pretty boy."

"No." Mackenzie took a sip of his beer to cool his temper, and when he spoke again, his voice was more level. "I'm a hell of a lot more than a pretty boy, overaged or otherwise."

Carson raised an eyebrow. "I meant professionally, dear. I'm sure you're a young man with a great depth of character and many wonderful qualities, but that's not what modeling is about. Modeling is about having the right look and the right attitude. And I'm wondering if your attitude is in quite the right place."

It wasn't really a threat, but Mackenzie heard a definite undertone in Carson's voice. Mackenzie sighed. He'd been with his agent for years, and Carson had put up with a lot from him. "Things aren't going too well at home," he forced himself to admit. "My boyfriend... there's a lot going on. This isn't a great time for me to be away."

"And with your *old* boyfriend, you couldn't work too much because he didn't like it." Carson shook his head sadly. "When are you going to let your life be about *you*, Mackenzie? When are you going to make your decisions based on your own interests instead of someone else's needs?"

Mackenzie frowned. "Wait. I'm not... I hope I'm *never* going to make my decisions that way. Not entirely. I mean, that's just being selfish, isn't it? Doing what's right for me without taking anyone else into consideration?"

"I think you *need* to be a little selfish, dear. Everyone *else* is, so if you're not, you'll just get run over."

"No," Mackenzie objected again. "With Nathan, yeah, that sounds right. But not with Joe. He's the complete opposite of selfish. I mean, if he was more selfish it would be *great*, because if he was doing what he wanted, he'd be spending more time with me."

"Okay," Carson said, holding his hands up in surrender. "Your boyfriend is wonderful. But maybe he's just not a good fit. Maybe this isn't the right time in his life, or your life, or whatever. Sometimes the universe doesn't align. Sometimes things don't work out." Carson sipped his drink and looked at Mackenzie speculatively. When he spoke again, his voice was hard. "It's time for you to shit or get off the pot, Mackenzie. I am moving heaven and earth, getting you jobs and opportunities that are honestly surprising even *me*, they're so good. I am putting a lot of energy into building your career, but I can't be the only one dedicated to your success. If you don't want to make this work, you need to decide *now*, before I waste any more time on you."

"When we started up again, you told me there wasn't going to be a lot of work. That's what I was expecting. A shoot here or there, enough to make some extra money so I could keep using my savings for the church. You told me *not* to expect a career."

"I gave you the worst-case scenario," Carson said defensively. "Things are working out better than that. You should be *thrilled*." He sipped his drink again. It seemed to be some sort of mean potion, because his eyes narrowed before he said, "There are lots of fish in the sea, dear. The crowd you're about to get in with? I'm talking New York, Milan, and Paris, not boring old Toronto. Those are the places you'll be going, and you'll be meeting rich, powerful, handsome men. Men you can build a life with, a life where you can *both* be selfish and still give each other what's needed." Carson shrugged nonchalantly. "I'm sure your farmer is lovely, but he's hardly irreplaceable."

A replacement for Joe. Mackenzie tried to imagine it. Another man, just as good, but with a more compatible lifestyle. Someone as caring, gentle, strong, and funny. Someone who could turn Mackenzie on just by looking at him and who could follow through on the promise of the look. Someone brave, solid, generous. Someone with shoulders as wide as a doorway and an ass so tight it could crack walnuts.

No. Mackenzie wasn't going to find another man like Joe. And a man *like* Joe wasn't going to be enough anyway. Joe was the one Mackenzie loved. There was no point trying to replace him.

So maybe he wouldn't be looking. Maybe he'd take some time for himself. There'd be travel, and he'd be working a lot. In his spare time he could take a course or start reading more. Go to galleries. He could go to the theater himself, damn it. He didn't need Joe to buy him tickets.

Of course, he *wanted* to go with Joe. He wanted to see Joe in his shirt and tie, his shoulders so broad Mackenzie'd had to get the shirt custom tailored. He wanted to drive to the theater together and hold hands in the lobby, then find their seats and keep their hands tightly clasped. For all his masculinity, Joe wasn't shy about showing affection, even in public. After the show, Mackenzie wanted to walk together, talking and laughing and sharing their favorite parts of the production. And Mackenzie wanted to go home with Joe, and undress him and climb into bed with him and let Joe make him feel perfect. There wasn't enough theater in the world to make Mackenzie happy if he wasn't with Joe.

And that was what it came down to, he realized. It didn't matter if he was unhappy with Joe, because he'd be unhappy without him too. He was in too deep to get out now. If he could go back in time and arrange to have never met Joe or to have walked away the first time Joe had tried to break them up?

No. He still wouldn't change anything. He wouldn't give up

the good just to avoid the bad.

He wouldn't give up at all. The thought came to him in what he was pretty sure was generally referred to as a blinding attack of the obvious. He wouldn't give up. That was all there was to it. Joe might be ready to quit, but he was just tired. Exhausted from the overwork, the stress, the guilt he insisted on carrying around with him. Joe wasn't thinking straight, so Mackenzie needed to step in and help him out.

"I love him," he said out loud. "I'm not going to replace him. And I think... I'm sorry, Carson, but I think I need to turn this job down. And future jobs too, probably. Anything I can't do in a day or two at the most, I think, is too big. I might need to get back to you on that."

Carson's squint turned into a glare. "No, dear," he said icily. "That's not how it works. If you aren't committed to your career, 100 percent, then I won't be finding jobs for you. I'll give them to someone else, someone who might actually use them as a way to build something bigger."

"I guess that's your call," Mackenzie said. He felt as if a tight band around his chest had loosened. He was going to fight for his man. He was setting his own priorities, making his own decision. He'd slid over into the driver's seat, behind the wheel, and he knew where he wanted to go.

Then he realized he had an overall plan, but no real idea of what steps he needed to take to make it happen. The band started tightening again. "I need to go," he told Carson. "Thanks for the beer."

He found his way to the sidewalk and started walking, then figured out what the first step needed to be and pulled out his phone. When Ally answered he said, "I need your help. Will and Sarah too. Lacey, I think. Probably some other people eventually, but I think that's good for now. Can you meet me somewhere, away from the house? Tomorrow, if possible."

"Are we doing a caper?" Ally asked. "I've always wanted to do a caper."

"Not quite. I don't think." Mackenzie frowned. "Well, maybe a bit. I have no idea, really. I guess I'll do whatever it takes."

"I have no idea what you're talking about, but I'm in. I'll bring Lacey. How about at Sarah's place tomorrow after school? About three thirty? I can call Will and get him to be there."

Mackenzie had been right to get Ally involved. The girl made things happen. "Sounds excellent. Thank you."

He shoved the phone into his pocket and walked down the street with a light step. He was *doing* something. He had no idea *what*, exactly, but at least he wasn't just sitting back and letting things happen.

"Look out, Joe Sutton," Mackenzie said aloud, ignoring anyone who might be giving him strange looks. "I'm on your trail, hunting you down. You can run, but you can't hide."

That was probably a bit more aggressive than he really wanted, but he'd adjust as the situation demanded. For the time being, he was happy to have at least the start of a plan.

CHAPTER SEVENTEEN

"VERY NICE, Kami," Joe said. "You'll be riding on your own in no time."

She didn't respond, too focused on her task. Joe had clipped two lead ropes to Devil's halter for Kami to use as reins, hoping to avoid painful jerks to the animal's mouth when Kami got too excited or became distracted. He had a third rope running between the halter and his own hands, ready to intercede if things went wrong. And Kami *was* pretty excited, but distraction wasn't a concern at all. Her attention was almost trancelike, and he had to halt the horse and touch her leg, then give her a while to respond every time he wanted to give her instructions.

Luckily, he wasn't finding he needed to do that many times. She'd ridden before the fire, although not often: the Waltons hadn't kept horses of their own, and Joe hadn't bothered to go out of his way to get Kami on the Sutton herd. One more way he could have made the girl's life less miserable, one more missed opportunity.

Still, she apparently remembered enough to handle the basics. And she was more confident on the animal than he'd expected. Given her fear of falling down the stairs, he'd worried she might panic at the increased height, but she'd shown no signs of anxiety. The whole experiment was a success.

It was about time something went right. Joe was trying not to think about his conversation with Mackenzie the day before. No good could come from thinking.

"Let's go to the end of the lane and back, and then we'll call it a day, okay, Kami? You're going to get cold if we go much longer." Joe had picked a warm day for this little adventure, the snow soft enough to not be slippery, but a dampness in the air seemed to drain heat out just as effectively as a cold wind would have.

Kami didn't argue, probably because she hadn't heard what Joe had said. He opened the gate from the yard, and the dogs trotted over from their observation posts by the railing. "She did pretty well, didn't she, guys?"

The dogs wagged their tails in agreement, and Kami smiled at them. Apparently only other animals could distract her from the horse.

"Do you want to try a jog?" Joe asked. As expected, he got no response, so he reached up and guided one of Kami's hands to the saddle horn. Devil's jog was smooth, and the horse was lazy enough not to go any faster than was absolutely required, so it was safe to push things a little further. "Okay, give him a squeeze," Joe instructed, and then he pressed Kami's leg against the horse. Devil yielded to the one-sided pressure rather than increasing his pace; Sutton horses knew the rules. Joe sighed and moved up to Devil's head. "You're going to need some retraining if you're going to be a therapy horse. Come on, now!" Joe tugged gently on the lead rope, quickened his own pace, and kept an eye on Kami as the horse finally broke into a reluctant, unsure jog. "Good boy," Joe said, and Devil seemed reassured. "Good girl," Joe said, but Kami wasn't listening to him. She had clutched the horn when Devil had first changed his pace, but only for a few strides before she found her balance and released her grip, sitting tall and happy in the saddle. She looked good. She looked free.

The end of the driveway came too soon. Joe slowed the horse to a walk and turned them back toward the barn. Devil went about two steps before breaking into a jog again. "No," Joe said, bringing the horse back to the walk. Another few steps and another jog.

Joe didn't think he'd ever seen this horse move voluntarily in his life. He slowed him again, then turned and looked back at Kami. She was grinning at him, and he squinted at her face, then her legs. "Are you doing it? Are you telling him to jog?"

"Jog," she said happily, and even through her snow pants he could see her legs tighten around the horse, urging him forward.

Joe let it happen. Devil wasn't going to work up much of a sweat on such a short ride, and Joe could cool him out afterward if needed. The key thing was that Kami was enjoying herself and taking charge of at least this one small part of her life. There was lots of time to help her learn about being a responsible rider. For this one time, he'd let her enjoy the freedom of being a little irresponsible.

So he jogged beside her, lead rope loose to give her freedom, and when she reached the barn and turned around for another trip down the driveway, he wasn't altogether surprised and didn't object. When they finished that loop, though, he held Devil's head and touched Kami's calf until she looked at him. "That's enough for today, Kami. You don't want to get too tired. I bet you're going to be sore tomorrow as it is." The ride hadn't been too intense, but Kami had been pretty inactive for about half a year, and her muscles must have lost a lot of their strength. "Come down now, and we'll give Devil a nice grooming, okay? He was a good boy, wasn't he? Do you think he wants to eat the apple you brought him?"

There was a little fuss as Kami realized how far she had to drop to get off the horse's back, but she calmed down when Joe put his hands on her waist and helped guide her to the ground. She staggered when she landed, her legs jelly after the exercise, and he helped her over to the bench by the side of the barn. "Okay, you sit. I'm going to walk Devil a little bit, then we'll untack him, and you can give him his treat. Okay?"

Joe loosened the horse's girth and took him for a short tour of the yard. He wasn't really hot, but it was good to remind Kami of the routines involved in caring for animals. He could imagine a world where she'd be able to do this herself. Maybe not the saddling, or at least not until she got a little stronger. Heaving a forty-pound western saddle up higher than her head would be a bit of a challenge for quite a while, and it wasn't fair to Devil to have someone throwing things at his back without any control. But maybe Kami could go for a ride along the tree line, giving herself a little space, a little freedom. Damn, Joe was glad he'd thought of this. He couldn't wait to see Mackenzie's reaction—Oh. Except Mackenzie might not be around long enough to even hear about this. Joe needed to not think about that. There was nothing he could do about it, so he should keep himself from being tortured by the possibilities. The inevitabilities.

He turned back toward the barn, and his stomach lurched a little when he saw the empty bench by the wall. Damn it. Where had Kami gone? Not far, at least. There hadn't been time for her to put much distance between them. And hopefully her legs were still tired. She'd probably just gone inside the barn or something. Nothing to worry about.

Still, Joe picked up the pace. He was almost back to the barn when he saw the bright red of Kami's jacket, and his stomach gave another lurch. "Kami!" he yelled, dropping Devil's lead rope. "Kami, no! Not that horse!"

The girl was bent over, working her way through the rail fence into Misery's paddock, and the gray mare was staring at the intruder with gleeful malice.

"Misery, don't you dare," Joe yelled, running forward.

But he was too far away. Kami straightened up and Misery came at her, ears pinned and teeth bared. Joe roared, but neither Kami nor Misery looked in his direction. That was when a beige blur streaked into the paddock, leaped through the narrow space between the rails, and charged at the mare, growling and barking like a demon. It was Griffin, and Red was behind him, heavier and slower but even more intimidating when he arrived, both of them diving into the space between the girl and the horse and driving Misery backward. Kami stood as if amazed by the show being put on for her amusement, squawking a little as Joe opened the gate and dragged her back through it. She was safe.

"Griffin," he croaked through a mouth that had gone dry. "Red. Come."

The dogs backed off with a few extra snarls, Misery following them with the clear intention of winning back the ground she had given up when she was surprised. Joe stepped back into the paddock and stared her down. "You get the hell away from them, you crazy bitch," he growled. And the horse might not respect the dogs, but she knew better than to mess with Joe. She pinned her ears but stopped moving forward, and when he stepped toward her, she dropped her head and took a step back.

If he pushed it any more, she'd turn her ass and kick at him, but that'd be defensive; he couldn't blame her for that. And damn it, now that the adrenaline was working its way out of his body, now that Kami was safe, he couldn't blame Misery for the initial problem either. Joe knew her temperament, he knew what she was, and it was his job to work with that knowledge and make sure she wasn't around anyone she could hurt. He eased out through the gate and latched it, then turned to the surprised girl crouching to receive kisses from Red and Griffin. "Not this horse, Kami. Never this horse. She's not safe."

She wasn't safe, but Joe kept her on the property. He had some weird affection for her antisocial behavior, and, God, he loved riding her, the two of them working cattle as if they shared one athletic body and one focused brain. Riding a horse like her made the mundane task of moving stock into an adventure and a privilege.

But he could do the job almost as well from an ATV, and a four-wheeler wouldn't attack an eleven-year-old girl just because the child wandered into its territory.

Damn it. Joe had known what he needed to do, but he'd put

it off. It wasn't just the effort it required for him to look after Misery, it was also the requirements of safely keeping a dangerous horse. He didn't have the time or energy to do it responsibly, so he couldn't do it at all.

He looked over the fence at the mare and wondered if he'd be able to find a good home for her. Better to have her put down than send her to someone who'd try to beat her attitude out of her. Or to someone who wouldn't recognize the warning signs and take the proper precautions. "Damn it, Misery," he said. "Why you gotta be so mean?"

The horse gave him a contemptuous look and turned to take a nonchalant bite of hay. Nothing exceptional had happened, from her perspective. Attacking children and being chased off by dogs was just the way she liked to spend her afternoons.

Red had left Kami and come to stand next to Joe. "Good work, old man," Joe said. "You covered for me." He glanced over his shoulder and saw Griffin still leaning happily against Kami, Kami just as happy to lean against him in return. "You and the doodle. He's pretty quick, huh? Pretty brave."

Red didn't look totally convinced about that, but he wagged his tail in Griffin's general direction as Joe walked over to Kami and the dog. "Come help me put Devil away, okay, Kami?"

She reached up and quietly took his hand. She trusted him and was willing to be led. He needed to be sure he didn't abuse that trust. It was his job to keep her safe.

So when he got back to the house he put in a call to a horse behaviorist he'd brought out to work with Misery when she'd first come to the farm. Sherri had helped him figure out some of the horse's quirks, but she'd said it was always going to be a challenge with a horse so determined to be dominant. Misery would respect individual humans, if they earned it, but she wasn't the sort of horse that would submit to the entire species. "She knows how strong she is," Sherri had said, sounding almost admiring. "And in order to do her job right, she has to know she's faster and smarter than the cattle. She's not going to be too impressed with someone just because they walk upright and happen to wear clothes."

"I think I need to reassess," he said now. "Can you come out and give me an opinion on her, where she is now? And maybe help me find her a new owner, if you think that's safe."

They made an appointment for early the next week, and Joe tried not to think about it as he put the phone down. No Mackenzie, no Misery. All his guilty pleasures, the relationships he couldn't justify but couldn't abandon. He needed to be strong. And he needed to not think about any of it, not if he was going to have a chance of getting through the day.

"I'm going to start dinner, Kami. Can you help set the table? Here, let's start with forks. Put a fork at each place, please."

Kami shuffled off toward the table. They left the placemats out most of the time, and Kami would set places at all of them, regardless of whether there was someone expected to fill that place. It was just easier than trying to predict who'd be there and then trying to communicate that to Kami. They'd build up to that, someday.

Joe was slicing vegetables and Kami was placing napkins when the mudroom door banged open. Joe glanced over, then set down his knife. Ally had borrowed the truck to get to school that day since she'd had some appointment in the afternoon. Lacey had gone with her, and they'd agreed to pick up the kids at the day care where they went after school. So he wasn't too surprised to see the four of them coming inside. But they weren't alone. Will was there, and Sarah, and Jean the social worker, and was that Lorraine, the woman who lived across from the church, who'd taught Mackenzie to play euchre? And Vince Deacon, the captain of the volunteer fire department. Andrew Stark, wearing his OPP uniform, and Kathryn Webb, the principal at the elementary school. Clayton MacIlray was there too. He was a plumber, for Christ's sake. Was there something wrong with the plumbing?

And at the end of the parade, proud as a mother duck, came Mackenzie. They all crowded into the kitchen, and Austin ran over to be picked up for a hug. "Lots of people!" he said happily. He kissed Joe's cheek and then beamed at the visitors. "We should have cake!"

"I don't have any cake, little man. Sorry." Joe wasn't sure what else to say, and thankfully Mackenzie edged his way forward to take charge.

"I need to talk to Joe for a couple minutes. If you could all wait in the living room, that'd be great. We won't be long." He glanced in Joe's direction, as if aware that the truth of the final statement depended at least a little on Joe's cooperation, and smiled tentatively.

They stood without speaking, waiting as the procession shed boots and outdoor clothes and headed for the living room. Will and Sarah both frowned at Joe as they passed, and Sarah whispered, "If you don't listen to Mackenzie, you will damn well be hearing about it from me!"

Ally was a little gentler, clearly torn between trying to act like an adult and wanting to bounce with childish excitement. "It's going to be good, Joe. You just need to let it work!" Then she took Austin from Joe's arms and turned to gather Savannah and Kami. "Special treat today, guys! TV *before* dinner! Come on, we'll watch upstairs!" She looked over her shoulder at Mackenzie. "I'll get them settled, then come back down." Then she smiled at her brother. "Let it work, Joe. We can do it."

With the adults in the living room and the kids upstairs, Joe and Mackenzie were alone in the kitchen, staring at each other.

Joe was the first to speak. "What the hell's going on, Mack?"

Mackenzie smiled nervously. "Yeah. Good question. It got a bit out of hand. But I can explain." He stepped a little closer and reached forward tentatively, then drew his hand back. "I can explain," he said again. "Please let me."

As if Joe could ever say *no* to Mackenzie. He stepped back and leaned against the counter, and he waited.

CHAPTER EIGHTEEN

MACKENZIE KNEW he only had one shot at this. If Joe had time to get his defenses up, there'd be no chance to get through them. It was only this way, with surprise on Mackenzie's side, that he could make Joe hear him.

"I love you," he said. Always good to start with something positive. "And I'm not leaving you. No way. If you want me gone, you have to kick me out. Otherwise, I'm here for good. Okay?"

Joe just stared at him.

"Okay," Mackenzie said. He needed to keep the momentum up. "But things aren't working the way they've been going. We need to make some changes."

"Changes that involve having half the town in my living room?"

"Yeah," Mackenzie said calmly. "That's probably going to be part of it. Everybody in there is here for a reason. And they can all explain themselves better than I can. But the thing is, before we go in... I want you to *listen* to them, Joe. I need you to stop being a fucking martyr, carrying the whole world on your shoulders all by yourself." Mackenzie had thought up clever words for all of this, a coherent speech complete with literary allusions and rhetorical devices, but now the ideas were all dancing around and refusing to stay organized. "It's like in *The Little Prince*. Did you ever read that book? In French class, maybe, *Le Petit Prince*?"

Joe looked at him like he was crazy and slowly shook his head.

Not good. The allusion only really made sense if they'd both read the book. But Mackenzie didn't seem to be able to shake himself off the path he was on. "There's a fox. And the guy tames him. And then, once he's tamed, the guy's responsible for him. You know? Once you tame somebody, you have to take care of them."

"I'm trying to get rid of animals, Mackenzie, not tame new ones."

But Joe was just playing dumb. He understood the analogy. "You tamed *me*," Mackenzie said patiently. "I fell in love with you. I know you tried to run away at first, and I think you were maybe a little psychic on that one. If I'd known what was coming, I'm not sure I'd have had the guts to go through with it. But I didn't know, and I'm glad I didn't, because I'm glad I'm with you, and I plan to stay there." He stopped for a breath. Joe's face was unreadable, but that was about the reaction Mackenzie had been expecting. He plunged on. "Joe, I *know* the kids need you. I get that, and I respect the hell out of you for making them a priority in your life. But the thing is? *I* need you too. You're responsible for them, and it's wearing you down, so I know it's not fair to add a whole new responsibility, but that's too bad. You're responsible for me. I love you and I can't live without you and I need more from you than you're giving me. So there it is. That's the hard part."

Another deep breath, a chance for Joe to react if he was going to, and then Mackenzie spoke in a softer tone. "But the easy part? The easy part is in the living room, and they're only the tip of the iceberg. They're here to help with Kami and with whatever else you need help with. Because you're not the only person in the world with a sense of responsibility, Joe, and you're not the only person who's interested in helping other people out. And from talking to Jean and Andy, I can tell you that you're not the only person feeling guilty about not getting the kids out earlier. You do *not* have to do this alone."

Joe hadn't objected yet, so Mackenzie pushed a little further. "And you *and* them should stop feeling guilty. Remember what you told me after those rednecks tried to cause trouble after the movie? I said it was my fault they'd come after us, and you said it wasn't. You said that's what they want us to believe, but it's not true. You know whose fault it was that the girls' father was an abusive asshole? It was the girls' father's fault. That's it. You know who probably had a duty to get them out of there? Their mother. You aren't Superman, Joe. You're not in charge of the whole world."

Mackenzie took the chance now, stepping a little closer and reaching out to rest his palm on Joe's chest. "So you need to let go of that guilt. And you need to let me help you with that. Because we tamed each *other*, Joe. I'm just as responsible for you as you are for me, and one of the things that made me unhappy was realizing that and knowing I wasn't doing my job. I wasn't taking care of you. But I will now."

Joe was on the edge. Mackenzie could feel it. He wanted to believe, wanted to make this work, but there was his old fear, his old stubborn independence. Mackenzie forced himself to seem calm as he said, "I used to think it was stupid when people used the word *partner* to refer to their boyfriends. It sounded so sterile and passionless. But now I understand what they mean. I want us to be partners. If you take something on, I want you to count on me to help you with it. I want you to fucking *talk to me* about it before you take it on, but that's a fight for another day. For now, I want to be your partner. Your boyfriend and your lover and your sweet schnookums too. I want all of that, and I want you to give it to me, and I'm going to help you get yourself in a place where you *can* give it to me. Okay?"

"What exactly are we talking about, here?" Joe's hand moved as if of its own volition, sliding up and then wrapping its fingers through Mackenzie's. "I want this to work. I want to give you what you need. But, seriously, Mackenzie, why are all those people in my living room?"

Mackenzie felt a bubble of hope growing in his chest. Joe was listening. He was willing to try. "We can go find out, if you want."

"Wait. Why are you even here? What about that job? The American line, or whatever?"

"I cancelled it," Mackenzie said airily. "I don't really think I want to model anymore." He raised an eyebrow at Joe's surprised expression. "Oh. I suppose I could have discussed that with you first. In the postrevolutionary world, I will absolutely talk to you about that sort of thing. But this was a decision made under the old regime. Prepartnership. So I did whatever I wanted without bothering to talk to you about it. That must be really annoying, huh?"

"Is the new regime going to be a lot more sarcastic?" Joe asked mildly. "Because I'm not sure I'm in favor of that."

Mackenzie smiled at him and squeezed his fingers. "The new regime will be whatever we want it to be," he said. And he truly believed it. "Now, come in and be dazzled by the possibilities."

Joe did as he was told. Mackenzie was pretty sure the dazed compliance would wear off at some point, but at least temporarily Joe was playing along. He made his way into the living room and sat down where he was told, then waited quietly as Mackenzie settled himself.

It was strange to have all these people looking to him for leadership. One more innovation for the new regime, he supposed, and he tried to rise to the challenge. "We all care about the Walton kids," he said, nodding in Lacey's direction to acknowledge her special connection. "And we all want to help. So far, Joe's been doing most of the work, and he's been doing a great job, but he can't keep working that hard." He paused and gave Joe a hard, warning look. "It'd be pretty insulting to the people in this room to think he's the only one who could do a good job with the kids." He leaned back in his chair a little before adding, "But obviously continuity is important. The kids need to know who's in charge of them, need to come home to the same house and have the same routines. That's a job for Joe and me." He looked at Joe to see if he would object to the two-person team, but saw no reaction.

"I'm taking steps to be home more, and I'll play a more active role when I'm here." That earned him a warning look from Joe, and he hastened to add, "Because I'm an adult and I make my own decisions and I know what's important to me and what isn't. And I'm happy to let go of the unimportant in service of the important."

Joe still didn't look thrilled, and Mackenzie decided to get the rest of the bad news out of the way all at once. "And Ally's not going to do the science-exploration thing this semester. She says she wouldn't enjoy it if she was worried about things at home all the time, and she's got a line on a great job at the vet clinic that'll give her some real experience and look good on her vet-school application but that'll give her enough free time to still help out around the farm."

"No, Ally," Joe said. "This is a once-in-a-lifetime opportunity! The places you're going to see? The stuff you'll learn? You can't pass that up."

"I'll learn stuff here," she said nonchalantly. "And I don't believe in 'once in a lifetime.' I'll find something just as good and do it when the timing's better. Lacey and I are thinking about taking weekend trips—places closer to home that are still totally worth seeing. And for some of them we could bring Kami or Savannah, or maybe both of them. And I'm *psyched* for the vet clinic. They said I can help with surgeries! They wouldn't let me do that when I was just a co-op student." She beamed at Joe and wiggled her fingers. "These hands, inside an animal! It's going to be excellent!"

Joe didn't look too impressed. "We can talk about it later," he said threateningly.

Mackenzie decided to let that one go. "Lacey wanted to quit school and help out full-time—" Joe had his mouth open, but Mackenzie held up a hand to silence him. "But I said no because I'm not completely insane. We can discuss that decision if you want, Joe, but I was pretty confident you'd agree with it. Everyone finishes high school. That's the bare minimum. Right?"

"Of course that's right," Joe sputtered.

"Good, we agree. So Lacey's going to stay in school. She'll help out like she's been doing, and she'd like to learn more about the animals, if that's okay with you. When Ally goes to school in the fall, you'll need a farmhand, and Lacey's interested in giving that a try."

"You should be going to college too," Joe tried.

"I have absolutely zero interest in higher education," she replied. "At least not right now. I figure I can work for a while, get the family straightened out, and if something comes up that I'm interested in, I'll give it a try. There's no point in wasting money when I don't know what I want."

"We can talk about *that* later too," Joe muttered.

"Sarah wants to take over the paperwork," Mackenzie said quickly, before Joe got sidetracked. "For Kami's schooling, but for the farm and the house too."

"You've always hated it," she said calmly. "And I think it's fun. *So I'll do the bill payments, make the applications for bursaries or whatever for Kami. All that stuff. I've got it covered."

"You're a sick woman," Joe said, but he wasn't arguing.

"Will's going to be on call," Mackenzie said. Joe still didn't know about the impending baby, but that was one more conversation that could wait for another day. "We figured he's the one you're most likely to ask for help."

"And you'd better do it," Will said, "Or I'm going to come over and just start doing random shit. You'll come in from the barn one night and I'll have painted a room or something. Not a room that needed painting, not a color you like, just me, pretending to be useful. That's what'll happen if you don't direct my energies." He looked around the living room thoughtfully, then said, "Maybe a nice light peach."

"Don't paint the living room," Joe said. He turned back to Mackenzie. "I'm afraid to ask what everyone else is here for."

"We're here to represent the community," Vince Deacon said.

"I'm here to remind you that you've given a lot over the years, to a lot of different people. The fire department is just one way you've been of service to others. I want to tell you we'll be happy to have you back once your wrist is better. But if you can't make it back, that's okay too. You've done your time. You've served the community, and if you're busy serving in a different way right now, we want to help you with that."

"I'm president of the Rotary Club," Clayton MacIlray said. "We've already talked about finding a way to help the Walton girls out, and since Lacey apparently isn't going to need a scholarship, we're out of ideas. You need to help us find ways to help them."

"And I wanted to let you know that the school is absolutely dedicated to finding ways to make Kami welcome there," Kathryn Webb added. "We'll get her the help she needs. If the school board won't fund enough staff, we'll find volunteers or whatever else it takes. You need to know she's safe and happy from eight thirty to three thirty, and we can do that."

"And if the day-care center doesn't work out after school," Lorraine added, "I know people who are happy to step in so you can still do a full day's work on the farm." She nodded with the satisfaction of a well-intentioned busybody who'd found an outlet for her invasiveness. "I'll need to screen them and make sure they're dedicated to making a long-term commitment. Kami needs to get to know them, and they'll need to get to know Kami. If the day care doesn't think they can handle Kami on their own, maybe they'll change their mind if I can deliver them an extra couple volunteers each day."

"We all should have stepped in sooner," Andy Stark said. "Jean and me especially, but the whole community. Not just you. We couldn't have known there'd be a fire, but we knew things weren't good in the house. Now you need to let *all* of us have a chance to make things better for the girls."

"*All* the girls," Clayton MacIlray said. "Lacey, if you need help, you let me know. If Savannah needs something, I want to know about it." He looked at Joe. "We're a community, and we look after our own. It shouldn't be just one person taking it all on himself."

"We can make it work," Mackenzie said. He needed Joe to see that. If Joe could just find some hope, they could work together to figure out the details.

"It's what's best for Kami," Ally said, reaching out to take her brother's hand. "It's great that she had one person on her side, but it's even greater if she has more."

Joe swallowed hard and looked at Mackenzie. "We'd have a lot of details to figure out," he said.

Mackenzie felt the tension drain out of him, replaced with a buoyant hope. "We can do it," he said confidently. And then, quietly, "I need you to do it."

Joe stared at him for a long moment. Then, slowly but firmly, he nodded. "Yeah. Okay. Let's give it a try."

CHAPTER NINETEEN

"THERE'S A special harness," Joe explained to Kathryn Webb. "One end on the dog, the other end on the kid. I'm not sure we'd really need it with Kami and Griffin. They're pretty devoted to each other, so I can't see either one wandering off. But it'd make it clear that he's a service dog. The training place said we could get him a little... I don't know, it's like a little jacket. Like a cape that doesn't flap. It goes under the harness, and there'd be words on the side explaining his job."

"And his job would be primarily to lessen anxiety but could also involve keeping her from wandering away." The principal sounded thoughtful.

"Yeah. I mean, it wouldn't be, like, a job description. Not on the side of his cape. It'd just say 'Service Dog' or something."

"He could be a useful tool to help her reconnect with her classmates. Everyone likes a friendly dog."

"And he doesn't shed. Unlikely to cause allergies. Totally housetrained, no aggression at all. He's an excellent dog for the job."

"Let's give it a try," Kathryn said. She sounded relieved that Joe had come up with a plan. For all her dedication, she'd been having a lot of trouble making the school into the safe, welcoming place she wanted it to be. Well, at least she'd been having trouble making Kami *believe* it was safe and welcoming. It had only been a week since The Intervention, as Ally had taken to calling it, so nobody was discouraged yet, but finding a solution to the school problem was important.

Especially since Kami seemed to be almost as agitated at home. They'd started letting Griffin sleep on her bed, and that had helped some, but she'd still wake them with crying a couple times a night. Joe or Lacey would stumble into her room and find her sitting in her bed with her arms wrapped around Griffin, sobbing loudly into his ruff. They'd moved Savannah in with Austin so she wouldn't be disturbed.

That was what their lives were: constant upheavals and adjustments, never a good night's sleep or a time when they weren't trying to figure out a way to do one thing or another better than they'd been doing so far.

But it was okay, because it was both of them. Joe *and* Mackenzie. They still didn't seem to have the energy for a sex life, but now it was *both* of them falling into bed exhausted. A gentle kiss, maybe a little snuggling, then blessed sleep, at least for a few hours. And when they woke, it would be *both* of them hard at work.

Joe was pretty sure Mackenzie was trying to prove something, and surely he'd ease off eventually. But since the meeting, Joe had come in from the barn every morning to find a hot breakfast waiting for him, the kids washed and dressed, Kami carried downstairs and playing happily with the toys Mackenzie had brought into one corner of the kitchen. Austin would usually be with her, and when they squabbled, Mackenzie would be the one to decide whether intervention was warranted. Joe would go back out to work and come in to clean laundry and another hot meal. It was strange to sit there with Mackenzie, no kids in the house. The few times they'd gotten closest to sex had been during their afternoon naps—never actually taking things to completion, but at least making out a little, reminding themselves that their bodies *would* still work that way if only they had the energy to commit to it.

It was the dinners where Mackenzie was outdoing himself. He

seemed to have accepted that beef was cheap and easy, but he was using it the way the dieticians suggested, almost as a garnish. Beef stir-fry, beef stew full of vegetables, small, succulent steaks so flavorful they could dominate the meal without taking up that much space.

Joe had tried to make it clear that Mackenzie wasn't expected to turn himself into a fifties housewife, and Mackenzie had just grinned and said he was having fun. He'd back off when he got tired of it, and they'd go back to throwing whatever food they could find into a pot and hoping for the best. Until that happened, though, Joe was really trying to just enjoy it all without feeling guilty about any of it.

He checked his watch. The family had decided that on Fridays the kids would come straight home, no after-school program, so they'd be arriving any minute. Mackenzie was at the church, showing it to a pair of future grooms looking for somewhere quaint and special. Joe grinned, headed for the pantry, and pulled out oatmeal and chocolate chips and the rest of the ingredients for fresh cookies. Mackenzie didn't have a monopoly on showing affection through food.

He was sliding the first two cookie sheets into the oven when the mudroom door opened, but he didn't see the smiling faces of children when he looked over. Instead, Nick stood there, wearing a grubby spring-weight jacket about two sizes too small for him, shaking with cold. Joe looked out to the parking area and didn't see a car.

"I hitched," Nick said through chattering teeth.

"Get that jacket off and sit by the fire," Joe said, flipping the switch on the electric kettle. He had no idea what was going on, but he firmly believed in the utility of boiling water when in doubt. "What happened to your car?"

"They took it," Nick said. There was something in his face, a desperation that made Joe think the kid was being honest. "They took everything. My clothes, even. They just showed up at my apartment and made me sign over the car, and they loaded all my stuff into it and took off."

"They?" Joe said, trying to sound calm. He pulled down a mug and a tea bag, then got impatient with Nick's slow progress and strode over to unzip the jacket himself.

"I found that on the subway," Nick muttered.

Joe dropped it with distaste and bent down to pull off Nick's wet shoes. "Okay, go sit." He gently pushed his brother in the right direction. "I'll bring you tea, and you'll tell me who *they* are and why the hell they took your stuff and you didn't call the cops."

"You know who they are, Joe," Nick said. He was shuffling toward the fireplace, at least.

Joe sighed. Yeah, he supposed he did. Not the specifics, but the general idea. "You borrowed money from them?"

Nick nodded. "Nobody else would give me any."

"Nobody else would give you any because we didn't think you'd be able to pay it back. And if these guys came for you, that means you *weren't* able to pay it back." Joe tried to bite back the lecture he wanted to give. "Is the bar still running?"

Nick shook his head. "They closed it down, took all our equipment to pay the debts."

"And the guys you borrowed from... they're good now? Or are they going to come after you for more?" Joe poured the hot water into the mug and added a squirt of honey. He didn't want to think about his baby brother getting into this kind of trouble, but he needed to know whether it was likely to spread to the rest of the family.

"I think they're good. They know I'm done, and the car is probably enough to pay off the capital, at least. I guess my stuff goes to pay for the interest."

Joe handed the mug to his brother, who wrapped his fingers around it like it was made of gold.

"Okay. So you're safe. That's good." They sat quietly for a while.

"It's weird that I came *here*, isn't it?" Nick sipped his tea, winced as it burned his lips, then looked innocently at his brother. "I mean, I'm not exactly welcome here. And there's no room for me. But still, I didn't go to Will or Sarah's. I came here."

"This is your home, Nick." But Joe should be honest. "Although there *isn't* actually a bed for you, unless you want to share a room with a girl who gets the night sobs. We moved Savannah into the spare bed in Austin's room."

"I've slept on this couch before," Nick said. Apparently failure, terror, and cold made him much easier to get along with. Joe would have to remember that for future occasions.

"Mack's going through some sort of gourmet-chef phase, so the eats will be good."

"Nice. If I'm full enough, I can pass out anywhere."

Then the door banged open again, and this time it *was* the kids. They dropped their school stuff and trooped inside, and Joe fed them warm cookies with cold glasses of milk. It was too precious for words, really, but nobody complained.

Mackenzie came home with fish from the market, and Joe forced himself not to make a face. Maybe they'd take the kids ice fishing over the weekend, and Mackenzie could learn it wasn't necessary to spend money on things the farm could provide. Or maybe Mackenzie was just following Joe's aborted plan to simplify their lives and buying some stuff instead of having to produce it all at home.

"I'M JUST glad he came home," Joe said softly to Mackenzie as they lay in bed that night. "If he hadn't thought he could come here...."

"He knew he could." Mackenzie ran a comforting hand over

Joe's back. "And he's being an angel, so far. Is that likely to last?"

"Of course not. And even now, I wouldn't leave anything valuable lying around where he can see it."

"He wouldn't steal from you," Mackenzie objected. "He really loves you. He looks up to you. Wants to be like you. That's a lot of pressure, you know. On him. You're a lot to live up to, Joe Sutton."

Joe propped himself up on his elbow. "Where are you getting all that from? Are you just making it up?"

"Well, he never said it outright, maybe. But I'm pretty sure it's true."

"Is that how it was with you? Did you want to be like your dad, or your brother?"

"Me?" Mackenzie's laugh was incredulous. "Hell, no. I was *never* going to be like them."

"If you'd gotten in trouble when you were Nick's age, would you have gone to your parents?"

Mackenzie didn't answer right away, but finally Joe saw him nodding in the dim light. "Yeah, I guess so. I wouldn't have wanted to, but I would have."

"That counts for something, right? I mean, whatever it is between you all, you would have gone to them if you'd needed to. And they would have tried to help you."

"They would have lectured me until my ears bled."

"That's probably what Nick thinks I'm going to do." Joe wasn't sure if it was a good idea, but he decided to push a little further. "They love you. They miss you. I'm not saying you should start going over for Sunday dinner every week, but in the interest of our partnership and our sincere commitment to discussing each other's decisions, I think you should think about spending a bit more time with them. Invite them up to see the church. Something."

"I thought we were talking about *your* messed-up family,"

Mackenzie protested.

"We shifted topics," Joe said easily. "That's part of the new world order. We change topics pretty frequently. Get used to it."

"Can we change back? Can we talk about what your baby brother is going to be doing with his time? And are we *sure* things in the city are wrapped up tidily?"

"Maybe you could call your friend and find out," Joe suggested. After all, it had been Mackenzie who'd gotten Nick involved in the bar business in the first place. Of course, Joe had agreed to the whole plan and had been totally aware of the risks, so it wasn't like Mackenzie had anything to feel guilty for, but in terms of follow-up, he was in a good position to find things out.

"I will," Mackenzie promised. He was quiet for so long Joe was pretty sure he'd gone to sleep, but then he said, "Do you think my parents would *want* to see the church? I mean, they're not really interested in churches. Architecture. Whatever."

"They're interested in you," Joe said, and he kissed Mackenzie's temple. "Make it an open invitation. They should come up sometime, when they feel like it. I bet they have a date booked before you're off the phone. Seriously, Mack, I'm not good at understanding people, and even I could see that they were desperate to be part of your life."

"Do you think they'd want to move to the area and start a chain of tasteful B&Bs catering to the gay-wedding crowd?"

Joe grinned. "Maybe not quite *that* desperate. But it'd be networking, right? They must have friends with gay kids, or even just kids who don't want to get married in a regular church but still want a sense of tradition. All your target market."

"Damn, it's sexy when you talk business talk to me."

"Yeah? Are you thinking about your profit margin? Is it *rising*?" For the first time in weeks, Joe's cock was calling attention to itself, suggesting it might like a little something.

And at first, things seemed promising. "Maybe it's *going down*,"

Mackenzie said with a waggle of his eyebrows. But he didn't follow up with any actual down going of his own, just nestled into Joe's chest and shut his eyes.

That was fine. They were learning new rhythms. Mackenzie wasn't in the mood right now, just like Joe hadn't been in the mood at other times. They needed to resynch or something. It wasn't a big deal. *Not a big deal*, Joe told his cock, but as usual it didn't pay much attention to the messages his brain sent to it.

Joe flopped his head back into the pillow. He could feel Mackenzie's breathing change as he fell asleep, and it was enough. Sure, sex would be good, but they had other things to worry about right then. Sex could wait.

For a while, at least.

Chapter Twenty

"It turns out that Joe's great-grandparents were members of the congregation," Mackenzie said. He was nervous. He'd shown people through the church lots of times, but somehow, this tour was different. "So that's a nice bit of continuity. He actually has their wedding photos, taken right outside against the stone wall along the side. I'm planning to get them framed to hang downstairs in the reception area."

"That's a lovely idea," his mother said. "And this is an absolutely lovely building, Scott. It's so wonderful that you're keeping it for something close to its intended purpose."

"The original church owners didn't have a problem with you using their building this way?" his father asked.

Mackenzie tried not to bristle. *Don't go looking for trouble*, Joe had said. "Why would they?" he asked as sweetly as he could manage.

Mackenzie's parents exchanged a look. "Just horning in on their business, maybe," his father said quickly. "Nothing wrong with it, of course, just maybe they wouldn't want the competition."

"The building had been abandoned for almost a decade," Mackenzie responded. "On and off the market, with them dropping the price every time they relisted. I think they were just glad to get it off their books."

"Well, their loss is your gain," his mother said sweetly. She ran her hand over the polished wood of one of the gracefully curved pews. "I wonder if it could be used for other events, as well. We have a charity fashion show for the hospital each year. It would be so lovely to have it in a place like this."

"Your audience probably wouldn't want to drive quite so far away," Mackenzie said reasonably, and she laughed.

"No. Not *my* audience, and not just for a fashion show. But if there was someone in the area doing something similar, you could use it for that. Maybe even donate the space, if you can afford to do that. Get the exposure, and probably a tax receipt."

It was an interesting idea, but Mackenzie didn't want to get carried away. "I don't think they have the same kind of fundraisers up here, really. It's not a big fashion town."

His mother waved her hand airily. "Whatever. The equivalent."

Of course, there *was* no real equivalent. But he didn't have to argue with her. He realized that in an almost disorienting flash of clarity. He didn't need to win every conversation. She could say something he didn't agree with, and he could just let the words float by him. It was strange that it had taken him this long to realize it, but now that he had, he could feel the truth and the power of it. His parents didn't control his identity, and their opinions weren't an authority he had to either accept or rebel against. He could let go of the little things in order to make the big things work out.

"We had a little restoration work done on the stained glass," he said, walking down the aisle toward the colorful window. "Not much, though. It was in remarkably good shape, all things considered."

The tour continued, and when they'd seen the church he invited them back out to the farm for lunch. He'd decided not to extend that invitation until he saw how the first meeting went, but he felt pretty good making the offer. Joe was at home with ample food prepared, and Mackenzie was surprised by how eager he was to introduce his parents to his family.

The words hit him as he was easing behind the wheel of his car. His family. He'd thought it, and he'd meant it. Joe might be at the heart of things, but he wasn't the only person Mackenzie loved. Ally, of course, and Austin. They were Joe's blood, and Joe was Mackenzie's life—of course Mackenzie loved them. Anyone would love them. But Lacey and Savannah and Kami were in his heart too. They were more difficult to deal with, but not more difficult to care about. Mackenzie had a family.

He wanted to race home to share his epiphany with Joe, but he forced himself to drive sedately, his parents following behind in their own car. He slowed when they reached the entrance to the driveway and tried to see the farm through their eyes, or remember how it had seemed to him when he'd first arrived there, but he couldn't do it. This place wasn't about impressing his parents or being picturesque or even about being ragged and rough. This place was his *home*, and he couldn't see it as anything but the most beautiful spot on Earth.

He thought about bringing his parents in through the front door but realized he wasn't even sure it opened. And they should come through the mudroom, anyway, to get the full effect of entering the Sutton home.

And they absolutely *did* get the full effect. When Mackenzie pushed the door open there was a panicked scream from inside the kitchen. Not Kami, for a change, but Savannah. "Close the door!" she yelled. "Get inside and close the door!"

Mackenzie jumped to comply, his startled parents piling in on top of him as he reached behind them to pull the storm door shut.

Joe leaned into view from behind the fridge. "Zombies out there," he said calmly. Then he shot a look at Savannah. "At least, I can't think of any other possible reason to be screaming at guests like that."

"He could have gotten *outside*," Savannah protested, and she turned to run off to whatever she was in the middle of.

Joe caught her shoulders. "Could you please say hello to

Mackenzie's parents?"

She turned to him with wide eyes. "But Frank's in trouble!"

"If you can't be polite, he won't be the only one in trouble."

Savannah took a deep breath, then turned to Mackenzie's parents. "Hi," she said. "I'm Savannah."

"I'm Carol," his mother said, "and this is my husband, Michael. It's nice to meet you, Savannah." She glanced at Joe, then back down at the little girl. "Who's Frank? Can I help with him?"

"He's our *ferret*," Savannah said as if it should have been obvious. "He got out of his cage, and now he's lost, and if the dogs find him they'll eat him, and if he gets outside he'll freeze to death or some animal will eat him, and if he gets stuck in the sofa somebody might sit on him and squish him!"

"Oh my," Mackenzie's mother said. "That sounds serious."

"Savannah and Austin have been learning to take care of Frank," Joe said. "But they are really, *really* careless about keeping the cage door shut." As he spoke, he quietly pulled at the neck of his flannel work shirt, tugging it down enough so the newcomers could see a furry brown face peeking out with polite interest. Savannah was too short and too distracted to notice. "So now they're realizing why I nag them about that all the time. If they're going to take care of an animal, they have to be responsible." He made a face as if accepting the morally questionable nature of his deception. But he didn't show the ferret to the little girl. "Savannah, go look some more, please. We'll keep an eye out in case he comes in here."

He waited until Savannah was out of earshot, then said, "It's not like I took him out of the cage. He *was* loose when I found him. I'm just harboring the fugitive for a while, until they hopefully get it imprinted on their brain that they need to keep an eye on him."

"How much longer?" Mackenzie asked. This was Joe's show and he wouldn't intervene, but he felt pretty bad for Savannah. Not everyone could be as perfect at animal care as Joe was.

"It's only been about five minutes," Joe said a bit defensively.

"I figure they can make it another five." He looked apologetically toward Mackenzie's parents. "The living room kind of looks like a bomb went off in it. The search was enthusiastic, but not too controlled."

Mackenzie was startled by the boom of laughter coming from his father. "A ferret!" he said as if it were the most interesting thing in the world. Mackenzie wasn't crazy about sharing his home with a weasel, but apparently his prejudice was not based on anything he'd picked up at home. "He seems very friendly. Can I hold him?"

So Joe fished the animal out from his shirt and passed him over, and Frank was as charmingly curious as he always was, and even Mackenzie's mother reached out to cautiously pet him.

Joe eventually returned the ferret to his chastened handlers, and then the family sat down to lunch. The Sutton/Walton kids were as animated as ever, and Mackenzie felt himself tensing, waiting for his parents to roll their eyes and act as if children should be seen and not heard, but they seemed as engaged in the conversation as the children. Austin was happy to recount, in only slightly garbled fashion, the trials and tribulations of ferret care to Mackenzie's dad, and Ally discussed her career goals with Mackenzie's mother. Kami watched both newcomers through suspicious eyes, but she didn't act out, and when Joe prompted her she ate at least some of her meal.

When the meal was over and Joe had set the kids to cleaning up, Mackenzie invited his parents to sit in the somewhat-put-back-together living room, but they exchanged a look and then his mother said, "We'd better get going home. It's a bit of a drive. And we don't want to overstay our welcome."

"You wouldn't be." Mackenzie was surprised to realize that he meant it.

"Maybe we could have lunch again, sometime before next Christmas. Or if there's an event at your church, one that we could come to? I'd love to see that place filled with people." Mackenzie's mom smiled wistfully. It was hard to resent someone who shared his love of the church building.

"Absolutely," Mackenzie said. He wasn't quite sure what event his mom would be able to go to, but if it could happen, he'd try to think of her. Then he saw her quick glance toward Joe and realized what she was thinking. It wouldn't be polite to invite her to the wedding of a *stranger*....

"The gardens are really nice in the late spring," Joe said blandly. Mackenzie honestly couldn't tell if he'd picked up on his mom's hint or not. "Mackenzie spent a lot of time weeding them last year, and I guess he'll be spending almost as much this year, but I'd say it's a worthwhile effort."

"Sounds nice," Mackenzie's father said with only a little effort. He was not a man who generally had a lot of time for flowers.

They left then, without any further innuendos, and Mackenzie looked cautiously toward Joe, who raised an eyebrow back at him before saying, "We are not getting married just so your mom can go to a wedding in the church. Nope."

It was a good thing the kids had left the kitchen already so there weren't witnesses to Joe shutting down a suggestion Mackenzie hadn't even made. "You don't have the time, energy, or money to give me the wedding I'd deserve, anyway."

"Wait, you think *I'd* be putting time, energy, or money into that little project?" Joe looked suitably amazed. "No way, man. I think weddings are a waste of all three."

"This is my potential source of livelihood you're dismissing, you know."

Joe grinned at him and eased over so they were facing each other, standing close enough that they were touching from the waist down, leaning back from their waists so they could still see each other clearly. "You don't want to hear my thoughts on modeling either, probably."

Mackenzie ignored that crack. He had something more

important to focus on. "Wait. Are you saying you're against *marriage*, in general?"

"Marriage? No, I'm not against it. It's not a personal goal or anything, but if people want to get married, that's cool. If they want to have big weddings, that's fine too. It's just not my thing."

"What if it's *my* thing? What if I want to get married and have a big wedding?"

"Tell me when and where," Joe said seriously. "That goes for helping with organizing or whatever too." He grinned again. "If you decide it's important to you that you climb Mount Everest naked, you should tell me when and where I need to be to help you with that, too, and I'll be there. Especially for the naked part."

Mackenzie stared at him. "Wait. This is... I mean, I did *not* just ask you to marry me. That's not what happened. But, hypothetically...."

Joe reached past Mackenzie and selected an apple from the fruit bowl on the counter. "Hypothetically, I'd be in, if that's what you wanted to do."

"What, like, as a personal favor to me? Not because it's something *you* actually want." Mackenzie wasn't sure if this was worth getting upset about or not.

Joe was clearly choosing the *not* side. "Yup. That's about right," he said with a nonchalant shrug. He took a bite of his apple as he waited for Mackenzie's response, then looked at him a bit more closely, obviously realizing Mackenzie wasn't completely pleased with the conversation. "I love you," Joe said slowly. "I want to be with you. I don't need a piece of paper or a bunch of people staring at me while I say vows to know that. If you want the extra stuff, that's cool, I can go along. But...." He shrugged. "Yeah. It'd be a personal favor to you. One of many personal favors I'm more than happy to do for you."

"I can't decide if that's incredibly romantic or totally the opposite."

"The most important questions are the ones that don't have a simple answer," Joe said with a mockingly wise nod. He took another bite of his apple, then looked at it appreciatively. "This is really tasty, for this time of year. Want a bite?"

They'd just finished lunch, and Mackenzie didn't have Joe's constant appetite, so he didn't really want a bite, not for its own sake. But he liked the idea of sharing food with Joe. He opened his mouth a little, Joe positioned the apple just right, and Mackenzie took a bite. It *was* really tasty. He closed his eyes and let the tart juice wash over his taste buds, then opened his eyes and saw Joe waiting patiently. "Okay," he said.

"It's better than okay," Joe responded almost heatedly. "That's not a local apple! It came all the way from New Zealand or somewhere. And it still tastes almost fresh picked!"

"I wasn't talking about the apple, Joe." Mackenzie rested his hands on Joe's lean hips, then ran them around to link at the small of his back. "I meant the wedding stuff."

"Oh. And what does *okay* mean in that context?"

"It means I'm okay with it. I don't really want to get married, although a wedding *would* be a lot of fun. But I like hearing that you'd go along if I wanted you to."

"Don't forget about the naked Mount Everest offer. I think it's about time somebody upped the challenge level on that little hike, and maybe you're the man to do it."

"Okay," Mackenzie said again.

It *was* okay. Mackenzie had Joe. That was all he needed to make things good.

Chapter Twenty-one

The next night was Sunday dinner, and Joe came down from the barn early to get cleaned up and help with the cooking. He needn't have bothered, though. Well, getting cleaned up was probably a good thing, but there were plenty of workers in the kitchen. Sarah and Dave were there, Sarah organizing the kids into workforces with almost military precision. Dave had retreated to the living room, as he usually did, this time with Mackenzie and Will for company. Nick was the only adult male in the kitchen. He actually seemed like he was being useful for a change, but probably he was just working up to asking Sarah for some favor or another.

Joe didn't like thinking that way about his brother, and when he came downstairs from his shower, he made himself go into the kitchen and say, "Hey, Nick? Have you got plans for work? Anything on the horizon?"

He'd had good intentions but knew he'd chosen the wrong words when Nick's relaxed expression twisted into a sneer. "Plans for getting out of the house, you mean?"

"No. I didn't mean it like that." Joe was letting himself in for a world of hurt, but he made himself say it anyway. "I was wondering if you wanted to help me with the cattle. Well, with the beef, really. I know I could get better prices if I marketed it differently. Cut out the middleman and find restaurants and gourmet stores directly. Maybe even do some farm-gate stuff—

sales directly to individual people. But I don't have the time to do all that."

He waited for Nick's reaction but got none. "I know it's not as glamorous as owning a bar, but it'd be a lot less risky—hardly any start-up costs. If you want to be independent, you could set up your own company and buy the beef from me wholesale, or if you want a bit more support, you could just work for me." That was about all Joe had to say, but Nick was still staring at him. Joe shrugged. "It's an idea. Think about it, if you want."

"Yeah," Nick finally said. "I'll think about it."

And that was that. Joe had done his duty. He'd made one more attempt to keep Nick from feeling the way Mackenzie had. Maybe neither family had meant to banish their youngest sons, but if the kids didn't feel welcome, intentions didn't matter too much. So Joe would keep trying to make Nick feel like part of something and then keep trying to clean up after everything exploded all over.

With so many extra people the table was crowded, but nobody complained. They ate, and they laughed, and when dessert was finished, Will stood up and said he had an announcement to make. "Lindsey and I are expecting a baby, in about five months."

Sarah didn't look too surprised, but Joe felt like he'd been hit with a heavy stick. Will was having a baby. With Lindsey. It should have been strange that Will was announcing the event alone, but given Lindsey's historic disinterest in Sutton family gatherings, it was all too natural. And now she and Will were having a baby together. Will would be connected to this woman for the rest of his life even if they didn't stay together as a couple. They were going to be parenting a child together. Joe wanted answers, but this wasn't the time. "Congratulations," he said, and he tried to remember all the reasons he really meant it. "You'll be a good dad."

"I hope so," Will responded. He looked at Austin. "You ready for a new cousin? A little baby to look after?"

Austin didn't look too sure. "*I'm* the baby," he said petulantly.

"Nah," Joe scoffed. "You're a big boy now. Big enough to look after a ferret and to help look after a baby." Not that Lindsey was likely to be enthusiastic about that idea, but Joe would just have to find ways to make it happen. One more challenge. Maybe he'd see if Mackenzie wanted to take this one on.

But dinner was over and Joe had more important things on his mind. Or at least more *immediate* things. "You ready to go?" he asked Mackenzie as the table was being cleared.

"Go? Where?"

"I'm sure I mentioned it," Joe said. He reached for Mackenzie's hand and tugged him gently into the mudroom. Sarah nodded as they left, acknowledging the transfer of responsibility. The kids were hers for the night; Joe had plans.

"I don't think you did," Mackenzie protested.

"Huh. Well, get your coat on. Boots too. Let's go."

"Go where?" Mackenzie asked again, but he did as he was told.

"Well, if you've made it this far without knowing, you might as well make it a little farther. I won't ruin the surprise."

"You're annoying."

"Careful, or I won't *give* you the surprise, and that'd be even more annoying. Right?"

"So I'm choosing the lesser of two annoyances?"

"Yup." Joe pulled his own boots on and checked that Mackenzie was properly dressed before pulling the door open and heading for the truck.

"We're driving somewhere?"

"Did you think the surprise was in the barn?" It was a funny thought. "Here, Mack, enjoy your new calf."

"I'm not going to talk to you anymore. Not until we get to where the surprise is."

That was probably an okay idea. Joe didn't want Mackenzie pissed off before they got to their destination. So he pulled out and headed down the long driveway, turned onto the road, and drove about a minute before his headlights found the reflective markers Will had installed the day before.

"We're going into the forest?" Mackenzie asked. "Because, you know, a new *bear cub* would be just as absurd as a new calf."

"Well, there goes my idea for Valentine's Day." They drove along the rough road toward the lake. "We need to get a couple loads of gravel for this. It's on the to-do list," Joe explained.

"Okay...."

Joe didn't bother to respond to that, because they'd reached their destination. He pulled around so the headlights lit up the outside of the building and looked at Mackenzie for a reaction.

It wasn't exactly favorable. More like confused. "The old cabin?" Mackenzie said. "You told me your grandpa bought this property and the house was already on it, but nobody's lived in it for a long time?"

"And what else did I tell you?" Joe prompted.

"You said you wanted me to climb Mount Everest naked."

"What did I tell you about this cabin?"

Mackenzie frowned, then tentatively said, "You thought it was something that could be fixed up. You said the structure was still good, and maybe it'd be worth trying to save it."

"What did I think we could do with it?"

"You said...." Mackenzie turned quickly to stare at him. "You said it could be a honeymoon suite for the people getting married at the church! You said it has its own little lakefront and a good view and it could be really cute! But there's no *way* you've had time to do that!"

"You don't need time when you've got a brother in the contracting business," Joe said smugly. "Will's got a couple crews he really likes, and he wants to make sure they're getting steady work so somebody else doesn't hire them away. So when he didn't have a job for them, he'd send them here." He wished the light in the truck was better so he could see Mackenzie's expression more clearly. "You want to go see?"

"Are you kidding me?" Mackenzie demanded. "Seriously, you guys fixed this place up? I can refer people here if they want to rent it? Joe, this is…."

"He didn't actually tell me about it until yesterday. I mean, we talked about it in theory, and I agreed it sounded like a good idea, but I didn't know he was actually working on it. It's all him. Come see it. Maybe you'll think it's ugly, so you'd better not get too grateful too fast." Joe pushed his door open and met Mackenzie at the front of the truck. Neither of them had bothered to put his gloves on, so their skin was cool as their fingers entwined.

"We'll need to get better outdoor lighting," Joe said thoughtfully. "The place is rewired, so it can handle the demand." He led the way toward the front door and unlocked it. There was a temptation to sweep Mackenzie up and carry him across the threshold, but Joe resisted. Mackenzie could sometimes be a bit touchy about which stereotypes they perpetuated, and Joe didn't want to ruin this night with a fight. So he took Mack's hand and led him inside, then flipped the lights on.

"Oh, Joe!" Mackenzie was clearly torn between pulling his boots off and looking around the room. He ended up not doing a great job of either, and Joe knelt quickly to deal with their footwear. "It's perfect," Mack said, stepping into the room as if in a dream. "All the wood, and it feels so open but so cozy!"

"Bed in the loft," Joe said. "Bathroom and sitting area and kitchenette down here." He didn't really need to explain all of that, probably, but it was fun. "And check this out." He tugged Mackenzie toward the french doors at the far end of the building. "You can't see it at night, but there's a really good view of the lake, and we'll build a little deck down there in the springtime. But until then...." Joe pulled the doors open and nodded toward the subtly lit, steaming pool built into the deck.

"Hot tub!" Mackenzie yelped excitedly. "Joe, I fucking *love* hot tubs."

"I thought you might," Joe said with a grin. He didn't mind them himself, if he was being honest. "You want to get in?"

"Do we have time?" Mackenzie asked wistfully. "How late can Will and Sarah stay?"

"All night," Joe said. "If you want." As far as he was concerned, this was the best part about the renovated cabin. "We can rent it out to your wedding customers, for sure. But when it's not booked, and when we can find someone to babysit...." He spun Mackenzie around and pulled their bodies together. "It can be for us." He kept his first kiss gentle because he was springing all of this on Mackenzie out of nowhere and needed to give the man time to catch up, but he'd been thinking about this night for a long time, and desire was hot and demanding in his gut. "I miss you," he said softly. "I want to hear the way your breath catches when you get turned on and the way you moan to tell me I found the right spots. And I want to hear you making all the noise you want to when you come, without worrying about a bunch of kids hearing you."

Mackenzie was the one to deepen the kiss, darting his tongue out to meet Joe's and start their sinuous dance.

It would be easy to just take it from there, but Joe wanted this night to be special, and he made himself pull away. "Hot tub," he almost ordered. "Strip down."

Mackenzie didn't waste any time, and they raced each other to get naked and slide into the almost painful heat of the steaming water. Joe reached over to turn on the jets, and at the same time pulled the bottle from where he'd stashed it in a pile of snow.

"Champagne?" Mackenzie said with a happy smile. "You didn't miss a trick, did you?"

"A jug of wine, a hot tub, and thou," Joe paraphrased. "What else could we need?"

"Not a damn thing," Mackenzie said, and he leaned back into the jets as Joe shot the champagne cork out over the snow. He'd find it in the spring.

It was nice to sit and relax. Sure, part of Joe's brain worried about how things were going back at the house, but he'd already checked to be sure he got cell coverage at the cabin, and his phone was in his jacket, which was right by the tub. Everything was fine. He clinked glasses with Mackenzie and they sipped their drinks, and Joe was reminded again of why he preferred beer. But champagne made Mackenzie happy, and a happy Mack meant a happy Joe.

"I really love you," Mackenzie said, taking one more sip from his glass before carefully finding a spot for it on the edge of the tub. He let the jets bounce him over toward Joe and then stabilized himself when he was straddling Joe's lap, facing him, their half-hard cocks making a reacquaintance that had been far too long coming. "This is perfect."

"Good," Joe said, and he stretched up enough to find Mackenzie's lips with his own.

There was something a little different about their kisses this time around. It took Joe a little while to realize what it was. Mackenzie was setting the pace. It was probably partly because he was on top, and he always got a little more active from that position, and partly because Joe was kept reasonably busy just trying to keep them stable in the water. But mostly it was because Mack seemed to *want* to be in charge, and Joe had no thought of objecting.

"We have all night?" Mackenzie asked when they paused for breath. "Because there's a *lot* of stuff I want to do to you, and it's gonna take some time."

"All night," Joe confirmed. "I'm yours."

"You're damn right you are." Mackenzie slipped his hand down to take a firm, possessive grip of Joe's cock. "This is mine." He braced his knees on the hot tub bench and raised himself a bit out of the water, pulled Joe's body up with him, then reached down to kiss Joe's nipples as they rose out of the steam. "These are mine." Then he slid his hands a little lower, down to grip Joe's ass cheeks. "And this is mine. Anytime I want it."

"Within reason," Joe agreed with a grin.

"No. No reason. No qualifiers." Mackenzie looked pretty serious.

Joe had no idea what was going on, but he nodded. If Mackenzie cared, Joe cared. "Okay," he agreed. "No qualifiers."

"I'm going to fuck you soon," Mackenzie promised, but he let their bodies relax back onto the seat, rubbing his ass tantalizingly along the hard length of Joe's cock. "Not tonight. Maybe next time we come here. I'll bring some toys, and I'll work you open and make you fucking desperate. I want to know how it feels to be inside you. I want to make you feel as good as you make *me* feel."

"We can do that," Joe agreed, roaming his hands over Mackenzie's slick body. "But I'll tell you, you make me feel pretty damn good the way we usually do it too."

"Do I make you feel *owned*?" Mackenzie asked between kisses. "*Claimed*? *Cherished*? Because that's how you make me feel when you fuck me." He slid his hand down to find Joe's cock and eased himself into position.

"Wait," Joe made himself say. "There's lube in my jacket pocket."

"Excellent," Mackenzie said, sliding himself across Joe's body to fumble through the pile of clothes. "I want to take this slow. I want to make it last."

Joe found his champagne flute while Mackenzie dealt with the lube, and he held the glass while Mackenzie took a sip, then drained the glass and dropped it somewhere behind him. He wanted to focus on Mackenzie's perfect body, lean and lithe, his skin so soft and unblemished, his eyes dark as they stared into Joe's, and, God, his ass, tight but yielding as he eased himself down around Joe's cock, making them both gasp with pleasure.

Mackenzie still seemed determined to take things slow, so it was a good thing he was in charge. After so long without sex, Joe's body was screaming at him to spin Mackenzie around, pin him against the side of the hot tub and fuck him hard and fast. He had to force himself to sit still as Mackenzie teased him. They were joined together, Joe's cock buried to the hilt, but Mackenzie seemed to have almost forgotten about that part of things, focusing instead on kissing and exploring Joe's body. There was a slight movement between them, the tiniest hint of ripples instead of the tidal wave Joe craved, but nothing more.

Mackenzie sipped from his glass then dripped the champagne into Joe's mouth. "Tastes better like that," Joe said with a wicked smile, and Mackenzie repeated the trick. When his glass was empty, he reached for the bottle but didn't bother to pour it into the flutes, just drank from it and then poured some into Joe's mouth. After he replaced it in the snowbank, he finally started to move a little. Everything was still slow, but each time he lifted his body he eased himself a little further off Joe's cock before sliding back down for a kiss. Eventually he pulled off so far the head of Joe's cock was squeezed by the tight ring of muscles at Mack's opening before he slid all the way back inside.

Joe fought to keep control, but he knew it was a losing battle. He fumbled to find Mackenzie's cock, squeezed it tight, and kept his hand still so that every time Mack rose off Joe, he pushed his own cock into a snug grip. He heard Mackenzie's breathing catch, heard him swallowing the sounds that wanted to come from his throat. "Let me hear you," Joe said, his own voice tight and breathless. "There's no one around. I want to hear you."

Mackenzie's moan sounded almost like a sob. He finally sped up, the sinewy grace of his earlier movements replaced by a desperation that more clearly matched Joe's needs. "God, Joe," he gasped, his eyes closed and his head thrown back as his attention was claimed by the sensations. Joe wanted the moment to last forever, but he also, desperately, needed to come.

"Come on, Mack. Come on," he urged. He used his free hand to tug almost fiercely on Mackenzie's nipple, then slid it down to caress his balls, and then further back to feel his own cock as it slid in and out of Mackenzie's body. Mack gasped as Joe slid one finger inside, his hand moving with Mackenzie's body to provide a constant pressure.

"Joe!" Mackenzie cried almost desperately. His eyes were still closed, but he had a tight grip on Joe's shoulders, his fingers clenched with effort as he worked both of them toward their orgasm.

Joe knew what he should do. He needed to think of kittens or dead things or baseball scores or whatever it took to keep himself from coming too soon, but he couldn't make himself do it. He couldn't tear his eyes away from the beauty before him, couldn't ignore how perfect his body felt, couldn't deny the desperate need activated by each one of Mackenzie's ecstatic gasps. He felt his orgasm building and couldn't stop it. He *needed* to come, needed to know Mackenzie was once more owned and claimed and cherished.

"Oh fuck!" Mackenzie groaned just in time, and it was the spasming of his body that pushed Joe right over the edge. They came together, Mackenzie still moving even as the arch of Joe's body pushed them both up out of the water. Joe grabbed Mackenzie's hips and tried to drive deeper into him, deeper than he'd ever been, and the thought of his seed filling Mackenzie was enough to bring one final spurt from his overwhelmed body.

They eased back into the water together without uncoupling. Mackenzie slumped forward, his body relaxed, and nestled his head into Joe's shoulder.

"That was perfect," Mackenzie finally murmured.

Joe wasn't going to argue with the sentiment. "Let's go inside and I'll show you the shower," he said instead. "It's big enough for two. We can rinse off, then sleep a bit, and when we wake up we can do it all again. Sound okay?"

"You know it does," Mack said, but he didn't move.

That was okay. They had a plan, but there was no rush. When Mackenzie was ready for the next step, Joe would be right there with him. In the meantime, though? He leaned back against the hot tub and let himself relax. In the meantime, there was nowhere he'd rather be.

ABOUT THE AUTHOR

Kate Sherwood, Cate Cameron, Catherine Dale... and probably a few new names, eventually. They're all one person.

One person who's lucky enough to get to live a bunch of extra lives through all the characters in her books, and who's trying desperately to keep all the lives organized into some sort of categories... so each name writes a different type of story.

But really, beneath the genre categories? All the stories will have some kind of humour, even in the darkest times. They'll all show characters who are far from perfect, but who are trying to be better.

Basic bio stuff? Kate/Cate/Catherine lives in Cottage Country, the water-filled world north of Toronto, Canada, the land where summers are sunny and crowded with visitors and winters are snowy and isolated. She loves it there. Not that she doesn't sometimes miss the city, especially when her internet is acting up or she wants something delivered!

She works full-time at a non-writing job but would love to shift into a more writing-centred life. There's a five-year plan. It might work....

OTHER BOOKS BY KATE SHERWOOD

For details, see www.booklives.com

Writing as Kate Sherwood (m/m)

All That Glitters – contemporary romance

Long Shadows, Embers, Darkness, Home Fires – four book
contemporary action

Feral, Lap Dog, Twice Shy, Pure Bred – four book NA contemporary
romance

Sacrati – fantasy/alt history

In Too Deep – NA contemporary romance

Chasing the Dragon – angst and adventure!

Mark of Cain – contemporary romance

The Fall, Riding Tall – two book contemporary romance

The Shift – contemporary fantasy novella – monster hunters!

Room to Grow – contemporary romance novella

The Pawn, The Knight – two book futuristic romance with plenty of
angst

Poor Little Rich Boy – contemporary romance

More than Chemistry – light contemporary novella

Dark Horse, Out of the Darkness, Of Dark and Bright – three book
contemporary romance with extras

Shying Away – NA romance

Lost Treasure – contemporary romance

Writing as Cate Cameron (m/f, YA)

The Billionaire's Forever Family – contemporary romance

Center Ice, Playing Defense, Winging It, Breakaway – contemporary YA hockey romance

Just a Summer Fling, Hometown Hero – contemporary small town romance

Shining Armor – contemporary romance (originally published under "Kate Sherwood")

Writing as Catherine Dale (YA, contemporary fantasy, general fiction—everything but romance!)

Dark Houses – Speculative YA